THE DEVIL YOU KNOW

THE DEVIL YOU KNOW

Robert Swartwood

RMS Press

For Norman and Rosemary Sargent

THE DEVIL YOU KNOW

Part I

THE BOOGEYMAN

1

The guard is short and stout, almost pudgy. He walks his section of the perimeter carrying an AK-47 at the ready. He's walked past this spot twice so far, taking his time, his focus mostly down at the beach. He pauses, straps the AK-47 to his shoulder, and pulls out a pack of cigarettes. He uses a match to light the cigarette, flicks his wrist to extinguish the match, then tosses the spent match aside. He takes a heavy drag off the cigarette, blowing the smoke out through his nose.

I give him the pleasure of one final drag before slipping out of the shadows, a knife in hand. His back is to me, so he doesn't see me, but he hears me at the last second. He turns, and I plunge the blade repeatedly into his chest.

The cigarette falls from his hand. He tries to reach for his rifle, but by that point it's useless. My blade has punctured his heart and lungs. Blood instantly stains his shirt. He issues his final breath. Not the noblest way of taking his life, but the quietest I could do under the circumstances.

From the transmitter in my ear, Atticus says, "You have two more heading your way."

I whisper, "How long?"

"Ten seconds. Fifteen if you're lucky."

Right now six quadcopters are quietly buzzing in the air above me, each equipped with an infrared camera, monitoring the area, the feeds bouncing back to Atticus in the States while I'm here on the Mexican coast, twenty miles from Culiacán, on Ernesto Diaz's compound. I've been in Mexico three days now, having done as much surveillance on the compound as could be done in that time. Ernesto Diaz is inside the house, with a bunch of guards. By now Ernesto knows his son is dead. He may not know this for certain—there's no way Javier's body has been found—but maybe a gut feeling a father has when his son disappears off the map.

Despite the fact it's the middle of the night, sunglasses are currently propped on my head. I check to make sure they're secure and then sheath the knife and grab the guard with both hands, drag him back into the shadows where I'd been hiding. I try to do this as quickly as possible, but my broken rib is causing me pain. I also try to do this as quietly as possible, but the guard's boots scraping against the ground sound like fireworks in my head. At least there's the sound of the ocean not too far away to muffle the noise, the surf hitting the sand and rocks.

I slip the man back into the shadows just as the two other men appear around the corner.

In my ear, Atticus says, "The cigarette."

Shit.

It's maybe fifty feet away, the cherry still glowing faintly. Maybe by the time the guards get close enough the cherry will be extinguished, but maybe not. I could easily take the guards out with one of my pistols—I have two strapped to my belt, both of them equipped with sound suppressors—but I want to wait as long as possible before I alert the rest of the guards. Because based on what Atticus has seen from the quadcopters, there are fourteen in all, counting the guard I just killed. Ten monitoring the outside perimeter, four others inside the house, all heavily armed.

One of the approaching guards whispers, "Hector, we know you have a fresh pack of cigarettes. Don't hold out on us."

The two guards move into my line of sight. Both of them are carrying identical AK-47s.

I could easily take them out right now, but again, I don't want to bring attention to myself. The pistols are silenced, but that doesn't mean the shots would be entirely silent. This isn't a movie. The shots would still make noise, enough that it might catch the attention of the other guards walking the perimeter. I'm going to have to start shooting at some point—there's no way I'll be able to do this without lead—but I want to wait as long as possible.

My left hand touches the stick on my belt. It's a foot long, black, and looks like a baton. But it's not a baton.

The same guard who whispered before whispers again.

"Hector, *mi amigo*, where are you?"

That's when the other guard spots the fading cherry. He pauses, taps his counterpart on the arm, and points.

Time to work.

I unsheathe the blade again and throw the knife at the closest guard forty feet away. The blade slams into the guard's back. He grunts, drops the AK-47, reaches for the knife stuck between his shoulder blades as he starts to fall to his knees. By that point I'm sprinting forward, the other guard turning toward me and raising his rifle. I throw the baton at him. It strikes him in his throat, stunning him just long enough for me to reach them both.

Swiping the baton off the ground, I use it to smash it against the side of the guard's face, then twist the baton and pull it apart to reveal its other purpose. I step behind the guard and wrap the garrote wire around his throat. The man struggles, attempting to reach back at me, but the wire is sharp and tears into his skin. Blood squirts out, and in seconds the man stops struggling as the life fades from his body.

The other guard, meanwhile, has stopped trying to extract the knife from his back. For the moment he ignores the AK-47 lying feet away, and even ignores the gun holstered to his belt. Instead, he reaches for something else clipped to his belt.

His radio.

In an instant, I calculate the distance between us. About twenty feet, but still more than enough space for him to access his radio before I make it over to him. And then what? Pull the knife from his back, slice him across the throat? Won't matter how I kill him, because by then he'll have already used the radio. Maybe he won't be able to alert the other guards to exactly what's happened, but any slight warning is more than I can allow.

I have no choice, I realize, and pull one of the pistols from my belt.

I place a bullet into the back of his head.

Despite the silencer, the single round shatters the night's stillness.

For a moment I don't move, just stand there staring at the dead guard.

Atticus says, "They're coming for you."

"How many?"

"All of them."

2

The Diaz compound sits on the top of a bluff overlooking the Pacific. A chain-link fence circles the compound, some trees and bushes lining spots of the fence. I can't see the men hurrying in my direction, but I can hear them—the heavy pounding of their boots on the ground coming from both directions— and I start to take a step toward the shadows where I'd been hiding before, when I pause.

Atticus says, "You've got less than ten seconds."

Ignoring him, I pull out the strip of firecrackers from my pocket—I'd purchased them from a kid selling fireworks on the street earlier today on a whim—and extract a lighter from my other pocket and prime the lighter as Atticus says, "Five seconds," and then once the fuse lights, I fling the strip of firecrackers toward the end of the bluff, right toward the narrow trail I'd used to climb up here.

I slip back into the shadows, right next to the first guard's body, and I watch as the other men hurry into view. There are five of them. Each carries an AK-47 at the ready. They pause when they see the two bodies on the ground. They look up at each other but say nothing. One of them notices the divots in the dirt from the dead guard's boots. He starts to look toward me, but right then the firecrackers go off.

All of the men turn and open fire at the end of the bluff. As they do, I step out of the shadows and, using the dead guard's AK-47, mow down the other guards, sweeping the barrel from left to right, right to left.

Six seconds, that's all it takes, and then all seven guards are down.

Atticus says, "Three others still inside the fence."

"Where?"

"Right by the entrance."

I toss the spent rifle aside and start running toward the entrance. As I run, I take a flashbang grenade off my belt, pull the pin, and toss it over the fence when I'm just ten yards from the entrance.

On the other side of the fence, the flashbang grenade goes off. I hear one of the men shout something, and then there's brief gunfire directed toward the explosion. By then I step around the corner, a gun in hand, and take out two of the guards who have their backs to me, two bullets each to the back of their heads, but where the fuck is the third?

Someone shouts behind me, ordering me in Spanish to stop and drop my weapon.

I start to turn.

The man shouts again, telling me to drop my weapon.

In my ear, Atticus says, "Give me a second."

I'm not sure what this means, and I'm not sure this guard will give me more than a second before he drops me.

The man behind me shouts again in Spanish.

"Drop the fucking gun."

It's the last thing I want to do, but I let the gun fall to the ground.

I whisper, "Atticus?"

In my ear: "Another second."

Behind me, the man says, "Where are the others?"

I say nothing.

"*Puta*, where are the others?"

My hands held up at my sides, I slowly turn.

The guard's young, almost a kid. Just like the others, he carries an AK-47, but it doesn't waver in his hands.

I answer in English.

"Only me."

"Bullshit."

I just smile—and watch as one of the quadcopters takes a nosedive into the back of the guard's head.

He stumbles sideways.

The distraction gives me only two seconds, but it's enough time for me to pull the other pistol from my belt and place two bullets in the guard's face.

As the guard hits the ground, I do a sweep of the area for any other surprises.

The compound sits one hundred yards away. Several pickup trucks and SUVs are parked beside it. The lights are on inside, but I can't see any movement.

I ask, "Anybody slip out the back?"

"Not yet."

"What side am I looking for?"

"The east side."

I start toward the house, moving on a diagonal to give me space. Almost every light is lit inside the house, and so far I haven't seen any movement, which is disconcerting. Ernesto Diaz is here, isn't he? From the limited surveillance I've been able to conduct the past few days, the answer is yes. I did take out ten of his men, but what if they were just decoys and the house is empty?

"Atticus, those nifty little toys of yours can't see the heat signatures inside the house, can they?"

"I'm afraid they cannot."

I've reached the pickup trucks and SUVs and carefully weave my way through them, my gun at the ready in case anybody's hiding inside one of the cabs. Underneath a few of the vehicles I leave surprises and then keep moving closer to the house.

I spot the electrical box on the side right where Atticus had said it would be. I leave another surprise and then swiftly move toward the front, keeping close to the house for cover. It's been a full minute now since I entered the fence and nothing's happened, and the stillness unsettles me. An alarm bell goes off in my head, but there's nothing with which to associate it.

At the edge of the house, I pause once again.

Atticus says, "What's wrong?"

"Something doesn't feel right."

"Do you want to abort?"

"No."

"Then get to it."

I do one more sweep of the front yard before hurrying around to the porch steps. The door is already open, which sets off another alarm bell in my head.

I step into the foyer.

It's what one may call a grand foyer. The ceiling two stories tall. The staircase split, moving up both sides of the wall. A small chandelier hanging above my head. The house isn't a mansion like you'd find back in the States, but it's impressive enough for an area full of poverty and slums.

Fuck this.

I shout, "Knock, knock! Is anybody home?"

Silence.

At least for the first couple seconds, and then I hear footsteps behind me as four men appear from side rooms, then two men appear at the top of the stairs.

The men don't say anything, just glare, so I decide to break the ice, pointing at the sunglasses on my head.

"I'm a tourist on vacation. I'm looking for the beach. Can anyone point me in the right direction?"

Still silent, the men aim their guns at me.

I whisper, "Atticus, now."

Somewhere in the States, Atticus presses a key on his keyboard, and outside, the surprise I attached to the electrical box—the quarter pound of plastic explosive—detonates. There's a magnificent *bang*, and then the house goes dark.

Party time.

3

The sunglasses on my head are not actually sunglasses. They're a kind of night vision goggles, designed to look like sunglasses, and once the lights go out, I drop to the floor and flick the glasses down on my face just as some of the guards open fire.

They're not entirely stupid, though. They know better than to shoot wildly in the dark. Fact is, it's not totally dark because outside the sky is clear and the moon is bright, but it'll take several seconds before their eyes start to adjust.

I hit a button on the side of the glasses, and the world turns green. Now I can see just as clear as day.

Only a few of the guards opened fire but quickly stopped, not wanting to shoot any of their friends. One of them shouts for someone to turn on a flashlight. I look back and forth, but it doesn't appear any of them has a flashlight. Someone pulls out his cell phone, no doubt planning to use a flashlight app.

I kill him first.

Because of the silencer, there's only a slight muzzle flash, barely even there, which doesn't give the guards much to aim for. A few shoot randomly, but their shots are high.

Okay, no more screwing around.

I move toward the closest wall, right beside one of the guards, and shoot him in the head. Then I turn and take out three more guards—*pop, pop, pop*—before sprinting toward the other end of the foyer because the two guards up at the top of the stairs now open fire in my direction.

They move down the stairs, slowly, taking their time as they wait for their eyes to adjust.

I don't give them the time—I take out the closest guard, two in the head, then hurry up the stairs as I fire across at the other guard.

My bullet hits him in the shoulder, causing him to twist back and fall down the stairs. He's still alive, though. He climbs to his feet, disoriented, looking around the foyer and shooting randomly.

Standing at the top of the stairs now, I place a bead on his head and pull the trigger.

His head snaps back, and he falls dead to the ground.

Satisfied all the guards are dead, I turn and walk straight into a wall of flesh.

Stumbling back, I have a moment to take in the three-hundred-pound man standing in front of me. I remember seeing him the other day, trailing Ernesto, clearly the old man's personal bodyguard. A massive guy, all muscle. His eyes haven't adjusted quite yet to the dark, but still he manages to hit me when he swings his enormous fist.

I fly into the wall. The gun falls from my hand on impact. I pick myself back up, reach for the gun, but the giant lashes out with both hands, gripping different parts of my body, until one of his hands finds my neck. He throws me up against the wall. I kick and punch at him, but it does little good. With the night vision, I can see the frenzied look on his face, the pure menace in his eyes, as he starts to squeeze my throat. When I try to kick him in the balls, he swats at me with his other hand, slapping me across the face, causing the glasses to go flying.

I can't see in the dark now, but that's okay. I still have one of the guns holstered to my belt. I try to reach for it but the giant seems to sense my intention. He grabs the gun himself, yanks it from the holster.

Fuck this.

Again I kick the giant in the balls, as hard as I can, and with my right fist I punch him in the throat. It doesn't drop him, but it does stun him long enough for him to release his grip. I don't have time to catch my breath as I struggle back to my feet and start kicking randomly in front of me, hoping that the tip of my boot connects with his face.

The giant lets off several rounds of the silenced pistol, the shots going straight up toward the ceiling. I'm close enough to see the muzzle flashes—only feet away from my head—and I dive forward, grabbing the gun and wrestling it from the giant's hand.

He smacks me with his other hand, but I elbow him in the throat, again and again, until he stumbles back, coughing, and lets go of the gun.

Taking possession of the gun once more, I turn and press the silencer into the giant's chest and squeeze the trigger repeatedly until the magazine is exhausted and the slide pops back.

The giant falls to the floor. He doesn't die right away—I can hear him gasping for air—but he will in the next minute or so.

I drop the empty magazine, load a fresh one, and then turn toward where the glasses fell.

The green glow catches my eye. I pick them up and put them on and see the world as clear as day again. I turn to check on the giant—and see that despite all the bullets in his chest he's in the process of sitting up. He has a gun in his hand, shaking with the effort, aimed in my general direction. I hurriedly step to the side as he shoots at the wall, stride up to him, and place a bullet in his head.

He falls back to the ground, dead.

Atticus says, "Are you okay?"

I wince at the pain from my already broken rib and the brand-new bruises.

"Peachy."

"You're almost done, Holly. Do what you do best."

I head deeper into the house.

4

Now that the gunfire has stopped and the power's out, the house is completely silent.

I'm taking a chance searching the second floor first. For some reason I feel that's where I'll find Ernesto Diaz. I probably should check the first floor first, then make my way up to the second, but I don't want to waste time. Because there's a very good chance one of the guards called for help once the gunfire started. More men could be here any minute. I've done well so far—I mean, hey, I am still breathing—but I'm not sure how much more I can manage, especially with my depleting ammo.

The hallway stretches out in front of me, doors lining both sides. All of the doors are closed.

I approach the first door and stay to the side as I turn the knob and push it open. When nobody fires at me, I peek inside.

Empty.

I do the same with the next room, then the next. All empty.

As I go to open the fourth bedroom, I hear a noise inside, what sounds like whimpering.

I push open the door but don't step inside, waiting for

somebody to take a shot. When nobody does, I slowly step inside the room, sweeping my gun from one corner of the room to the other corner.

The room appears empty—just a bed and chairs and a TV—but I can still hear the whimpering. It's coming from the closet.

Could that be Ernesto? No, because now that I'm crossing over toward the closet, the whimpering is clearly that of a child.

My heart seizes. My mission is to kill everybody—every living soul—in this house. During my surveillance, I hadn't seen any children out in the fenced-in area.

I step on a loose floorboard. The sudden sound in the silence is enough to cause the child to cry out in fear.

Only wait—that sounds like *another* child.

Jesus Christ, there are *two of them*.

I tear open the closet door and step back, aiming the gun inside. Thanks to the night vision glasses, I can see the two children hiding in the closet, just as I can see the woman crouched down between them, holding them fiercely. Both children start crying. One is a boy no older than five years old, the other a girl maybe a year or two older. Tears cover their faces. The woman stares out at me, fear in her eyes.

I whisper, "Where is he?"

The woman says nothing, just holds the children even tighter.

Part of me—a cold, calculating part—knows I should kill them right here and now. Just place a bullet between each of their eyes. When I came to Mexico, I came with the intent of killing Ernesto Diaz and his family and whoever else stood in my way. It was something I accepted, something I understood needed to happen to keep my mother and my sister and my sister's family safe. Because Javier Diaz had threatened them. And because Javier Diaz had threatened them, I killed him. And I knew once word got back to Javier's father, the man would see to it that his son was avenged. I needed to stop the cycle, and so that's why I'm here now, in Ernesto Diaz's compound, ready to kill every living soul inside.

But children?

No, this mission may have started out as one with coldhearted intentions, but I can't bring myself to kill children. Looking at these two now, I'm reminded of David and Casey, whom I last saw only days ago and whom I will never see again. When they had been taken, I'd killed to get them back, and now I'm killing to protect my own family, but fuck, I can't bring myself to kill children, I just can't.

"I'm not going to hurt you. But I need to know where Ernesto is."

When the little girl hears the name, her cries renew and she murmurs something in Spanish that immediately seizes my heart again.

Grandpapa.

Of course. These are Ernesto's grandchildren. And the woman, she may very well be the children's mother. If that's the case, that means this is Javier's wife, or at the least his lover. That alone would add her to my kill list, but I'm not about to end her life while she holds on to her two children.

"Are you their mother?"

The woman shakes her head and whispers.

"Nanny."

"You need to leave right now. Take the children. Get out of here."

The woman doesn't move. The children, held in her tight embrace, don't move either.

"Now!"

All three of them jump.

Atticus says, "There are children inside?"

"Yes."

He sighs.

"That is not ideal."

"No, it's not."

Atticus sounds like he's going to say something else but pauses.

I ask, "What's wrong?"

"Checking something."

Then, his voice urgent.

"Bedroom window at the end of the house just slid open. It looks like Ernesto is trying to escape."

I pull a penlight from my pocket, toss it at the woman. It hits her on the leg and she screams like she's been shot.

"Relax. It's just a flashlight. Use it to find your way outside. Leave as soon as you can. And keep it on, so I know not to shoot you. Understood?"

Atticus in my ear: "He's climbing out the window."

"*Understood?*"

The woman nods quickly. The children have started crying again. The little girl keeps saying *abuelo*, over and over, and the boy is so scared he pees his pants.

I shout, "Go!"

Without waiting for a response, I turn and hurry out of the bedroom.

5

"He's almost out."

Atticus's voice echoes in my ear as I sprint toward the door at the end of the hallway.

Because of the urgency, I don't bother being careful, which is of course stupid on my part. Instead of standing to the side when I open the door, I run at it full on and kick it open. I expect only Ernesto to be in the master bedroom, but there are two more guards inside. One is assisting Ernesto out the window, the other stationed across the room, his gun aimed right at me.

The second guard fires off a shot. Had the lights been on, his bullet would have taken me out, but because of the dark, he misses by a few inches.

I shoot him first, two bullets to the head, then swing my pistol toward the other guard. That guard has already let go of Ernesto—the old man issuing a strangled cry—and has grabbed the AK-47 strapped over his shoulder as he turns to-ward me.

This guard doesn't care about precision. He squeezes the

trigger and doesn't let go, spraying bullets everywhere in my direction.

I dive to the side and stay flat on the floor as I take aim at the guard's nose. My bullet shatters his face and he stumbles back, his finger still on the rifle's trigger, exhausting the rest of the magazine into the ceiling.

I jump to my feet and sprint over to the opened window. Ernesto is already hurrying away, back toward the front of the house. But he's limping, favoring his left leg, which he either sprained or broke from the fall.

Aiming carefully out the window, I fire off two rounds, one of which strikes Ernesto in his right leg. He falls to the ground and then lies there, motionless, before he regains some strength and uses his arms to start crawling forward.

Just outside the window, one of the quadcopters hovers midair, its camera pointed at me.

I ask the quadcopter, "Anybody else around the compound?"

Atticus says, "Not that I can see. Ernesto is the only one left."

I glance down at the ground two stories below. If Ernesto were more mobile, I would climb out and drop down, but why potentially roll my ankle if I don't have to?

I step away from the window and cross the bedroom to the door. Down the long hallway to the top of the foyer where the woman and the two children are already halfway down the one set of stairs. She carries the boy while she grips the girl's arm, pulling her forward. Mercifully for the children, the penlight's thin beam doesn't illuminate much of the carnage. But the children are still scared, the boy sobbing, the girl sniffing back tears.

The penlight swings in my direction when the woman hears me coming.

"Relax. Just keep focused on what you're doing."

The penlight stays on me for a moment longer before swinging back toward the stairs. The woman does her best to keep the bodies and the blood concealed by the dark.

I use the other set of stairs down to the foyer, stepping over dead bodies on my way out the front door.

Ernesto hasn't gotten far. Maybe ten yards, maybe less. He's nowhere near the pickup trucks and SUVs he seemed to have been headed toward before I shot him. The moon is bright enough that he sees motion off to his left. When he realizes it's me, he gives up and stops moving.

I stand over Ernesto, the gun in my hand.

He glares up at me. The muscles in his face ripple with pain. When he speaks, his voice is deep and stunted.

"My son?"

I raise my gun, point it at his head.

"Tell him I say hi."

Despite the silencer, the single gunshot sounds like an explosion in my hand.

Behind me, the little girl screams.

I turn to find them standing not too far away, the woman still holding the boy, her hand wrapped tight around the little girl's arm. The penlight is still on, but the woman holds it at her side, shining at the ground.

I don't bother trying to comfort the children. That isn't my job. Just like I'm not about to explain myself.

I take a step forward.

The woman flinches, gripping the girl even tighter.

"I told you, I'm not going to hurt you. I didn't come here for you. I came here for him."

I don't bother pointing at the dead man behind me.

"Get in one the SUVs and drive away. You want to be far away for what happens next."

The woman stares at me. Her voice trembles when she speaks.

"What happens next?"

"Actually, on second thought, make sure you don't use either that SUV or that pickup."

I point at the closest ones.

The woman keeps staring at me.

"Why?"

I don't answer. I step past her and the children and head back inside the house. It takes me two minutes to do what I need to do, and then I'm back outside and it doesn't look like the woman and children have moved.

"Goddamn it"—exhaustion in my voice, irritation—"you should be gone by now."

The woman shakes her head slowly.

"There is nowhere for us to go."

Atticus in my ear: "You've got company."

I turn away, looking around the compound frantically.

"What do you mean?"

"Heading up the drive to the house. Two pickup trucks."

I sprint toward the open fence. Ernesto Diaz's compound is secluded, which was why I knew it would be possible for me to breach it. The closest town is five miles away. Now two pickup trucks are bouncing up the rugged drive.

Behind me, I hear the woman approaching.

I glance back at her and the children but don't say anything at first, my mind reeling with all the different possibilities. This would have been a whole lot easier had the woman and children not been here. Hell, this would have been a whole lot easier had I not tried to help Rosalina in Las Vegas. Every action has a subsequent reaction, and it was my trying to help Rosalina that started this whole damn mess.

Atticus says, "You need to make a decision."

"I can't just leave them here."

The woman looks at me strangely, thinking I'm speaking to her.

Atticus says, "You can't take them with you either."

I'm silent, which is all the answer Atticus needs. He hasn't known me very long, but still he understands my nature.

He sighs.

"Do what you must, but hurry."

The pickup trucks are closer now. They'll be here within thirty seconds. Time is running out, so I turn to the woman and the children and I tell them that they need to follow me.

The woman only stares at me. The boy starts sobbing.

I aim the gun at her, shout, "Now!" and that seems to do the trick.

We're in motion at once. I lead the woman and the children around the corner toward the trail that leads off the bluff and down to the beach. Out here the moon is bright, exposing the dead bodies.

The woman murmurs something that may be a prayer, and the children start sobbing again, and around the corner the sound of the two pickup trucks' engines growl as they reach the end of the drive and tear through the open gate.

I motion for the woman to start down the trail. It's narrow, and she needs to grip the girl even tighter to make sure she doesn't stray.

On the other side of the fence come voices as men pile out of the pickup trucks.

Atticus in my ear: "My eyes are on the men. Are you clear?"

Because this is part of the plan, I know that right now the three remaining quadcopters are hovering near the house, close enough that there won't be any trace of them come tomorrow.

I check to make sure the woman and children are making good progress, and then I start down the trail after them.

"Do it."

In my mind, I can see the men from the pickup trucks hurrying into the house. These men are better prepared, so they have flashlights which spotlight all the bodies littering the floor. Maybe a few have even found Ernesto Diaz. What any of those men thinks in this moment is impossible to say, but what's for certain is that they don't think long. I've set several charges around the house, as well as those I had previously set by the vehicles, and wherever Atticus is in the States, he presses several keys to send the signal that will detonate those charges.

As I hurry down the trail, following the woman and children, the world behind me explodes.

6

A minute later we're off the trail and on the beach, and the woman sets the boy down momentarily on the sand. But the boy doesn't like this, and grips fiercely at the woman's leg, clamps himself like he'll never let go.

The woman stares up the trail. A fireball had bloomed behind us as we hurried down to the beach, and now black smoke fills the night sky.

She says, stunned, "You blew it up."

I nod, surveying the empty beach.

"Why?"

I look at her but say nothing.

The woman stares back at me, completely stunned. In the moonlight I now see she has a pretty face but her hair is disheveled. She wears no jewelry—no earrings, no necklace, nothing on her fingers. Her place of employment—probably the only thing helping to makes ends meet—has just been destroyed and she's trying to wrap her mind around the reason why.

Both children hold onto her, each taking a leg. The girl has stopped sobbing—maybe she's run out of tears—but the boy still hasn't let up.

I motion past them, up the beach.

"Let's go."

The woman's eyes go hard.

"We are not going anywhere with you."

"Fine. I'd just wanted you away from the blast anyway. I don't give a shit where you go."

This isn't quite true—my heart aches at the thought of leaving the children behind—but the simple fact is I can't waste any time. Those reinforcements had come pretty quick, and there's no telling how long before more reinforcements arrive. I've used up almost all of my ammo, and besides, I no longer have Atticus in the sky keeping an eye out for surprises. Right now it's just me, and if I want to stay alive, I have to move.

I step past the woman and the children and start up the beach. I've only gone ten paces when the woman calls out.

"Wait."

I turn back.

The woman says, "Where are you going?"

"I'm leaving."

"But *where?*"

Desperation tinges her words. It's not complete desperation yet, but it's getting there.

"Up past those rocks and trees is a boat. I'm going to take that boat and head a couple miles up the coast."

I pause, waiting to see what she'll say to this.

She doesn't say anything and just stands there, watching me.

I say, "I don't have time to mess around. I need to leave."

"Can I—"

She pauses, swallows.

"Can *we* come with you?"

Atticus says, "I don't advise this, Holly."

"I'll call you back in a bit."

I pull the transmitter from my ear and flick the switch to turn it off.

"I can take you a couple miles up the coast, but that's it."

The woman stares at me. She doesn't speak. Doesn't look like she has any words yet. Maybe shock is starting to set in. If that's the case, there's no way I can leave her alone with the children.

"Hey."

I clap my hands to get her attention.

"Did you hear me?"

She blinks, looks at me again as if seeing me for the first time.

She asks, "How far up the coast?"

"A couple miles. But we need to leave now."

The woman still doesn't look convinced.

I say, "If you come with me now, I promise to keep you and the children safe."

It's not quite a hollow promise, but it's not exactly a sincere promise either. I don't want to leave the children here, but I also can't stay here much longer. If promising the woman their safety is what it takes to get them moving, then so be it.

The woman takes another moment to process this, then nods and looks down at the children. She scoops the boy up again, grips the girl's arm, and starts toward me.

I hold up a hand to stop her.

"What's your name?"

"My name?"

"Yes, your name."

She takes a moment to think about, like she doesn't remember her own name.

"Maria."

"And the children?"

"This is Jorge and Ana."

"Well, Maria, the boat we're about to get on is a boat you've never been on before. It's very important that you secure your-self and the children so that they don't fall out."

Her eyes widen at this.

"We might … fall out?"

"If you don't hold on, yes."

I turn and start toward the trees and rocks when Maria speaks again.

"What is your name?"

I shake my head.

"You don't want to know my name."

"Why not?"

"The less you know about me, the better."

I lead them past the private section of the beach, past the trees and rocks, and two minutes later we enter another small clearing. The Combat Rubber Raiding Craft is right where I left it.

The CRRC is a specially fabricated rubber inflatable boat often used by Navy SEALs and Marines. There's no outward protection, so it's mostly used for night missions.

I drag the CRRC to the edge of the water and help Maria and the children into the boat. Maria uses some of the ropes to strap herself and the children in.

I push the boat farther out until the water gets up to my waist, and then I crawl onto the boat and position myself near the back by the outboard motor.

"Hold on."

I pull the cord to get the motor going, and steer us out deep-er into the darkness.

7

I don't go too far out into the water, but just far enough where I can still see the coast. It's maybe five o'clock in the morning now, and the sky is starting to grow brighter minute by minute.

Maria sits at the front of the CRRC, holding both children. Neither child is sobbing now. They look too preoccupied trying to figure out what's happening and where they're going.

I have a GPS device that shows where we are in relation to the coast. I used it to find Ernesto Diaz's compound from the ocean, and I use it now to get us back to where I had launched. It's ten miles away, and takes nearly thirty minutes before I veer us inland.

I kill the engine right before we hit the sand. We come in smooth enough, just a slight jerk, and I immediately hop out to push the CRRC forward.

I help the children out, the girl first and then the boy, and then Maria climbs out of the boat onto the sand.

Keeping the CRRC where it is, I hurry over to the rocks several yards away. The gas canister is still there, along with a backpack. There are only two bottles of water in the backpack. My throat is parched, but I hurry back and offer the two bottles to the children.

The children don't want to take the bottles from me. Now that we're back on land, they look ready to start crying again.

"Are they thirsty?"

Maria takes the bottles from me and hands them to the children. She encourages them to drink. Jorge seems more eager than Ana, twisting the cap off and gurgling half the bottle before Maria tells him to slow down.

I return to the CRRC and slosh the gas in the canister all over the thing. I set the canister inside and open the backpack. The only other item is another block of plastic explosive. This one's charge is a bit different. I went old school and triggered it with an egg timer.

Back in the water now, I position the CRRC so its tip is pointed back out toward the ocean. Using bungee cords, I secure the outboard motor. I set the egg timer for sixty seconds, then think better of it and make it ninety seconds. I replace the timer and the block of plastic in the backpack, step behind the CRRC, pull the engine's cord, and let it tear away.

I'm worried that the lack of weight will cause the thing to tip up and flip over, but it travels at a good speed, heading farther and farther away from shore.

I stand in the water and count down the seconds in my head, visualizing that egg timer in my mind, and right when I get to ninety, there's a sudden *boom* and the CRRC erupts into flames. From this distance, it's hard to tell what's even on fire, but the gas works fast, devouring the manufactured rubber, and within a minute the whole thing disappears.

I turn back to find that Maria and the children haven't moved. Jorge now grips an empty bottle, but Ana doesn't look like she's even opened hers yet.

"Let's go."

For some reason I expect Maria to refuse again, or for the children to start sobbing, but they follow me without a word.

I lead them up a trail away from the beach onto another bluff. Unlike the bluff that Ernesto Diaz's house once occupied, this one is mostly deserted except for a brick building. I'm not sure *what* the brick building is for, exactly, but it's small and rundown and empty and sits a good quarter mile from the main road.

An El Camino is parked behind the building. I stole it late last night.

"Do you know what this building used to be?"

Maria nods slightly.

"Yes. Many years ago an old man opened it to rent surf-boards to tourists."

"What happened?"

"No tourist in their right mind wants to come here. The man lost all his money and died broke. And the building"—she shrugs—"nobody ever did anything with it."

The windows and door are boarded over. Graffiti stains the weathered outside.

I ask, "Where do you live?"

Maria stares at me like she doesn't understand the question.

"Where is your home?"

No response.

"Do you know where the closest town is?"

She frowns, looking out at the main road.

"A few miles south, I think."

"Do you know anybody who lives there? Friends, family?"

Maria looks down at the children. Jorge has dropped the plastic bottle somewhere along the way, but Ana still grips the unopened bottle tightly in her hand. Both children watch me with a mixture of fear and hatred.

"Believe it or not, Maria, I'm trying to help you. What I did tonight ... I can't explain why I did it other than I had no choice."

Maria looks at me again, her eyes now hardened into a glare. "You killed Ernesto."

"Yes."

"You killed all those men."

"Yes."

"Why?"

The children watch me, wanting to know the same question their nanny just asked, and it causes me to pause.

"Are these Javier Diaz's children?"

Maria nods slightly, unsure the purpose of the question.

"Where is the children's mother?"

Maria shrugs.

"She travels."

"Do the children speak English?"

"No."

I speak in English.

"I killed their father because he threatened my family, and I knew the only way to keep my family safe was to come here and kill their grandfather."

I glance at the children to see whether they understood any of that, but they only stare back at me with a kind of hollow listlessness that pierces my heart.

"Tonight I intended to kill everybody at that compound. Everybody. But I couldn't"—I shake my head—"I wasn't about to kill them. And as you're their nanny, I needed to get you out too. Do you understand?"

Maria just stares at me.

"Do you understand?"

She blinks, nods slowly.

"I have to leave now. I've brought you much farther than I probably should have. But I'm hoping you can take care of these children a little bit longer. Can you do that?"

"You promised to keep us safe."

"I brought you up the coast. There's nothing more I can do."

I look at the children one last time. I want to say something to them, apologize somehow, ask them for forgiveness, but they will never understand why I did what I did tonight, nor will they ever forgive me. To them, I am a monster. The boogeyman. They'll never forget what happened tonight. They'll never forget I was the one who killed their grandfather.

Without a word, I leave them by the deserted building. I climb into the El Camino, hotwire it once again, and then steer past them down the dirt drive toward the main road. As I drive past, I see Ana sobbing again. Part of me wants to stop, tell them to get in the car, and that I'll drop them off at the nearest town. It's the least I can do, isn't it? After everything I've done—all the terrible things they've witnessed tonight because of me—the least I can do is not leave them here in the middle of nowhere.

A payphone stands near the end of the drive, rundown just like the building behind me. It doesn't look like it works, but maybe it does. I could turn the car around, pick up Maria and the children, and drop them off here. At least then Maria could call somebody to come help them. Some person who could add some certainty to the children's already haphazard lives.

After a moment of hesitation, I make a left onto the main road and drive north.

8

I head up the coast, using the main road most of the way. The sun is starting to rise, the sky getting even brighter. I keep checking the rearview mirror, but nobody seems to be following me. In fact, the highway is mostly deserted this early in the morning.

When I'm several miles away from my next stop, I dig the transmitter out of my pocket, flick the tiny switch on the side, and put it in my ear.

"Atticus."

Silence.

I give it a couple seconds before trying again.

"Atticus, are you there?"

More silence. It lasts maybe ten seconds, and then there's a crackle of static followed by a tired sigh.

"What did you do with them?"

Straight to the point—that seems to be Atticus's style, at least from what I've been able to gather in the limited time I've known him.

"Relax. Everything's okay."

Another sigh.

"Holly—"

"I left them behind, okay? I took them up the coast and then I left them behind."

"You're saying they accompanied you in the CRRC?"

"Yes."

"That was very unwise, Holly."

"The craft's been destroyed."

"And? The idea was you would disappear. Yes, you may have destroyed the CRRC, but that doesn't matter because now there are witnesses."

"The woman's not going to say anything."

"How do you know?"

"I saved her life."

"Are you even listening to yourself?"

"What did you want me to do, Atticus? Kill the woman and the children? Just put a bullet between their eyes and move on? Is that what you would have done?"

Atticus is silent for a moment. I can't tell whether it's because he's actually considering the questions or giving me the extra moment to vent.

He says, "You could have left them behind."

"And then what would have happened to them? More narcos would have shown up, and God only knows what they would have done to the woman and children."

"Where did you leave them?"

Now it's my turn to be silent.

Atticus says, "Based on where you launched the CRRC, I'm guessing that's where you left them. And if that's the case, you essentially left them in the middle of nowhere."

I smack the steering wheel with my fist.

"Goddamn it, Atticus, what would you have had me do? I couldn't leave them behind, and I couldn't bring them with me. So yes, I left them in the middle of goddamn nowhere. Was it the most ideal situation to leave them in? No, but it was my only choice."

The highway stretches out ahead of me. A town stands off in the distance, several miles away. I check the rearview mirror once again to make sure nobody's behind me before I turn off into a field.

Atticus says, "Where are you now?"

"I'm about ready to make the switch."

"Very good. When do you anticipate you'll cross the border?"

"It's, what, a twelve-hour drive from Culiacán? I plan to head straight out. I'm going to stop by my room first and take a quick shower. I got some blood in my hair that didn't come out in the ocean. My luck, the border guards will notice it, so I might as well cross the border looking presentable. As we discussed, I'll purchase a burner phone and call you and set up a time and place to meet James."

"James is already on the road. He has everything you'll need. A new ID, new social security card, new bank card, new credit cards, everything. We've liquated all your accounts, paid off all your debts."

I say, "Goodbye, Holly Lin. What is my new name, anyway?"

There's a smile in Atticus's voice when he answers.

"Guess you'll just have to wait and see."

"I still think it's bullshit I'm not able to pick my own name. Ever since I was a little girl I've wanted to change my name to Madonna."

"Good thing the choice isn't up to you."

The car bounces up and down over the rugged terrain. I'm moving at a slow enough clip that not too large of a dust cloud spreads.

"Thank you, Atticus."

"Of course, Holly. Good luck."

I pluck the transmitter out of my ear and flick the switch to turn it off. I toss it on the seat beside me as I steer the El Camino over a rise and down into a ditch. The dirt bike is still where I left it. I park the car beside it, kill the engine, and step out.

I strip out of my clothes, put on new ones, and throw the dirty clothes into the car.

In the back of the El Camino is another plastic container of gas. I douse the car, including the interior, and light a match and throw the match onto the driver's seat.

Wearing a new pair of gloves, I climb onto the dirt bike, start the engine, and drive back up the incline out of the ditch.

I pause at the top of the rise to glance back down at the El Camino. The fire is going strong. The car will be found at some point, but by then all trace evidence—including my clothes and the transmitter—will have long been destroyed. Maybe a connection will be made to Ernesto Diaz, but most likely not. The nice thing about committing crime in Mexico is that it happens all the time. It's almost impossible to connect dots when there are an infinite number of dots.

The plan now is to ride to the next town. I'll abandon the dirt bike and steal another car and drive that another twenty miles up the highway to the hotel I'd checked in two days ago. It's not a nice hotel, but it's not a shitty one either. It's an anonymous hotel, one of hundreds. Assuming it hasn't been stolen, my car is parked in the lot. I'll drive north and cross the border and meet James, who has my new ID and other essentials to start a new life.

Holly Lin will cease to exist.

About time.

9

I park ten blocks away from the hotel. I'm wearing gloves, but I do my best to wipe the car down anyway—the steering wheel and gearshift and door—though part of me knows it won't matter. The car will either get stolen again or it will remain abandoned for days and then stripped for parts. Doubtful the owner will ever find it. The old Holly Lin would worry about such things—maybe the owner needs the car for work, to get groceries—but the new Holly Lin (the Holly Lin that will soon no longer exist) has become much more selfish.

It's early morning and the sun is rising, the city starting to wake up and go about its day.

I keep my head down the whole way to the hotel, trying to remain as inconspicuous as possible while also keeping an eye out for any danger.

I note the car I drove into Mexico is still in its spot. It's not stolen—Atticus had arranged it for me, with clean tags and registration—but once I drive it back into the States it will be swapped with the car James is currently driving toward the border. He'll take it and probably have it demolished. Not that it's been used in any crime, but better safe than sorry.

The Do Not Disturb sign is still on my door. Good. It's been that way the past two days. I'm sure the cleaning people love the fact they get to skip this room.

I unlock the door and enter quietly, my gun now held at the ready. I check the bathroom, then check the window overlooking the parking lot to make sure it hasn't been tampered with. When I'm confident everything is secure, I chain the door, set the gun aside, and begin to strip out of my clothes.

I keep the gun in the bathroom while I take a shower. The water is warm and pulsing and I'm so exhausted I could fall asleep under the spray, but I stay focused, washing my skin and hair clean, then step out of the shower, steam thick in the air, and wipe at the mirror to look at myself.

Less than a week ago I had come face to face with a man who I had believed was dead. Zane, my boyfriend, my lover, the man who I thought my father had killed, had turned out to be a complete and utter asshole. He had taken David and Casey Hadden because I had messed up his operation and he wanted a flash drive, and I had to go to some pretty extreme lengths to retrieve that flash drive. Zane, unsurprisingly, was planning to kill the kids anyway, but I had managed to kill him. Not before he kicked the shit out of me first, which explained the bruising on my face and the broken rib. The rib will heal eventually, as will the bruises on my face. If I'm lucky there won't be any scars, and if there are scars, then so be it. They won't be my first, and they most certainly won't be my last.

I dry off and put on shorts and a T-shirt and light hoodie, socks and sneakers. Atticus had given me a fake ID for entering the country. My alias has everything: social media profiles, a job history, credit history, even transcripts from school. My name is Samantha Lu. I'm a graduate student on vacation using my time off to study the Mexican culture or some such bullshit.

Once I'm dressed, I wipe down the room, even though, again, I doubt anything will come of it. I'm paid up for two more days, and I plan to keep the DO NOT DISTURB sign on the door. I'll leave the keys on the bed along with a nice tip. If anything else, the cleaning people will be happy.

I keep my gun secured to the back waistband of my shorts. I throw the backpack over my shoulder and exit the room, looking up and down the hallway. Nobody around except the cleaning cart propping a door open several rooms away.

The car outside is a Honda Civic, maybe ten years old. Completely anonymous. When I had originally crossed the border, the CRRC was hidden in the trunk along with a suitcase. The weapons I had—the two pistols and garrote and knife—were hidden underneath the car. There hadn't been much concern about being stopped and searched on my way into the country—nobody gives a shit what goes into Mexico—and I had been waved through with barely even a glance.

Now I know leaving Mexico will be a piece of cake. Even if they search the Civic from top to bottom, nothing will be found. Most likely, I'll just be waved through like before. I'll meet up with James, swap out the cars, get my new identity, and start my new life.

I keep thinking about Maria and the children. The girl holding that water bottle, having not even cracked the cap yet.

For all I know, they're still at the place I left them. Or maybe they've walked to the closest town. Or maybe somebody came and picked them up and gave them a ride home.

Or maybe somebody came and raped them, left them beaten and battered by that abandoned building to bake as the sun rose higher and higher in the pale sky.

You promised to keep us safe.

I close my eyes. Take a deep breath.

The woman and the children are fine. They're not my concern, anyway. I did all I could for them.

I put the Civic in gear. I go two blocks when I spot the kid from the other day. He's an early riser, apparently, already on the street corner hocking his fireworks.

I stop the car, power down the passenger side window.

"Hey, kid."

He smiles at me, already a natural salesman as he runs through his pitch.

"Good morning, *senorita*. Would you like to buy some fireworks?"

"Not today. But those firecrackers you sold me? They came in handy."

I toss him some pesos and power back up the window and keep driving down the street.

A stop sign looms at the corner. I pause for traffic, and as I wait there I glance at the rearview mirror and see the kid still on the sidewalk with his fireworks. He can't be more than thirteen years old, much older than Jorge and Ana, much older than even David and Casey Hadden. For the moment I wonder if the kid has a loving family, whether his parents treat him right, and what inspires him to get up so early every morning to sell fireworks on the street.

I close my eyes and shake my head.

"Goddamn it."

Twisting the steering wheel, I pull a U-turn and head back the way I came.

10

I spot the smoke a quarter mile away.

It's late morning now, forty-five minutes since I'd pulled that uey, and the main road has been busy except for this deserted patch. A few cars ahead of me, a few passing me by, and a quarter mile away I spot the smoke and something with sharp claws grips my heart.

It could be nothing, of course, but deep down I know that's not true. My foot grows heavy on the gas pedal, pushing the Civic faster. Very soon that quarter mile turns into a tenth of a mile and I spot the brick building off the main road, that deserted relic, and as I had guessed the smoke is coming from there.

I take the turn hard and accelerate down the dirt road. Because of my speed, the rutted drive causes the Civic to bounce and jump all over the place. I grip the steering wheel tight, trying to keep the car on the drive, and when I reach the building I slam on the brakes and throw open my door.

A dust cloud hangs in the air behind me, connecting the Civic to the main road. Not very inconspicuous, but I don't care as I hurry around the building, calling for Maria and the children.

The door at the back of the building stands open. It looks like someone had taken a crowbar to it. The edges are ragged and blistered.

Black smoke pours out of the doorway.

I sprint toward the edge of the bluff to check the beach below, hoping maybe Maria and the children ventured back down there for some reason.

Empty.

I return to the building and the black billowing smoke. I stare into the smoke but can't spot any flames.

How much time has passed since I left Maria and the children here? Three hours? Four? If it weren't for the smoke, I'd think they had walked on to the next town over. But I hadn't seen Maria or the children anywhere as I'd driven through that town. There's a chance they may have gone south, toward whatever town lay in that direction, but still, what explains the smoke?

Leave. That's what part of me thinks. Just get back in the Civic and head north. Cross the border in Nogales and meet up with James and start my new life. That's the plan, after all. That's the *end* of the plan, really, the thing that will put all of this to rest. I can get on with a normal life, or as much of a normal life as somebody in my situation can. Find a job. Meet a guy. Get married. Have children. That's what you're supposed to do with your life, right?

I pinch the neck of my T-shirt and pull it up to my nose. I take in one large gulp of air and cup the T-shirt to my nose and run into the smoke.

For the first couple feet the smoke is thick and dense. But as I move deeper, cautiously leading with my right foot so I don't run into anything, the smoke starts to clear.

The building itself is all but deserted. No forgotten chairs or table. Nothing.

Which makes it easy to spot the bodies.

They lie in the corner. The woman in the middle. The children flanking her on each side.

I don't bother rushing forward. I know it won't make any difference. The bodies are no longer on fire. Their clothes and flesh have become charred. Now all that keeps going is the smoke. There's nothing at all for me to do, so I duck back outside.

Stumbling several paces away from the building, I take in the fresh air, drawing in large gulps. My heart is pounding. Blood screams in my ears. It's almost enough that I don't hear the approaching vehicle at first. It's only after a couple seconds I realize there's something wrong and turn to see the police car heading my way.

My hand automatically reaches for the gun pressing against the small of my back.

But no, I can't have a shootout with the police. Killing Ernesto Diaz and his guards was one thing, but killing police is a whole different thing.

The car is almost here. I step toward the building, enough so that my view of the car is blocked, and I pull the gun out and raise it above my head and throw it as hard as I can toward the bluff. There isn't much of a beach, so hopefully it drops into the water. And hopefully, fingers crossed, the surf doesn't push the gun back toward shore. Because once the cops get here and see what's happened, they're going to search the area, and the last thing I want them to find is a gun with my fingerprints on it.

On the other side of the building the car has come to a halt. I hear doors opening and slamming shut.

I stick my finger back deep in my throat. I've only ever done this once before, and even then it didn't really work right, and I realize there isn't much in my stomach now but that shouldn't matter.

I start gagging, picturing vomit, forcing myself to remember what it smells like, and it's enough to do the trick.

I fall to my knees right as I throw up.

Right as the policemen hurry around the building and shout at me in Spanish to put my hands on top of my head.

Part II

THE BEACON

11

By the time they arrived at the scene, the smoke had cleared and there were now five police cars parked around the brick building, as well as a dark blue Honda Civic.

Ramon parked the pickup truck, killed the engine, and then reached for his mask. He only paused when he noticed Carlos grinning at him.

Ramon said, "What?"

Carlos adjusted his sunglasses.

"Nothing. I think it's cute."

Ramon held the mask for a beat, suddenly embarrassed.

Carlos said, "I'm just busting your balls. You have a young wife and baby at home. I would wear a mask too. But I'm an old man whose wife is gone and whose children have moved out. I have nobody to protect."

Without another word Carlos stepped out and met up with one of the officers coming their way. That officer also wore a mask. The fact was, over half the officers at the scene had masks covering their faces. Ramon had always thought it silly, though he understood the reasoning behind it. At the time he hadn't had a wife and daughter. Now he did, and the last thing he wanted to do was put them in danger.

He hurriedly secured the mask over his nose and lower half of his face and stepped out of the pickup truck. He met up with Carlos and the other officer as the officer pointed at the brick building.

"Three bodies inside, what look to be two children and one adult."

Carlos said, "Where's the woman?"

The officer stepped a few paces past them to point toward the building. Ramon and Carlos shuffled closer to the officer to see a young woman sitting on a rock by the bluff. Two other officers stood near her.

"She was throwing up when we arrived."

Carlos said, "She have identification?"

The officer nodded eagerly, pinching a notepad from his shirt pocket and paging through.

"Samantha Lu. Twenty-seven years old. A graduate student from California."

"What is she doing here?"

"Vacation."

"Is she with friends?"

"No."

Ramon and Carlos traded glances.

Ramon said, "Did she say what made her decide to travel through Sinaloa by herself?"

"She said she needed to get away for a while. There's bruising on her face."

Carlos said, "What do you mean, bruising?"

"Bruising. Like somebody beat her up."

"Does the bruising look recent?"

"I don't know. Maybe a week or so."

"Did you ask her about it?"

"No. At the time I didn't think it was relevant."

Ramon and Carlos traded another glance.

The officer said, "It didn't happen here, if that's what you're thinking. I asked her if she'd been mugged or attacked since being in the country. She said no."

Ramon said, "Even if she had been, there's a chance she may not have told you the truth."

Carlos said, "Where is she staying?"

The officer named a hotel in Culiacán.

"We contacted the manager and he confirmed she has a room there for the next two days."

Ramon said, "What brought her this way?"

"She said she was driving south and noticed the smoke. She said she was worried so she pulled in to make sure nobody was hurt."

Carlos said, "You arrived not too long after she did?"

"Yes. Maybe only minutes after."

"She saw the bodies?"

"We think so. She was definitely inside the building. We know she saw something, though we're not sure if she saw the bodies because of the smoke. But she did throw up."

Ramon and Carlos looked at each other again.

Carlos asked him, "What do you think?"

Ramon said, "It's probably nothing, but I'll speak to her. First let's check inside."

They waved off the officer's offer to lead them into the building and entered to find three other officers standing around the charred bodies. They were young, probably at their first murder scene. One of them had his phone out to take pictures.

Carlos cleared his throat.

The three officers froze, turned to look at them. The one taking pictures quickly pocketed the phone, his face burning.

Carlos said, "Get the fuck out of here."

The officers hustled outside.

Ramon and Carlos approached the charred bodies. Just as the officer outside had said, two children and an adult.

Ramon glanced at Carlos.

"Do you think it's her?"

"After what happened last night at the Diaz compound, it has to be."

"But how would they have even gotten here? The Diaz compound is at least ten miles away."

Carlos's only answer was a slight shake of his head.

They were silent for a long moment, staring down at the bodies, when footsteps crunched the dirt behind them. They turned to find the officer who had spoken to them outside standing in the doorway.

"Another car just arrived."

Carlos said, "Do you know who it is?"

"I believe it is Comandante Espinoza."

Ramon closed his eyes, muttered a curse.

Carlos thanked the officer and turned to Ramon.

"He shouldn't be here."

"I know."

"We told him he shouldn't come."

"I know."

Before anything else could be said, their commanding officer filled the doorway. Geraldo Espinoza was in his late-fifties but looked much older. He wore dress pants and a dress shirt, typical office attire. He had dark close-cropped hair sprinkled with gray, a thin goatee, and glasses perched on his weathered face. Normally he looked calm, composed, completely in control, but now it looked like he was about to fall apart.

Carlos stepped forward, blocking the older man's view of the bodies.

"You don't want to see her. Not like this."

The desperation on the comandante's face was so palpable at that moment Ramon could feel it.

"Can you even tell—"

Carlos shook his head.

"No."

"Are you sure?"

"The bodies are too badly burned. They're just"—he hesitated, clearing his throat—"remains at this point."

The comandante took another unsteady step into the room.

"I need to see her."

Carlos shook his head again.

"Sir—"

"*I need to see her, goddamn it.*"

Ramon and Carlos didn't need to exchange glances this time to know what the other was thinking. They both stepped out of the comandante's way. The older man went forward. But he stopped short before dropping down next to the bodies as protocol kicked in. He stepped back, his body trembling, though strangely there were no tears in his eyes when he turned back to them.

"I shouldn't be here."

Saying it as if the thought had just occurred to him.

Ramon and Carlos said nothing.

The comandante nodded, as if just now hearing his own words.

"I shouldn't have come. I know I shouldn't have come, but I—"

His voice cracked, and he shook his head.

"We're going to find the son of a bitch and we're going to make him pay."

Ramon and Carlos only nodded.

The older man looked down at the bodies one last time before he turned and hurried outside.

For a moment, there was complete silence in the cramped building. The smoke may have cleared, but the stench of burned flesh still hung heavy in the air. Even the mask covering

Ramon's nose did little to slow the stink. Ramon didn't know about Carlos, but it was causing his stomach to churn.

He said, "Let's get some fresh air."

They walked outside. Comandante Espinoza had returned to his car, but he hadn't gotten back into it yet. He stood beside it, now smoking a cigarette, all the other officers avoiding him.

Carlos asked, "Remember the payphone on the way in?"

"What about it?"

"I'm going to see if any of these officers were smart enough to check it out."

"You think he would have used it?"

"Not the Devil, no. But maybe she did."

The Devil. Ramon hated the name given to the killer, but it was the one the newspapers had given him and it had stuck ever since.

Ramon said, "We don't even know if it's a she in there. We don't even know if those bodies are related to the others."

Carlos sighed.

"I think at this point it's safe to assume we know who those bodies are and who killed them."

"Something about it doesn't feel right."

"All of it doesn't feel right. Now I'm going to check on the payphone. Why don't you talk to the woman and see if there's anything one of the officers may have missed."

"And then what should I do with her?"

"Cut her loose."

12

I can't see the gun.

Not from where I am at least, sitting here on this rock, my back to the building and all the police.

I can see the ocean but I can't see the beach down below, and it's because of that I can't see the gun.

I mean, yes, I don't *want* to see the gun. If I threw it hard enough, it should have splashed down into the water. If luck is on my side, the tide would have taken the gun out far enough where it would have sunk to the bottom.

But if luck *isn't* on my side—if I didn't throw the gun out far enough or the tide somehow washed it back onto shore—then I'm screwed.

There's no telling how long they intend to keep me here. I've given them my information, answered questions, played the part of a worried, frantic tourist the best I could, but maybe it wasn't enough. Because they told me I couldn't leave yet, that I had to wait, and just what the hell am I waiting for? To give them time to canvas the area? So that somebody can make their way down to the beach and maybe stumble across the gun I'd thrown. If it hasn't touched water, there's a good chance my prints will still be on it. And if it did manage to get in the water ... would that be enough to scrub my prints? Even if they find the gun, there's a good chance they won't immediately link it to me, but still I don't want it to get to that point.

So I'm sitting on the rock, staring at the edge of the bluff, trying to spot the gun, when I hear footsteps approaching from behind.

A man clears his throat and speaks accented English.

"Miss Lu?"

I twist to look back over my shoulder. A man wearing one of those masks stands several yards away. His eyes are dark. He's not wearing a uniform like the others—he has on khakis and a blue polo shirt—but it's clear he's a cop.

"My name is Ramon. I would like to ask you a couple questions."

He motions at the two officers watching over me, and the two officers head back to the others without a word.

Ramon says, "What state?"

"I'm sorry?"

"You are from America, yes? What state are you from?"

"California."

"Where in California?"

"San Diego. I go to school there."

Is the man trying to trip me up? It's hard to say. These questions can simply be an icebreaker of sorts before he starts to really dig in. I gave the other officers my basic information—I'd memorized the entire cover, even the insubstantial bullshit like who I went to prom with in high school and the name of my favorite professor—and those officers no doubt shared that information with Ramon.

Speaking of which ...

"Are you a detective?"

"In a way. I am a crime scene investigator."

"Am I free to leave?"

"Not yet. I need to ask you a couple more questions."

"Like what?"

"Like what happened to your face."

Direct. I like it.

I look away from him for a couple seconds, showing my irritation but also my discomfort. Because this, too, is part of my cover story. Not added to the Samantha Lu cover that Atticus gave me, but my own cover story because I always knew there was a chance it would come up.

"I'd rather not talk about it."

Ramon is quiet for a beat.

"I understand."

"It's just"—I shake my head—"I don't want to talk about him."

Ramon says nothing.

I give it another couple seconds, staring past the man, before I look back up at him. And now, to add the finishing touch, a tear rolls down my cheek.

"My boyfriend did it, okay?"

This isn't technically a lie. Zane is responsible for what happened to my face, not to mention my broken rib. The only thing is, of course, for two years I had believed Zane was dead, killed by my father, until he showed up recently to kidnap the Hadden children.

I sigh, shake my head again.

"He sometimes got jealous, but he never did anything about it other than shout at me. Like, I never even flirted with other guys, but one night he thought I had hooked up with this guy at a bar and then he ... well, he did this."

I don't bother pointing at my face to indicate what *this* is. I let the bruises speak for themselves.

Ramon asks, "Where is your boyfriend now?"

If we're talking about Zane, the answer is dead. But if we're talking about Samantha Lu's boyfriend …

"I don't know, and I don't care. I left him. I hope I never see him again. I should have"—I hitch my voice for dramatic effect—"I know I should have pressed charges but I … I just didn't, okay? I know it was stupid, but I didn't feel like dealing with it. And so I just wanted to get away. That's why I got in the car and drove south. I didn't even realize I was planning to come to Mexico until I'd crossed the border."

Ramon is silent again. He glances out toward the ocean, then back toward the building and the crowd of police, before turning back to me.

"What brought you out here?"

"I told you, I didn't plan on coming to Mexico. I had to get away from—"

"No. I mean what brought you out *here*, to this specific location?"

He gestures at the building as if his words aren't specific enough. Like he thinks I'm not focused right now. Which is good. That means my act is working.

"I saw smoke."

"You saw smoke."

"Yes. From the road. It seemed … wrong. Like it wasn't supposed to be there."

"So you turned off the highway."

"Yes."

"What did you intend to do once you found the source of the smoke?"

"You mean like the fire? I don't know. Probably call 911. Though, like, is 911 even the emergency number down here? I guess first I just wanted to make sure nothing was wrong. Like, maybe it was some people burning trash or something. But then I saw the building was on fire and I just—"

I let it hang there, closing my eyes and shaking my head.

Ramon says, "Why did you go inside?"

"I don't know. It was stupid of me, I admit that, but at the moment I worried that maybe somebody was inside. I mean, there wasn't any fire at that point, it was just smoke, so I went inside and—"

I shake my head again, forcing pain into my face at the mere memory.

"It was awful. I mean ... what *happened*?"

"That's something we're still investigating."

He doesn't say anything else, just stands there staring at me with his greenish gray eyes. I'm pretty good when it comes to staring contests, but today is not a day when I want to challenge this man.

I look away from Ramon, back toward the building.

"Am I in some kind of trouble?"

"Why would you be in trouble?"

"The other officers told me I had to wait here. They said I couldn't leave. I'll be honest—I'm scared."

"What is there to be scared about?"

Now it's my turn—Samantha Lu's turn, really—to not answer.

Ramon says, "You no doubt hear stories about police corruption here in Mexico. I am not going to lie to you and say it does not exist, but you have nothing to worry about."

"Why are you wearing a mask?"

I know the answer, but am curious to hear Ramon's response.

He says, "It is to protect myself and my family."

"I noticed some other officers wearing masks too. Who do you need to protect yourselves from?"

He pauses a beat, as if giving it much thought, before answering.

"Mexico is not always safe for law enforcement."

I say, "Because of the cartels?"

Ramon offers up a half nod.

Now I play the part of a scared-out-of-her-mind tourist.

"Jesus Christ, I'm not wearing a mask! Do I need to be worried about anything?"

He shakes his head but says nothing.

I take a breath, let the fear slowly drain from my face.

"Then … am I free to leave?"

"Not quite yet. First, was there anything you noticed when you drove up to the building?"

"Such as what?"

"Such as anything out of the ordinary."

I give it a couple seconds before shaking my head.

"I'm sorry, nothing comes to mind."

"That's okay. I am sorry we kept you so long."

I wait a moment in case he has anything else to say, and when he doesn't, I stand up from the rock. I don't start walking toward the building and the Civic, though. Instead, I stare out at the ocean.

"It's such a beautiful view."

Ramon says nothing to this.

I take a couple steps forward.

Uneasiness enters Ramon's voice.

"What are you doing?"

I stand on the very edge of the bluff to look out over the ocean. And down at the beach. Nothing glints in the sunlight, so hopefully the gun did hit the water when I threw it.

I turn back and force a smile.

"Like I said, it's a beautiful view."

Ramon leads me back to the building without a word. He collects my ID from one of the officers and returns it to me. Among the officers milling around is an older man, who looks to be in his late-fifties. He stands by a sedan and smokes but doesn't say anything. He gives me a brief look before turning away and lighting another cigarette.

Ramon says, "Take care of yourself, Miss Lu. Be safe."

I just nod and start toward the Civic. As I do, another older man leaning against a pickup truck closes his phone and shouts excitedly at Ramon.

"My contact at the phone company confirmed a call was placed on the payphone three hours ago."

Ramon says, "To where?"

"A motel."

They speak Spanish but I'm able to understand them without any trouble. I don't want to be too obvious that I'm eavesdropping, of course, so I slide in behind the Civic's steering wheel and start the engine.

Ramon and the man with the cell phone climb into the pickup truck and seconds later they're speeding back up the dirt drive, disappearing into the dust cloud.

I throw the Civic into gear but don't drive as fast as the truck ahead of me, despite the fact I don't want to miss where it turns. There's a chance it may be gone by the time I make it through the dust cloud, and I want to know whether it turns left or right onto the road. Because despite the fact I should know better—despite the fact I should drive straight toward Nogales to cross over the border—I need to know where these men are going. I need to know who Maria called this morning, hours before she was burned to death.

13

The Paraíso Motel was located near the outskirts of Culiacán. It was two stories tall, painted a faded lime green, and looked as if its neon sign announcing the motel's name hadn't been updated in thirty years.

A police car was already parked out front when Ramon and Carlos arrived. The two officers inside didn't notice them as they walked up to the car from behind.

Carlos slammed his hand down on the car's roof, causing both officers inside to jump.

He said, "What the hell are you doing?"

The officers quickly collected themselves, and the driver said, "Very sorry, sir. We were told to wait outside."

"So there's nobody around back?"

Both officers said nothing, only traded nervous glances.

Carlos gritted his teeth.

"Somebody should be covering the back."

The two officers didn't move, too unsure what to do next.

Carlos said, "Goddamn it, get out of the car!"

The officers scrambled out of the car. One of them hurried

around to cover the back of the motel while the other lingered by the car.

Carlos told the officer, "Cover the front and don't fuck it up."

The officer nodded quickly.

Ramon surveyed the street. It was quiet for this time of morning, only a few cars coming and going. A skinny woman stood near the corner, leaning against a building. She was watching them, but she didn't look like somebody they should be worried about. In fact, even from this distance, it was clear she was a prostitute.

Carlos tapped him on the arm.

"Let's go."

They climbed the front steps and entered a dank lobby. Two box fans ran on either end of the lobby, pushing the warm air together into a vortex of humidity. The lobby was deserted save for a kid no older than nineteen sitting on a stool behind the counter. The kid stared down at his cell phone, his thumbs rapidly punching the screen. He only paused and looked up when Carlos smacked the bell on the counter.

"Help you?"

Carlos took the lead, flashing his badge at the clerk.

"A call was made to this motel at 3:47 this morning. We need to know who took the call and where the call was sent."

The kid stared at them, his eyes shifting from Carlos to Ramon and back to Carlos.

"Huh?"

Carlos repeated himself, talking slowly this time, but the kid still didn't seem to get it.

He said, "Maybe you should talk to the manager."

Ramon said, "Where is the manager?"

"He's not here right now."

"When will he be back?"

The kid shrugged.

"Don't know. He doesn't come in much."

Carlos reached forward, grabbed the back of the kid's neck, and slammed his face down on the counter. Blood squirted from his nose.

"Say that again?"

The kid whimpered, "What do you want from me, man? I don't know what you're talking about!"

"Somebody called this piece of shit motel at 3:47 this morning. We need to know who took the call."

"I don't know! I wasn't here! I wasn't here!"

"Who, then? Who was here?"

The kid said nothing.

Carlos grabbed the kid's neck again.

The kid cried out.

"It wasn't me!"

"We know that, asshole. You keep saying that. Who was here?"

"If I tell you, will you let me go?"

"That depends on how good your answer is."

"I don't want to go to jail."

"Why would you go to jail?"

"I don't know! Why won't you let me go?"

Carlos took his hand away from the kid's neck. The kid didn't move for a couple seconds, as if he thought it was some kind of trick.

Ramon said, "This is important. We need to know about the call that came in this morning at 3:47."

The kid touched his nose gingerly.

"Man, I think you broke my *nose*."

Ramon said, "Tell us about the call."

"I wasn't working. I got here two hours ago."

Carlos said, "Who did you relieve?"

"That's the thing. I'm not entirely sure."

"What does that mean?"

"When I got here nobody was at the counter."

"Who was scheduled to be here?"

The kid looked again from Carlos to Ramon and back to Carlos.

"He's not going to get in trouble, is he? He's a good guy."

Carlos leaned forward. His body language made it clear he had no problem slamming the kid's face against the counter again.

"Who's a good guy?"

14

A minute after Ramon and his partner enter the motel, the girl detaches herself from the side of the building at the corner and starts to make her way up the sidewalk.

She takes her time, repeatedly looking back over her shoulder like she's being followed. The officer standing in front of the motel sees her coming but doesn't seem to care. Then the girl, looking back over her shoulder one last time, steels herself and approaches the officer.

I can't hear what she says to him, not from where I am in the Civic parked a block away, but it looks like she's desperate as she motions frantically at the motel. She has something in her hand, I realize, and she tries to give it to the officer who shakes his head and waves her off. He's not being very patient with her, and it only takes a couple more seconds before he snatches whatever it is from the girl's hand, crumples it, and tosses it past her into the street. The girl screeches, staring at the crumpled thing as if it were her own child. She turns back to the officer, steeling herself even more, and it's clear that she intends to do something stupid—strike the officer, maybe, or spit at him—

but the officer isn't having any of it. He rests his hand on his holstered gun without a word, but the action speaks volumes. The girl hurriedly retrieves the crumpled object from the street and starts back down the sidewalk. She's facing me now, so I can see the tears streaming down her face, and she takes the crumpled object and tries to uncrumple it the best she can, but clearly the damage has been done.

I slip from the Civic and cross the street. The girl's desperation has piqued my interest.

The girl is so shaken up that she doesn't even see me until I'm a few feet away.

"Are you okay?"

The girl jumps, startled. She wipes at her eyes. She tries to speak but the words don't come and so she just shakes her head.

We're at the end of the block. I've stationed myself behind the corner of a building so the officer down by the motel can't see me.

"May I see that?"

The girl holds the crumpled thing in her hands. It's clear it's a photograph. Despite this, I can't see it from how she's holding it, so I start to reach for it.

The girl shakes her head, snatches the photograph to her chest.

"It's okay. I'm not going to make it worse. I just want to look."

The girl still doesn't look convinced. She's in her early twenties, but she looks maybe ten years older. Thin and frail, she doesn't even bother trying to hide the needle marks. Instantly I'm reminded of Rosalina and all the other girls who had been locked up at the ranch outside of Las Vegas. This girl is also a prostitute.

I keep my hand out, welcoming.

"Please, let me take a look."

Up the sidewalk, Ramon and his partner emerge from the motel. Ramon's partner says something quickly to the officer, who nods, and then Ramon and his partner climb back into their pickup truck and drive away. The officer climbs into his car a couple seconds later and drives around to the back of the motel, where he'll no doubt pick up his partner.

It all happens within a matter of seconds, and while I watch them I'm also aware of somebody stationed up the block across the street. Another young girl, only this one doesn't look like a prostitute. She has a cell phone raised up to her head, but it's not to her ear. It's clear even from this distance that she's taking pictures.

Ramon and his partner have turned the corner two blocks up. I should be in the Civic right now, following them, but it's at that moment the girl decides to trust me enough to place the crumpled photograph in my hand.

"My sister."

The girl's voice is barely a whisper.

The photograph shows a girl about the same age as the one standing right here in front of me. In fact, they look almost like twins, though the one in the picture isn't quite as frail. She wears short shorts and a halter-top that exposes her thin belly. She's alone and smiling at the camera, a real sincere smile. The lighting was bad enough that the camera needed a flash, which illuminates her belly ring.

"Where is she?"

The girl shrugs.

"She did not come home this morning. She *always* comes home."

"She was working last night?"

The girl nods.

"We both were. She was on this block."

"That's why you approached the police officer."

The girl nods again.

"I was hoping he could help. I was hoping he saw her or knew somebody who did."

I look once more at the photograph. The girl captured there looks happy. Hopeful. Excited at the prospect of life. I wish I could do something to help this girl find her sister, but right now there's just too much on my plate. I hand the photograph back to the girl.

"Good luck finding your sister."

The girl doesn't take the photograph. She isn't even looking at me. Her gaze is directed at something over my shoulder.

I glance back to see an old BMW coming up the street, two men in front, both wearing sunglasses.

I turn back to the girl but she's already moving away from me, hurrying up the sidewalk.

"Hey."

The girl doesn't answer, just keeps walking.

"Hey!"

The girl starts hurrying her pace.

Behind me, the BMW's engine growls as it shoots forward.

The girl is sprinting now, turning into the alleyway beside the motel.

The BMW's tires screech as it makes the hard turn into the alleyway, following her.

I shove the crumbled photograph in my pocket and hurry up the sidewalk. I notice that girl across the street again, the one taking pictures with her cell phone. Because of the commotion, her attention shifts toward me, and across the two blocks our eyes meet. She holds her phone up again, only for a moment, but I'm certain that she just took a picture. My picture.

Oh hell no.

Part of me wants to stray off course, head directly to this girl and take the phone from her, smash it so hard the memory card shatters into a hundred pieces, but before I can, the girl in the alleyway cries out.

The BMW is parked at an angle, its front bumper kissing the side of the building and making it impossible for the girl to escape. Both men are out of the car now, and one of them has grabbed the girl, shoved her up against the wall.

I glance back once more at the girl across the street. This girl now looking up and down the street, as if looking for something, and then hurrying over to the other side. For some reason I think she's coming to the prostitute's aid—maybe she herself *is* a prostitute as well—but instead she climbs the steps and disappears through the motel's entrance.

The girl in the alleyway cries out again.

I start down the alleyway, and don't speak until I'm only a few feet away.

"Hey, do you guys smell something?"

Because of their sunglasses, it's impossible to tell whether or not these men are glaring at me, but I'll bet five bucks they are.

I take another step closer, overdramatically suck in air through my nose.

"Yeah, it definitely doesn't smell good. Do you want to know what it smells like?"

Neither man answers.

I say, "It smells like two assholes."

One of the men turns to me, his hands clenching into fists.

"Bitch, you better get the fuck out of here before we turn you out."

I take another heavy sniff and then nod, pointing at the man.

"Yeah, you especially smell like a dirty asshole. When was the last time somebody wiped you?"

The man is clearly not used to having a woman talk back to him. His anger turns to rage, and he rushes at me at full speed. Which makes taking this one out too easy.

I duck and move to the side when he comes at me, stepping behind him and grabbing the back of his head and smashing his face straight into the nearest wall. Blood geysers from his nose. He stumbles back. Tries to take a swing at me. I duck this attempt even more easily, grab his arm and twist it behind his back, pulling up hard enough that his body becomes mine, a simple puppet, moving in whatever direction I want.

The other man has let go of the girl. He pulls a switchblade from his pocket, starts toward us.

I jerk the man's arm up and turn him toward his friend.

The man with the knife pauses, considering his options.

I say, "I'm going to dislocate your friend's shoulder because nobody likes a smelly asshole. You want me to dislocate your shoulder too?"

The man with the knife snarls.

"Fuck you, bitch."

"Suit yourself."

I twist the man's arm enough to hear something pop. The man screams. I push him forward at his friend. He stumbles a bit, almost falls into his friend. With the other man's attention focused on his friend for that instant, he doesn't see me coming. Within seconds, I've snatched the knife from his hand, stabbed him in the stomach, then grabbed his other arm and jerked it back until I hear that pop again.

He screams too.

I look up at the girl, who's staring at me in horror.

"Leave. Pack your things and leave town. Leave the city. Leave the state. Start a new life."

"But—but—but my sister—"

"Is not coming back. You know that. Whatever happened to her, she's gone."

The girl again looks to be on the verge of tears. She stands frozen for an instant before shaking her head as if waking from a dream. Immediately she squeezes between the wall and the car and hurries down the alleyway.

The knife is still in the man's stomach. I lean down and pull it out. Blood starts to ooze from the wound.

"Might want to put pressure on that."

The man's hand scrambles to find the wound.

I wipe the blade on the man's shirt so it's clean and then close the knife and slip it into my pocket.

"Think I'm going to keep this as a memento of our time together. Thanks, fellas. It's been swell."

Both of them swear and call me names, but it's hard to take them seriously when they're lying on the ground groaning in pain.

I reach the end of the alleyway just as the girl with the cell phone emerges from the motel's entrance.

I step back before she notices me. Peeking around the corner, I watch as she looks up and down the block again and then hurriedly crosses the street. She goes up the block and climbs into a car. Fortunately, the car faces this direction, so once she has it out on the street, she heads my way.

I'm already halfway down the block when she passes. From the corner of my eye it doesn't look like she sees me.

I cross the street and climb into the Civic, maneuver a quick three-point turn, and manage to catch up with the girl three blocks later.

I let her keep a two-block lead.

By now Ramon and his partner are long gone, but this girl, well, something tells me wherever she's going could be just as interesting.

15

Carlos banged his fist against the apartment door, and when there was no answer, he banged his fist again.

Ramon said, "Maybe he's not home."

They stood alone on the third floor of the apartment building, the hallway narrow and musty.

Carlos tried the doorknob. It didn't turn. He looked at Ramon.

"Did you stretch this morning?"

"Why?"

"Because I'm too old to kick down this door."

Ramon looked at the door.

"Maybe we should just try to find the manager or somebody else who might have a key."

Carlos said, "In a few hours agents from Mexico City will be coming here to take over our investigation. Do you want to look like an asshole who didn't do any work tracking down a lead?"

Ramon said nothing.

"I'm close to retiring, so it doesn't matter much to me, though

I would love to help bring the Devil down. You … you're just starting out. Think about how capturing the Devil would look."

Carlos pointed at the door.

"Now, are you going to do this or not?"

The door itself was thin and cheap. It took only two kicks before it broke away from the lock.

Carlos pushed the door open, his gun now in hand, and entered the apartment.

"Miguel, if you're in here, you have three seconds to come out with your hands up."

Silence.

Carlos said, "Three."

More silence.

"Two."

Nothing.

"One."

Ramon stepped up next to Carlos, his gun at his side.

"I guess he's not here."

"I guess so."

But Carlos and Ramon kept their guns out as they moved about the apartment. The place was as cramped and shitty as the outside of the building looked. The bedroom just a mattress on the floor and some boxes of clothes scattered about. Same with the rest of the place. A ratty couch and TV. The sink in the kitchenette full of dirty dishes.

Ramon said, "You think he took off?"

Carlos said, "I can't tell if the place has been ransacked or if this is how it always looks."

Out in the hallway an angry voice shouted.

"What the hell is going on here?"

A fat bald man stood in the doorway. He stared at the broken door as if in shock, then glared at Carlos and Ramon.

"Who the fuck are you?"

Carlos kept the gun held at his side.

"We're looking for Miguel. Are you Miguel?"

The fat man snorted.

"Do I look like Miguel?"

Carlos said, "It's impossible for me to say because I don't know what Miguel looks like."

The fat man seemed to notice their guns for the first time. His large brow creased as he frowned.

"Are you police?"

"Yes."

"What are you doing here?"

"We can't tell you that. Who are you, anyway?"

"I'm the landlord. I live on the first floor. I got a call there was a disturbance up here so I came to check it out before calling the police. Who's going to pay for that door?"

"Do you know where Miguel is?"

"No. What did he do?"

"How long has he been living here?"

"I don't know. A couple years."

"When was the last time you saw him?"

"I can't remember. I don't socialize with my tenants. But he always paid his rent on time, so I never had any problems with him."

"Does he have any friends in the building?"

The fat man shrugged his heavy shoulders.

"Again, I don't know. What's this about? Is he in some kind of trouble?"

"We're worried about his safety. It's important we track him down as soon as possible."

This was a lie, but they weren't about to tell the landlord the truth.

The fat man shrugged again, now looking about the place.

"That's all I can tell you. He always paid his rent on time. That's the only thing that matters to me. Never had any complaints about him."

Ramon said, "Do you know where he works?"

"Some motel. I couldn't tell you which one."

"Any other job?"

"Not one that comes to mind. Seriously, what is this about?"

Carlos and Ramon traded glances. It didn't look like they would get much more out of the landlord.

Carlos said, "Thank you for your time."

He and Ramon started past the fat man into the hallway, ignoring the landlord as he sputtered after them.

"Wait. What about the door? Who the hell is going to pay for that door?"

16

Ramon and his partner stand on the sidewalk for a minute, talking to one another, and then they drift over to the two cops parked along the street.

Ramon's partner leans down to speak to the driver. The driver nods. Ramon's partner leans back, and then he and Ramon walk to where they had parked their pickup truck down the block. They slip inside the truck and are gone seconds later. The two cops start their car and drive down the street where they make a U-turn and coast to a stop by the corner.

They're pointed right at the apartment building, keeping an eye out for whomever Ramon and his partner clearly didn't find inside.

I wonder how the girl is going to handle it. She's still sitting in her car a block away. She's been sitting there ever since she arrived ten minutes ago. As far as I can tell, she didn't notice that I was following her. No doubt too focused on the task at hand to be aware of her surroundings. Which makes me suspect that whatever she's up to she's a novice.

Two minutes pass before the girl finally opens her door and

steps out. She stands there for a moment, staring down the block—probably at the parked cop car—and then closes her door and starts to make her way down the street.

I watch her, curious how she's going to handle this, and am surprised when she just goes for it.

She slips her cell phone out of her pocket and stares down at it. From where I am I can't tell what she's doing with the phone, but my guess is she's trying to be inconspicuous. Texting, playing a game, whatever—she keeps her head bent as she works her way up the sidewalk and then, all at once, turns and enters the apartment building.

I step out of the Civic and cross the street. I don't have the luxury of a cell phone to act like I'm distracted. Besides my ID, passport, money, and the pimp's knife, all I have is the crumpled photograph the frail prostitute gave me. I slip it from my pocket and act like I'm looking at it as I walk down the sidewalk. I pause before the apartment building's entrance, looking up and down the block with a confused expression. I allow a quick beat to glance toward where the cops are parked. They're still there, and they're watching me, but my gut says it's just because I'm one of the few out on the street right now and standing right in front of the building. I look back down at the photograph, mumbling to myself, and then turn toward the entrance. Slipping the photograph back into my pocket, I pull open the glass door and enter.

The foyer is deserted. There is no elevator in the building, only a set of stairs. Judging by the closed doors along the first floor, I figure the girl took the stairs.

I start up the stairs, quietly, trying to hear the girl's footsteps, but a loud TV in one of the first-floor apartments makes it difficult.

As I reach the end of the stairs and turn a corner, a fat man nearly barrels into me. He's mumbling about a broken door and how much it will cost and the police are goddamned corrupt. He barely even notices me, lost in his own thoughts. I'm the one who needs to step out of his way, and then he's past me, headed downstairs.

I hurry up to the second floor. Peer down the hallway. All the doors are closed. None are broken.

I head up to the third floor.

Bingo.

The third door down from the left is open, kicked in.

I pause outside the apartment.

Somebody's inside. The girl? Most likely, but I can't be too sure. Only one way to find out.

I step inside the apartment.

The girl isn't here. At least, that's what it looks like at first. But then I hear movement coming from the next room—maybe the bedroom?—and a second later the girl appears, her cell phone in hand.

She doesn't notice me at first, too focused on taking pictures, but then she turns and looks up and gasps.

I say, "What the hell are you doing in my apartment?"

The girl stands there for an instant, frozen in shock. Then she frowns.

"This isn't your apartment."

"Did you break down my door?"

The girl shakes her head as if to clear it.

"This isn't your apartment."

She pauses, studying my face. Recognition lights her eyes.

"You were outside the motel."

I say, "Who are you?"

The girl throws it right back at me.

"Who are you?"

She holds up the phone, snaps a picture.

I say, "I can't let you keep that picture. Or the one you took back outside the motel."

The girl says, "Too bad. They're already in the cloud."

I can't tell if the girl's bluffing or not. The phone doesn't look advanced enough to be hooked up with some web cloud where all her pictures are stored, but maybe it is. And if that's the case, then that will make this a bit harder.

We're at a stalemate, both of us staring at one another, so I do the first thing that comes to mind.

I reach into my pocket and pull out the pimp's knife.

Eject the blade.

The girl's eyes widen.

"I'll call the police."

Her voice now a tremulous whisper.

"Call them. There's a car right outside. You saw it before you came in here. It was the same one that was back at the motel."

The girl just stares at the knife.

I ask, "Why were you at the motel? Why are you *here* now?"

The girl says nothing.

"Hey, look at me."

The girl blinks. Shifts her eyes up to meet mine.

"Are those pictures really sent to a cloud?"

The girl's nod is almost imperceptible.

"Then we have a problem. I'm going to need you to delete them. Right now."

The girl starts to shake her head.

"I can't delete them from my phone once they're sent, and they're sent automatically."

"Then how can you delete them?"

No answer.

I take a step forward.

"How. Can you. Delete them."

The girl takes a deep breath.

"Back at my house. On my desktop."

I nod, looking around the piece of shit apartment.

"Then you and I are going to have to go there."

The girl says, "Are you going to hurt me?"

"Not if you delete those pictures. That's all I want."

For an instant she looks relieved. Then she squints at me again.

"Why were you at the motel?"

"It doesn't matter. Why were *you* there?"

The girl licks her lips, considering. She stares at the knife for a long moment before shifting her eyes to look back at me.

"That's where the call went."

"What call?"

"The call that—"

She pauses, really looking at me again.

"Oh my God. You're her."

Now it's my turn to say nothing.

Excitement tinges her voice.

"You were at the scene. You were the one who found the bodies."

Something's not right. The girl shouldn't know that. What is she *doing* here, anyway? She's not police. She made that clear when she threatened to call them. So who is she?

The girl says, "Can I ask you some questions? What was it like finding them? It will be great for the story."

"Are you a journalist?"

The girl shrugs, grinning.

"You could call me that."

"Then you want a quote? Let's get out of here and go to your place and delete those photos from the cloud and I'll give you a quote."

Her eyes widen with surprise.

"Seriously?"

"Seriously."

I'm not telling the whole truth, of course. I have no intentions of giving the girl a quote or anything about who or what I am. I just want those pictures deleted. And I also want to know what she knows. Obviously she has a contact in the police force that tipped her off to the call. That's why she was waiting outside the motel. And once Ramon and his partner took off, she hurried inside and managed to sweet talk the same information out of an employee. Which led her here to … what, exactly?

I close the knife, slip it back into my pocket.

"Whose apartment is this?"

The girl looks like she doesn't want to say at first. Then she sighs.

"Miguel Dominguez."

"And who is he?"

"He worked last night at the motel. Whoever called there most likely spoke to him. That's why the police are now trying to find him."

"Do they think he killed and burned those people?"

The girl shakes her head like the answer is obvious.

"Of course not. Not unless he's the Devil."

I frown at her.

"The Devil?"

The girl says, "You don't know about the Devil?"

"You mean … like Satan?"

The girl frowns at this, and looks at the time on her cell phone.

"Shit. We've been here too long. We should leave."

Sounds good to me.

I follow her out into the hallway. She says the door was mostly closed when she arrived, so we close it the best we can and then head back down to the first floor. Through the glass door, I can see the fat man sitting on a plastic chair smoking a cigarette. Just the sight makes me crave some nicotine, so that's what I'm thinking as I follow the girl outside. A breeze wafts some of the exhaled cigarette smoke my way, and all I want to do at that moment is get a sniff.

That's when I hear somebody shout.

"There she is! Kill the *puta*!"

A familiar BMW is parked across the street. The two men I assaulted earlier are inside. The driver leans out his window, pointing at me.

Directing the two young men on the sidewalk with guns to kill me.

17

For an instant I'm aware that the two young men are much younger than I at first took them for. They're seventeen at the oldest, fifteen at the youngest. Which is why in that instant I decide not to kill them.

The girl is in front of me, having pushed open the door, and she sees the kids with the guns but doesn't move at first. Just like she had up in Miguel Dominguez's apartment, she freezes.

The kids raise their guns.

I grab the girl and yank her back into the foyer as the kids open fire. The glass door shatters. The kids give no regard to the fat man in the lawn chair. The man is simply in the way. His body bucks in the chair as bullets tear into it. I push the girl onto the floor, covering her with my body until there's a brief lull, and then I glance over my shoulder to see the kids advancing.

I jump to my feet, pulling the girl up with me, and push her toward the stairs. To her credit, the girl doesn't hesitate—she sprints up the steps.

I follow her up the steps just as the kids enter the foyer and keep firing. The wall spits up plaster. I reach the spot where the stairs twist, and pause around the corner, slipping the switch-blade from my pocket.

Two sets of footsteps hurry up the stairs. I wait until they're only a few feet away—right around the corner—before I step forward and jam the blade into the first kid's shoulder. The kid cries out in both pain and surprise, and I leave the blade in his shoulder as I easily disengage the gun from his hand. The other kid is following too close behind, and I kick him in the chest and send him tumbling back down the steps, the gun clattering away from him as he falls.

I pull the knife out of the kid's shoulder, shoot him in the ankle, and then start back down the steps toward his friend.

I lean down and press the barrel of the gun against the kid's forehead.

"Why?"

At first it doesn't look like the kid is going to answer, but then he issues a heavy breath.

"They paid us."

"How much?"

"Fifty each."

Jesus Christ. A hit on my life is only worth that much?

I keep the barrel pressed against the kid's forehead.

"How old are you?"

Again, it doesn't look like the kid is going to answer, but then he does.

"Sixteen."

I nod.

"You keep this up and you won't see seventeen."

I step back, shift the gun down toward his leg, and place a bullet in his knee. I kick his gun farther down the hallway, then turn and shout up the stairwell.

"It's clear!"

At least I think it is. I watch the street as I wait for the girl to reappear down the steps. She stares at the two kids with wide eyes. She turns to stare out at the street.

"It's safe out there too?"

"I'm not sure yet. Let me head out first. You don't hear any gunfire, hurry out and get in your car."

I step outside, the knife in my left hand, the gun in my right. The two men in the BMW are still parked across the street. Their expressions change the moment they see me. I glance up the block at where the two cops had been parked earlier, but they're long gone.

The BMW's driver starts the engine and throws the car into gear. Before he can peel out, though, I shoot out his front and rear tires as I advance across the street, and then I'm standing right beside the car aiming the gun at the two men.

"What did I tell you before? Nobody likes a pair of smelly assholes."

The men just glare at me.

I hold the knife in my left hand. There's still some of the kid's blood on it.

"I know I said I was going to keep this, but I changed my mind."

I lean into the window and stab the driver in the leg. The driver cries out in pain. The passenger scrambles to open his door, but before he can make much progress, I aim the gun once more and shoot him in the leg. He too cries out.

"Quit your crying."

The men glare up at me again.

"I let you off easy the first time. This time was a bit more rough. The next time? I'll kill you."

I step back, surveying the street. Some people are out now, watching the action, but that's it. The girl is already in her car and headed this way.

I lean into the car again.

"By the way, you paid those kids fifty each to take me out?

I'm offended. I'd like to think a hit on me would cost a bit more."

The driver keeps glaring at me. He spits and mumbles.

"Fuck you, *puta*."

I shake my head.

"How many times do you want to get hurt?"

I press the barrel of the gun against his shoulder and pull the trigger.

The driver howls in pain.

The girl pulls up next to us. I start toward her car but pause, turn back toward the BMW.

"Remember, assholes. The third time will be the last."

I open the door and slip into the passenger seat, and within seconds we're gone.

18

The back doors to the ambulance slammed shut and then the ambulance started away, its lights flashing but its siren muted.

Ramon and Carlos watched until the ambulance disappeared around the corner before they turned toward the BMW and the two wounded occupants sitting on the ground beside it. Three officers stood around them, weapons in their hands.

Carlos pulled out a cigarette from the pack in his pocket and lit it.

"You guys look like shit."

The BMW's occupants didn't carry any identification—even the BMW had no papers—but one of the officers knew them well enough to inform Carlos and Ramon of their first names, Hector and Pedro. Hector now glared up at Carlos and Ramon.

"Fuck, man, we're in pain here. Why are you treating us like criminals?"

Carlos puffed on his cigarette.

"Oh, I don't know. Maybe because you are criminals."

"No way, man. We're no criminals. We're good citizens."

"We know you two are pimps."

"*Pimps?*"

Hector forced an expression of confusion.

"No way, man, we ain't no pimps."

Ramon said, "We also know you deal drugs."

Now it was Pedro's turn to force confusion.

"*Drugs?* No way, we don't sell no drugs. We don't even *do* no drugs."

Carlos took one last drag on the cigarette, dropped it on the street, and then crouched down so he was on eye level with the two men.

"Let's cut the bullshit, all right? We know who you are. We know what you do. Now tell us, what happened here today?"

Hector's eyes widened.

"We told the other cops, man, this girl came out of nowhere and attacked us."

Carlos said, his voice flat, "Attacked you."

"Yeah, man. She came out of nowhere and started stabbing and shooting us. She's crazy, man. Hope somebody catches her before she kills somebody."

Ramon pointed across the street at where the dead landlord lay on the sidewalk.

"You mean like that?"

Hector and Pedro said nothing.

Carlos said, "So let me get this straight. Your story is that you two were parked here minding your own business when this girl came out of nowhere and *attacked* you. Is that right?"

Again Hector and Pedro said nothing.

"And then she, what, just happened to kill the old man over there too?"

Still nothing.

"And what about those two kids? You know, the ones who left in the ambulance? Either of you want to guess what it is they told us?"

Pedro shook his head and muttered.

"They're kids. Probably made shit up."

Carlos sighed and rolled his eyes at Ramon. He stood up and stepped aside so Ramon could take a shot. Ramon stared hard first at Hector, then at Pedro, and shook his head.

"Don't know why you guys are making this difficult on yourselves. Like my partner said, we know who you are, what you do. We know you hired those two kids to kill the girl. We know that the landlord got caught in the cross fire. Hell, we spoke to the man a half hour ago. So why don't you save us all some time and tell us why you wanted to take the girl out."

It didn't look like either man was going to answer, but then Hector turned his head to spit and glared back up at Ramon.

"We don't talk to scared cops who wear masks."

Ramon glanced up at Carlos, then pulled down his mask to show his entire face. He leaned toward the pimps, his voice going low.

"I'm not scared of shit. Now tell me why you wanted to kill the girl."

Hector said, "We told you, she came at us first."

"Yeah, and like I told you, we know that's bullshit."

Hector shook his head.

"No, not here. Earlier."

Ramon traded glances with Carlos. He frowned at Hector.

"Where earlier?"

"The Paraíso."

Ramon said, "What were you doing there?"

"One of our girls, man. She hadn't come home. We went looking for her, tried to get her back in the car. And then out of nowhere this *other* girl shows up."

"The one you paid those kids to try to take out."

"Yeah."

"What did she do that made you want to have her taken out?"

Hector just shook his head, looked away from Ramon. Pedro did the same.

Carlos said, "We're going to find out eventually. Might as well tell us now."

Hector turned his head to spit again.

"Shit, man, it's fucking embarrassing."

"What's embarrassing?"

"She came at us in that alleyway. She hurt us."

Ramon echoed it: "She hurt you."

"Yeah, man. And then she let our girl get away. We couldn't let that shit stand. We saw what kind of car she drove off in, so we called around. We heard from one of the taxi drivers where she went. That's when we found those kids and gave them the pieces to take her out."

Ramon glanced back up at Carlos, who nodded to him that they were done for now. Without a word Ramon stood back up, and they drifted down the street toward the empty Civic. The two officers who had been parked two blocks down keeping an eye on the apartment building stood next to it.

One of the officers said, "You wanted to talk to us?"

Carlos said, "Where were you?"

Both officers played dumb. The other one shrugged, shaking his head.

"What are you talking about?"

Carlos said, "How much did those pimps pay you?"

One of the officers looked down at his feet, then looked back up.

"We were hungry, okay? That's all. We left to get some food."

Carlos glared hard at them, and then shook his head.

"Get the fuck out of here."

The two officers scurried away.

Ramon watched them and said, "You really think Hector and Pedro paid them off?"

"Don't you?"

Ramon shrugged.

Carlos said, "It seems Samantha Lu is more than what she appears."

Ramon nodded.

"If that's even her real name."

"Good point. No college student can do what she did."

"Assuming it's really her."

Carlos gestured at the blue Civic.

"That's her car, isn't it? And the one kid said that she was Asian. I think it's safe to assume it's our girl."

Ramon stared at the Civic for a moment before he glanced up the block at the apartment building.

"So she managed to follow us to the Paraíso, then followed us here to this apartment building. Why?"

Carlos shrugged, lighting himself another cigarette.

"I guess we'll have to ask her the next time we see her."

"When do you think that will be?"

Carlos looked up and down the block, exhaling smoke through his nose.

"After what we just learned about her? I wouldn't be surprised if she's watching us right now."

19

The girl turns a corner and eases the car to a stop along the side of the street. She keeps her hands on the steering wheel, sitting ramrod straight, her eyes on the rearview mirror.

I ask, "What's wrong?"

She keeps watching the rearview mirror.

"I want to make sure we're not being followed."

"We're not."

She breaks her stare with the rearview mirror to glance at me.

"How do you know?"

"I just do. I've been keeping an eye out ever since we took off. Nobody's following us."

Almost a half hour has passed since we raced away from that apartment building. We haven't spoken once. The girl drove us through the city, away from the ghetto, toward a more respectable part of town.

I gesture at the houses along the street.

"You live in one of these?"

She shakes her head, puts the car in gear, and steers us back out into the street. She goes up one block, turns a corner, goes up another block, turns another corner, and the next thing I know she hits a button and a garage door farther ahead starts to open and she coasts right into the garage.

I'd caught a glimpse of the house before we entered the garage and was impressed.

"This your place?"

She shuts off the car.

"My grandmother's. I've been staying with her now the past two years."

"What happened to your parents?"

Somehow I know the answer even before she answers in a soft voice.

"They're dead."

She turns to me, her face all at once serious. She's in her early twenties, with dark eyes and long dark hair. She has a striking kind of beauty that makes me think she should be on the set of a *telenovela* instead of being chased by teenagers with guns.

She says, "Who are you?"

"Just a girl."

"What you did to those men back there"—she shakes her head—"where did you learn to do that?"

"YouTube videos. Just search 'kickass kung fu' and you'd be shocked at what you can find."

The girl stares at me.

I say, "What's your name?"

She hesitates, clearly not sure she wants to tell me, and then says, "Gabriela."

"I'm Samantha."

The girl smiles.

"That's not really your name, is it?"

I look around the garage. A Mercedes is parked next to us.

"I see your grandmother does well for herself."

"Yes, she does."

We step out of the car and I follow Gabriela into the house. The place is spotless. A TV plays from one of the rooms. Gabriela leads me into the room where an old woman sits in a chair swiping at a tablet.

"Grandmother, this is a friend from school. We're going up to my room."

The old woman smiles at me, says hello, and goes back to swiping at her tablet.

I follow Gabriela upstairs. Her room is bare. Besides a bed and a desk, there are two bookshelves filled with books but that's it. No pictures on the walls.

She sets her phone on the desk to charge, drops into her chair.

"I know it's not much to look at it. After my parents died and I moved in here, I didn't unpack most of my stuff. I guess"—she shrugs—"I guess part of me felt that this would only be temporary. Like if I didn't unpack, what had happened to my parents didn't really happen."

She shakes her head as if to clear it and turns to her computer. Powers it up, enters a password, and then brings up a browser. Seconds later she's on the site that gives her access to the cloud. All the pictures she took today—at the motel and then at the apartment building—are right there on the screen.

I'm in only three of the pictures. Gabriela deletes them with a few easy clicks and then glances up at me.

"There, they are gone for good. Happy?"

I just stare at the pictures.

Gabriela says, "Are we done now?"

"What are these pictures for?"

Gabriela doesn't answer.

I look at her.

"Why were you at the motel in the first place?"

She doesn't look like she's going to answer this question either, but then she frowns and sighs.

"Answer my question first."

"Okay."

"Why are you in Mexico?"

"I'm on vacation."

"You're lying."

"I'm a college student. I came down here to see the sights."

"You were the one who found the bodies. And then you followed those investigators to the motel. And then you followed *me* to that apartment building. That's not normal college student behavior."

"Really? Then what exactly was it you were doing? You said you were a journalist. Who do you write for?"

She opens a tab on the browser, types at the keyboard, and brings up another page.

La Baliza, the headline of the webpage reads.

I say, "What's *The Beacon*?"

"An independent news publication. It's outsourced by people like me all over the country. Most news nowadays won't tell the truth because they're afraid of the cartels or the government or sometimes both. We work in anonymity so we have nothing to fear."

"How did you end up at the motel?"

"There's an online portal where people can anonymously leave tips. Many police officers do. They keep me updated when something big happens. Today one of them left a tip that an American tourist found three bodies burned to death. They also mentioned the phone call sent to the motel. I went straight there."

"After those investigators left and you went inside, how did you know where they were headed next?"

"I gave the clerk inside twenty dollars. He was happy to give up the information anyway. He said one of the investigators assaulted him."

"So what's your story about so far?"

"I haven't decided yet. Somebody's already posted about the attack at the Diaz's place."

"Somebody?"

She shrugs.

"We all act as separate units. None of us knows who the other is. That way we can move about safely."

"So you're writing about these burned bodies."

"Yes."

"And the police believe this Miguel Dominguez is the killer?"

"No way he's the killer. But a call was made from the payphone to the motel, and Miguel was working there last night, so the police want to question him."

I frown, glancing at the computer again.

"Why are you so certain he's not the killer?"

"You saw his apartment. I'm no cop, but he doesn't strike me as somebody who could pull that off."

"You mean burning a woman and two children alive?"

Gabriela frowns at me.

"Why do you think the bodies belong to a woman and two children?"

Whoops.

I say, "I feel like there's something you're not telling me. Something I'm missing. You don't seem too shocked to find out those people had been burned to death."

"I'm not. This isn't the first time it's happened."

Now it's my turn to frown.

"What do you mean?"

Gabriela says, "He's been doing this now for over a year. This is the sixth time he's struck."

I think about Maria and those children, leaving them there at the brick building by themselves in the dark.

You promised to keep us safe.

I stare hard at Gabriela.

"What are you talking about?"

"Nobody knows his name, but everybody calls him *el Diablo*. The Devil. He's a serial killer taking out the mothers and children of cartel families."

20

Ramon stood on sand, inches from the incoming surf, and stared out at the ocean.

Behind him, Carlos said, "Tell me why we climbed down here again."

Ramon turned to him.

"I told you already."

"Yes, and it didn't make much sense then, so why don't you try it one more time?"

Ramon stepped back, surveying the small beach.

"After I spoke to Samantha Lu and told her she was free to go, she stood up and stared out at the ocean for a couple seconds."

Carlos lit a cigarette, blew out smoke through his nose.

"And?"

Ramon glanced up toward the top of the bluff, then back down at the beach.

"And I think she was looking for something."

"Like what?"

"I have no idea. I didn't think much of it at the time. I

thought maybe she was just looking at the ocean. But after what we now know about her ..."

Carlos said, "We don't know much."

"No, but what little we do know is suspicious enough."

"If she was looking for something down here, what do you think it was?"

Ramon was quiet for a moment, surveying the beach once again.

"I'm not sure. But we're, what, ten miles down the beach from the Diaz place?"

"Give or take, sure."

"How did the victims get here so fast? I mean, assuming they left around the time of the attack."

Carlos was quiet for a couple seconds, thinking it over. He took one last drag on the cigarette, flicked it out into the water, and sighed.

"I hate it when you start to make sense."

Ramon said, "You see my problem with this, don't you? Not to take away from the fact that a woman and two children are dead, but how did they *get* here? They could have driven, yes, but not down the drive from the house and then onto the main road. Narcos were headed to the place while it was being attacked. The woman and the children would have been seen."

"So the other options?"

"Walk down the beach is one that first comes to mind. But it would have taken too long. How long do you think it would take a woman and two children to walk the beach in the middle of the night? And let's not forget they're being forced against their will. The kids were probably crying. From the time of the attack to when they were—"

Ramon paused, the image of those three charred bodies flashing in his mind. He cleared his throat, tried again.

"From the time of the attack to when they were murdered, it doesn't give us a very large window."

Carlos nodded.

"I agree. So what's the next option?"

"They took a boat."

"A boat."

"Makes much more sense than flying. There's a possibility this guy has a helicopter, but it doesn't seem too realistic."

"So you think they took a boat."

Ramon paused a beat, giving it some more thought, and then nodded.

Carlos said, "Okay, but there's a problem with that theory."

"Which is?"

Carlos spread his arms, motioning at the beach.

"There's no evidence of a boat."

"He obviously took the boat with him."

"That's not what I mean. Look at the sand. Any trace of a boat being docked here?"

"Maybe he kept it farther out. Dropped an anchor. Forced the woman and the children back onto the beach, had them walk up to the bluff, and then—"

Flash of those three charred bodies again.

"—and then did what he did."

Carlos stared at him, not saying anything.

Ramon said, "I know I sound crazy."

"No, you don't sound crazy. That's the troubling part. A boat makes the most sense. The question is where did he go afterward?"

"Maybe we need to start looking at places along the coast."

Carlos looked out at the ocean and issued a heavy sigh.

"So you think Samantha Lu was looking for something down here."

"I do, yes."

"But you have no idea what she might have been looking for."

"No."

"It could be anything."

"Yes."

"I saw an empty water bottle on the trail leading down here. And over there by the rocks is a deflated soccer ball."

"Your point?"

"My point is the only thing I see down here is junk. Do you think she was looking for junk?"

Ramon said nothing.

Carlos sighed again and said, "Do you think she had something to do with the murders?"

Ramon just gave his partner a look.

Carlos said, "Yeah, I'm having trouble on that point too."

"Seeing the smoke from the highway and coming here to try to help and finding the bodies. Okay, I'm willing to believe that. But then she follows us into the city? And beats up those two pimps? And *then* takes out the kids those pimps sent to kill her? She doesn't sound like any graduate student I know."

Above them on the bluff, an officer called down to them.

"They're here!"

The officer waved to them to come up and then disappeared.

Carlos said, "About time. The sun goes down in another hour."

Ramon looked at his partner and took a breath.

"Ready for this?"

"Not climbing back up that hill, no."

They started back up the trail that they had taken down twenty minutes earlier. Ramon was barely thirty and in shape and the climb didn't faze him at all. Carlos, much older and overweight, needed to rest three times to catch his breath. When they reached the top they saw the building and the police cars still parked around it. As well as a new car that hadn't been there earlier.

Carlos said, "Looks like they're already inside."

They were. There were two of them. Both males wearing

khakis and polo shirts, their pistols holstered to their belts. They were crouched around the charred bodies which hadn't been moved yet (they had been given strict orders from Mexico City not to move the bodies until somebody arrived). They glanced at Carlos and Ramon when they entered the building but didn't give them more than a couple seconds' attention before directing their focus back on the bodies.

Carlos said, "You're the PMF agents?"

The *Policía Federal Ministerial* was a federal agency tasked with fighting corruption and organized crime. Once the Devil started targeting cartel families, President Cortez ordered a task force to lead up the investigation. Cortez wanted to stop the cartels, but he also wanted to make it known it was still illegal to murder the wives and children of those cartel families.

The men stood up and approached Carlos and Ramon. Each of them held out his hand.

One of them said, "Sorry about that. We thought you were just officers."

Carlos introduced himself and Ramon to the men and the men introduced themselves to Ramon and Carlos. Their names were Ibarra and Serrano and they had been tracking the Devil for over a year. When they heard about the bodies being found this morning they got on a plane as soon as possible.

Ibarra said, "And now we're here. What can you tell us about this?"

Carlos and Ramon told the agents as much as they knew. They didn't hold back. They even went so far as to tell them about Samantha Lu and how she had evidently been following them into the city.

Serrano said, "So you don't know where this young woman is now?"

Both men shook their heads.

Ibarra said, "What about this Miguel Dominguez?"

Both men shook their heads again.

The agents traded glances and then turned to look once again at the bodies.

Ramon said, "It doesn't sound like you're too worried about either Miguel Dominguez or Samantha Lu."

Ibarra shook his head.

"We're not. We would certainly like to speak to both of them if possible—the phone call to the motel is especially interesting—but right now they're not our focus."

Carlos said, "Why is that?"

"Because neither of them is the Devil."

Now it was Carlos and Ramon's turn to trade glances.

Carlos said, "How do you know that?"

Serrano crossed his arms and turned back to the bodies. When he spoke next his voice was low and hushed, almost conspiratorial.

"Because by now we think we know who the Devil is. And he's a ghost."

21

I rip open the plastic packaging as I exit the corner store and slip the disposable phone out and power it on. It takes about a minute before everything is up and ready. As it's brand-new, the phone has little battery life, but it's more than enough for my purposes. I dial the number on the card to add minutes to the phone, then dial the number I had memorized days ago before coming to Mexico. I toss the packaging in the nearest trashcan as I walk down the street back toward Gabriela's house five blocks away.

After three rings, a female voice answers.

"Thank you for calling Scout Dry Cleaners. Our normal business hours are Monday through Friday, seven a.m. to seven p.m., and on Saturday eight a.m. to three p.m. We are closed Sundays."

Then there's a beep and at first I'm not sure what to do, thinking maybe I have the wrong number. I even glance at the screen to double-check the numbers in case I'd somehow mixed a few up. But no, that's the number Atticus had me memorize.

Then thinking about Atticus and Scout Dry Cleaners, I shake my head and roll my eyes.

"Call me back. I don't know the number—this is a disposable—but hopefully it shows up on your end."

I disconnect the call and pause at the end of the block, surveying the street to make sure I'm not being followed. Gabriela loaned me one of her hats, so at least my face is somewhat hidden from those keeping an eye out for a young Asian woman.

A minute passes before the disposable rings.

I hit the green button and place the phone to my ear. "Atticus?"

Silence for a moment, and then Atticus's quiet voice.

"How far out are you?"

"Yeah, about that ..."

He sighs and says, "What happened?"

I'm quiet for a moment, but that moment is all Atticus needs.

"You went back for them, didn't you?"

I close my eyes, not wanting to get into it. Instead, I try to change the subject.

"Scout Dry Cleaners. That's pretty clever. I didn't know you were a Harper Lee fan."

Atticus says, "Holly, I may not know you very well, but I knew your father quite well, and despite what you want to believe, you are your father's daughter. So please don't waste my time any further than you already have."

It's true—Atticus doesn't know me very well, just as I don't know him very well. The only reason our paths crossed was because, despite being retired, Atticus is still somehow wired into the system. And when my father—who I thought was dead—needed me to steal something, he sent me to Atticus, the man who had once trained my father to kill, and Atticus, because children's lives were at risk, agreed to help me. And then, when it was clear my own family's lives were at risk, Atticus had agreed to help me again. So really, when you come right down to it, I have no reason not to tell this man the truth.

"I'm sorry, Atticus."

"What happened?"

"Like you said, I went back for them."

"And?"

"And"—I swallow, clear my throat—"and they were dead. Murdered. Burned to death, actually. Can you believe that, Atticus? *Burned to death.*"

He says nothing.

"So yeah, I'm still in Culiacán. Which means James is right now wasting his time heading to the rendezvous point. I would have called you sooner but this was the first chance I had to get away and find a disposable phone. But I want you to know I had *planned* to head straight for the border—I was even driving in that direction—but I just … I couldn't leave them like that. I wanted to make sure they were in a better place before I took off. But then I saw smoke from the highway, and when I got there …"

I trail off, not sure what more I want to say. I glance at the phone to check the battery life. Ten percent remaining.

Atticus says, "I'm sorry about what happened, Holly, I truly am. And I know for some reason you blame yourself for what happened. But right now you—"

I cut him off.

"No, Atticus, you don't get it. I *took* them there. I *left* them there. I practically delivered them to whoever the fuck killed them."

Atticus says nothing.

"And this isn't about some kind of guilt on my part. Yeah, I do feel guilty about what happened, but that's not all. From what I've been able to figure out, the person who did this has done it before. Several times. He's a serial killer, Atticus. Do you understand me? There's somebody out there killing the wives and children of cartel families."

Atticus says, "Yes, about that."

I realize I've been stationary too long and start up the block. "About what?"

"Something about this morning didn't feel right to me and I couldn't put my finger on the reason why. I had done as much research as possible on Ernesto Diaz, so I had believed I had all my bases covered."

I pause for a beat.

"But you didn't?"

"Not necessarily. It's just, well, based on Ernesto Diaz's status, he seemed to have had an abnormally large number of guards protecting him."

"What do you mean?"

"You said that this serial killer is going around killing the mothers and children of cartel families, correct?"

"Yes. Only the woman wasn't Javier's wife. She was the children's nanny."

"Then what happened this morning to the woman and children you left behind really doesn't make sense. The Diaz family is not part of the cartels. They don't do much in the drug trade, only the sex trade."

"Maybe this guy is branching out. Assuming it's even one guy."

"Yes, well that's not what has been bothering me."

"Then what has?"

"How many men did you take out at the compound? Almost twenty? It would make sense that Ernesto would have some guards—your surveillance of the compound the last two days proved that—but this morning there were just too many."

"He knew something had happened to his son, Atticus. He wanted to protect himself. Maybe he hired additional guards for a couple days."

"That's my thought. He must have hired additional men. The question now is who did he hire those additional men from, and will there be retaliation?"

I pause again, now two blocks from Gabriela's house, and ask, "Retaliation on who?"

"I haven't a clue, and right now that's what concerns me the most."

22

Fernando Sanchez Morales stepped out onto the patio to find his wife and seven-year-old son in the yard. His wife sat at the table, paging through a magazine, while his son kicked a soccer ball back and forth across the grass.

His first impulse was to shout at them, tell them to hurry inside. Blood started pounding in his ears. He wasn't aware his hands had curled into fists until he felt his nails digging into his palms.

Two of the bodyguards stood close by, sunglasses propped on their faces, rifles strapped over their shoulders. They kept their attention on the fence and the trees beyond it.

His wife glanced up at him and smiled.

"Do you hear them?"

He paused, the blood still pounding in his ears.

"Hear what?"

"Church bells."

She nodded toward the fence and the trees and the town down the hill. It took him a moment but he heard them then past the blood singing in his ears. Distant church bells.

His wife smiled again.

"There must be a wedding. Which reminds me, our anniversary is next month. What will you get me?"

Out in the yard, his son kicked the soccer ball a bit too hard. It sailed through the air and struck the fence. His son started running after the ball, but Fernando called after him.

"Ignacio, come here!"

The boy paused at the intensity in his father's voice.

His wife noticed it too, and the smile faded from her face.

"Why are you yelling at him?"

Fernando redirected his glare at his wife.

"Don't question me. And besides, you know better than to come outside."

His wife sighed, gesturing at the bodyguards.

"They're watching after us."

"That doesn't matter. You need to listen to me. It's for your safety."

She tilted the sunglasses to stare at him over the tops of the frames.

"You worry too much."

"This isn't a joke, Araceli. We've had this discussion already. You both need to stay in the house until I tell you it's okay to go out again."

She issued an overdramatic sigh, turning back to her magazine.

"It's a beautiful day. Let your son play with his ball."

He was moving before he even realized it. Crossing the short distance between them within a second. Snatching the magazine from his wife's hands and flinging it away while he grabbed a clump of her hair and yanked her to her feet.

Araceli cried out, gripping his wrist.

"Let go of me!"

He leaned down so his nose was almost touching hers. He growled between clenched teeth.

"Never disrespect me in front of my men. Do you understand me?"

From the yard, Ignacio called, "Mama?"

Araceli struggled for only a few more seconds before she settled. She knew the drill. This wasn't the first time Fernando became physical to make a point with his wife.

She glared up at him over the tops of the sunglasses.

"You've kept us locked up for over a year."

"Yes, for your goddamned protection. I would think you would be more grateful."

"We're prisoners in our own home."

"But you're still alive. Or would you rather the Devil get you?"

She said nothing to this. Fernando hadn't expected her to. He'd shown her the pictures early on when she said she didn't believe him. He made her keep the pictures on her phone as a constant reminder.

Ignacio hurried over to the patio, the soccer ball forgotten behind him. He ran straight to his mother and wrapped his arms around her waist and glared up at Fernando.

"Stop hurting her!"

This was his son, his own flesh and blood, speaking to him like a stranger. It made the blood start pounding in his ears again, his body going tense, but no, he wasn't going to hurt his son, at least not right now. Too much had happened in the past twenty-four hours that needed his attention that he couldn't get distracted by this.

He let go of his wife's hair and stepped back.

"Go inside and don't come out until I tell you it's safe."

Ignacio was sobbing now, gripping his mother like he thought she was going to disappear.

Araceli picked him up and kissed his cheeks, told him that everything was okay. She didn't look at Fernando as she hurried back inside the house.

The bodyguards started to follow them.

Fernando said, "Stop."

The men stopped.

"What did I tell you about them being outside?"

Neither man said anything.

"Don't make me repeat myself."

One of the men swallowed, cleared his throat.

"Sir, she asked us if they could—"

"Shut the fuck up. You should know better. She's not in charge. I am. Do you understand me?"

Both men nodded.

"I said, do you *fucking* understand me?"

The men said that they did.

Fernando dismissed them and the men hurried into the house.

A moment passed, and Jose Luis Guillen, Fernando's right-hand man, stepped outside. Fernando knew the man was there—he always knew when he was nearby—but he didn't turn away from staring off the hill toward town.

"What did you find out?"

Jose Luis cleared his throat before he spoke.

"Our people in the police confirmed the woman and children were burned. PFM agents arrived to the scene less than an hour ago."

Fernando turned to look at his right-hand man.

"Anything else?"

"Yes. Two investigators followed up on a lead that took them into the city. Apparently a payphone had been used sometime this morning to call a motel there."

This made Fernando frown.

"Are they sure it's him?"

Meaning the Devil.

Jose Luis said, "Right now all signs point that way, yes."

"But the Diaz compound. No single man could have killed all of those men."

"He's made attacks before."

"Yes, on bodyguards. On convoys. But nothing to this extent. Besides, it doesn't even make sense why the Devil would target them. Ernesto Diaz and his son weren't even at the meeting."

"That had occurred to me as well. But there is, um, something else."

Fernando noticed the pause and frowned at Jose Luis.

"Spit it out."

"Apparently a drone was found just inside the entrance to the compound."

"A drone."

"Yes, a small one. Part of it was destroyed from the blast, but it's still clearly a drone."

Fernando tried to picture it and frowned again.

"What kind of drone are we talking about?"

"Like I said, a small one. One of our people in the police thinks maybe it was being used for surveillance."

This stopped Fernando cold. He stared at his right-hand man for a long moment and shook his head.

"This doesn't feel like it was the Devil's work."

"What are you thinking?"

"I'm thinking that we lost, what, a dozen of our men? Ernesto wanted to pay for the extra protection, and I was happy to oblige him because he and my father were good friends. But fuck, now we're down a dozen men."

Fernando went quiet for another long moment, and then shook his head again.

"No, I don't buy that the Devil was responsible for this."

"But the bodies—"

"Yes, I know the bodies were burned. I can't explain that. Maybe the Devil was responsible for that. Maybe he's branching out. As for the attack on the Diaz compound, as for the dozen men we lost, I feel that we need to make some kind of statement."

Jose Luis looked at him curiously. He had been working for Fernando long enough to know in which direction his boss was headed, but he needed to hear the words first before acting.

"What statement?"

"That this family is not to be fucked with. That we are not to be intimidated. That when someone comes at us, we stand our ground. That we—"

Fernando cut himself off, shaking his head.

"No, it's much simpler than that."

Jose Luis asked, "What is?"

Fernando turned away again and stared down at the town off the hill. La Miserias, a small town of only a few hundred people. The small town with the church in the center, and its bells finally having gone silent from ringing. A wedding, Araceli had said.

Jose Luis cleared his throat.

"Sir?"

Fernando turned back. He felt the nails digging into his palms again and released his fists.

"Get some men together. It's time to make a statement."

23

Gabriela leans back from her computer and gestures at the screen.

"Want to take a look before I upload it?"

I step over to the computer and lean down to read what she's been working on the past hour. She's a good writer, there's no doubt about that. Short, declaratory sentences. Straight to the point. No filler. The girl definitely knows her stuff.

She writes about how the bodies of a woman and two children were found dead, burned today, by a tourist—thankfully she doesn't give any further detail about me—and how police determined a phone call had been made at a nearby payphone to a motel in the city. How the call was made to a motel and how the person working that shift was now a person of interest. She even provides pictures she snapped with her phone—one of the motel, the other of Miguel Dominguez's cluttered apartment. She ends the article stating that while the investigation is obviously ongoing, it's clear that the Devil has struck again.

I lean away from the computer, nodding.

"Impressive."

Gabriela beams as she moves the mouse around to hit the button to upload the article. Within a minute, she says, the article will be live on the site for the world to see.

I say, "You said *La Baliza* is an independent online publication?"

"Yes."

"Who runs it?"

She shrugs.

"I have no idea. I just think of him as the publisher. Nobody knows who he is."

"How many other people contribute to the site?"

She shrugs again.

"No clue."

I frown, looking back at the computer screen.

"So essentially it's just a free-for-all blog—would that be a good description?"

Gabriela shakes her head adamantly.

"Absolutely not. The reason I don't publish the articles under my name—the reason nobody publishes under their own names on the site—is because that's the only way we can protect ourselves."

"So you're hiding behind anonymity."

"No, it's not like that. I mean, yes, it is like that, but *La Baliza* isn't some gossip website. It publishes real news. Oftentimes news that major publications in this country are too afraid to publish for fear that there will be retaliation from either the government or the cartels. I don't know how it is in America, but journalists are not protected citizens. They may not be murdered by the government for speaking out against them, but when they create enemies, those enemies know the right people to call to have them eliminated."

"Is that what happened to your parents?"

Gabriela pauses, and at first I'm not sure whether or not I've struck a nerve. Well, of course I struck a nerve—I just asked about her dead parents, for Christ's sake—but while her body tenses, it's only briefly, and she shakes her head.

"No, their deaths were not nearly as interesting."

"What do you mean?"

She shrugs again, her face somber.

"They were in the wrong place at the wrong time. They were in the city, out at dinner, when a gang drove by and opened fire at a restaurant. Apparently the restaurant was owned by the parent of a rival gang member. Thirteen people died that day, all of them customers. None of the gang members were even at the restaurant, and neither were the gang member's parents."

"I'm sorry. How long ago did this happen?"

"It's been two years. My grandmother took me in right after. She's a good woman, though I think she's starting to show signs of dementia. You saw her on her tablet? I keep encouraging her to play those puzzle games to keep her mind active. But, well, she's getting old. She loves to cook, but her food isn't nearly as good as it used to be. Speaking of which, would you like something to eat?"

I haven't eaten in over twenty-four hours—my stomach completely empty—but right now I don't want to stop this conversation so I force a smile and wave off the offer.

"Thanks, but I'm okay right now. Were either of your parents journalists?"

She smiles that somber smile of hers.

"No, and they would think I'm crazy doing what I'm doing. But … I think they would understand, too."

"No offense, Gabriela, but it is crazy what you're doing. You could get yourself killed."

She shrugs again, this time almost listlessly.

"Anybody can get killed doing anything. I could slip walking down the steps and break my neck. I could step out into the street and get hit by a bus tomorrow. Or a gang could shoot up the café I'm in next week. The way I see it, we all have limited time here on this earth, and we should make the most of that time. For me, I want to get the truth out there to the people who care."

"What truth?"

"Just the truth. People need to know about the crime and corruption that happens in this country. I mean, I *know* they know about the crime and corruption because they see it every day, but most times it doesn't get reported by the news media for one reason or another. People have turned to social media to find out what's really going on. They use Twitter and Facebook to communicate. *La Baliza* isn't the only news hub in the country that does the kind of reporting we do. But it's become one of the best. You can't just sign up and start writing for them. There's no email addresses on the site. For me to even use it I needed to download Tor. Are you familiar with Tor?"

I nod. I'd heard Scooter talk about it once. I rarely used the Internet myself—in my previous life I had no time for social media let alone much else—but Scooter had always told me that if I use the Internet I needed to use Tor. Essentially, from how I remembered Scooter explaining it, Tor is a free browser that helps defend people from network surveillance and traffic analysis. By using Tor, Gabriela is able to post her stories without fear some hacker the cartel hired can trace her. Which is good, considering the stuff she says *La Baliza* publishes.

The somber expression on Gabriela's face somehow deepens. She stares past me, off into a distance only she can see, and speaks softly.

"There was this woman a couple years ago, she was an online journalist kind of like me. She lived in Tamaulipas, which was controlled by the Gulf Cartel and Zetas. The cartels had final say over what got printed or broadcasted. Probably *still* do, to be honest. But this woman, she would post danger alerts on Twitter that pinpointed the locations of violence as it was happening. People would send her information and she would help it get out there for everybody else. She also encouraged victims of crime not to remain silent and to report what happened to the police even with the knowledge that there would probably be reprisal. She understood that the only way to defeat the fear the cartels had brought to the people was for the people to finally stand up."

Gabriela shakes her head slowly, still staring off into that distance.

"The cartels put out ransoms on her. And not just her, but others who worked for the news hub and tried to defy them. The founder of the site even shut it down and left the state because he feared for his life. But this woman ... she kept doing what she had always done, which was to help the people of Tamaulipas stand up to the cartels. And it wasn't just helping people stand up to the cartels—she did so much more. She helped raise money for the community, organized blood donations, and helped people find affordable housing and free medical care. She was a hero, to be honest. A true hero."

Tears have begun to well in Gabriela's eyes. She wipes them away, focusing once again on me.

"The cartel found her. I don't even know which cartel it was. And the cartel ... killed her. But before they killed her, they tweeted from her phone, first outing her as the citizen journalist who had defied the cartels, then sending a message that the cartels would be coming for the other citizen journalists next. They posted a picture with her hands folded in front of her staring at the camera, and then a picture of her lying on the ground with a bullet hole in her head. The founder of the news site confirmed that it was her, and Twitter eventually shut down her account."

Gabriela goes silent again, wiping at her eyes.

"She was truly a hero. A role model, I guess you would say. Her fearlessness was absolutely spellbinding. She knew what she was doing was dangerous, that it would some day get her killed, but she did it anyway. I guess that's why I do what I do. I know it's dangerous, that it will probably get me killed some day, but if I don't do it, who else will?"

Gabriela stops there, letting the question hang in the air between us.

I nod and glance again at the computer screen.

"So tell me about the Devil."

24

Nobody knows when the Devil first started killing, Gabriela says. Cartel families are not like celebrities. They're not in the public eye. Drug lords yes, but not all drug lords. The government offers rewards for many of the drug lords, but the drug lords have too much power politically that the rewards don't matter. Oftentimes it's the politicians and law enforcement who must rely on those drug lords that they're supposed to be hunting to make ends meet, so of course they won't turn them in even though sometimes the rewards can go up to 30 million pesos. They know that once they turn in a drug lord, there will be a target on their backs.

The Devil has been killing for over a year now. Sometimes several months will pass between his kills. Sometimes weeks. The Devil, Gabriela says, is unpredictable. The first cartel the Devil attacked was the Juarez Cartel. One of the drug lord's wives and children were found burned to death out in a field. It was first reported on *La Baliza*, which had launched maybe a month earlier. From there, the rest of the news hubs picked it up, though the major newspapers were hesitant to carry the news for fear of retribution from the Juarez Cartel.

La Baliza didn't give the Devil his name. They had simply reported the events. Several months passed, and most people forgot about what happened, until another woman and her three children were found burned to death several miles outside Matamoros. It was reported that another drug lord's family had been targeted. This time it was the Gulf Cartel who had been hit.

Now more and more people started paying attention. The first time may have been a fluke, they reasoned, but now another drug lord's wife and children had been found burned to death.

Gabriela asks me, "Are you familiar with the cartels?"

I shake my head. While much of my work for the government had been all over the world, I hadn't done any work in Mexico.

Gabriela says, "There are seven major cartels. Each of the cartels has several different leaders, and many times they fight with each other over product or territory. But families are usually off limits. The fact that somebody had taken the wife and children of one of the leaders from the Juarez Cartel and burned them alive was an act of war. But from what I heard, all of the families immediately claimed they had nothing to do with it."

Over the course of the next year the Devil struck two more times. This time the cartels affected were the Beltran-Leyva and the Tijuana. Each time the mother and children were found burned to death. The sights were more public, in the middle of cities. Whoever was killing these women and children wanted to make sure the public knew.

For that first year, the cartels started fighting each other again. The truce they had agreed upon was over. It was an outright war, with gangs attacking other gangs in towns and cities, leaving hundreds of civilians much like Gabriela's own parents dead in the cross fire.

The cartel leaders began hiding their wives and children. Some even sent them off to hide away in various countries. They were all convinced their families were next. That the Devil would come for their wives and children and burn them alive.

The cartels didn't like the press attention, though. They threatened many of the major newspapers from publishing stories about the Devil. They didn't like the idea that somebody—*one person*, if that was to be believed—had managed to do so much damage to them. So it became the task of *La Baliza* and other news hubs to make sure they learned as soon as possible when the Devil struck again. And when he did, they made sure to get the news out there for the country to see.

Gabriela pauses her story, looking at me closely.

"From what I heard there's a reward for the Devil. Several of the cartels have vowed to put in 30 million pesos each. Combined, the bounty is up over ten million dollars US."

I ask, "Dead or alive?"

"They want him alive. That's the only way they will know for sure the person brought to them is really the Devil."

"And let me guess—they're going to torture the shit out of him."

Gabriela doesn't answer, at least not verbally. She looks away from me, her face becoming all at once troubled.

I ask, "What's wrong?"

"When I first realized that there was somebody out there doing this, I was happy. It sounds terrible of me, I know, but the cartels in this country are vicious. They kill people as if they are nothing. They rape women and children. Sometimes they even keep women and children as sex slaves. They're awful people, and the idea that somebody was coming at them, attacking them that way, was in a strange way … uplifting."

Gabriela frowns at me.

"But he's killing children. They may be the children of the drug lords, may one day take after their fathers, but they're still children. It's ... tragic and deserved at the same time. Like I said, it sounds terrible of me."

I shake my head and say, "No, it doesn't."

"Yes, it does. I know it does. But sometimes ... sometimes I don't care."

There's a silence then, both of us sitting in her bedroom, staring at one another.

I ask, "Was Ernesto Diaz considered part of the cartel?"

Her frown deepens.

"How do you know his name?"

I say nothing.

Her eyes narrow.

"What are you really doing here?"

"I told you, I'm on vacation."

"Yes, and I don't believe you."

The computer on the desk chimes. The screensaver has come up, and Gabriela moves the mouse to make the screensaver disappear.

I ask, "What is it?"

"An email came through from *La Baliza*."

"How can you be so sure?"

"I only use one email address to communicate with them."

She moves the mouse around again and opens a window. There isn't much text in the email.

"That's weird."

I stand up from the bed and step closer to the computer.

"What's weird?"

"He says he needed to make a change to my story."

"Who says?"

"The publisher."

"What did he change?"

"Almost everything. He took out all reference to the Devil."

"Why would he do that?"

Gabriela shakes her head, frustrated, and types back an angry response asking why this change was needed as the murders were obviously done by the Devil.

A response comes back a minute later.

Until we have more evidence, we do not know for sure the Devil is responsible. Don't let it get you down. You did great work.

Gabriela doesn't move for several long seconds, staring at the screen, and then she speaks between clenched teeth.

"This is fucking bullshit."

I say nothing.

Gabriela smacks the mouse to delete the email and stands up from the chair, begins pacing around the room.

"Such bullshit."

I watch her for a while, letting her vent, and then ask another question.

"How did you even know about the murders?"

She pauses, glancing at me with startled surprise.

"What?"

"The murders. How did you know about it?"

"I told you, there's a website where people can leave tips. Today I received a tip about the murder and then how the call had been placed to that motel. It would have taken me too long to go to the murder scene, so I went to the motel and waited. I figured if after an hour nobody showed up, it would have been a crank tip. Sometimes those come through, and we need to be careful of traps. But then Ramon and Carlos showed up."

"You know their names?"

She nods.

"I know almost all of the police officers around the area, at least the ones with authority. It's the same with local politicians. I usually write about the corruption in the city, so of course I need to know who these people are."

I step over to the window and look out through the shades. The sun is starting to set. I turn back to her.

"Gabriela, I don't know you very well, but you are one brave *senorita*."

She smiles.

"I think I could say the same thing about you."

Her cell phone on the desk vibrates. Gabriela picks it up and looks at the screen. She stares for a long moment, and then little by little her face starts to fall.

I ask, "What's wrong?"

"A new tip came in. Gunmen just killed over twenty people at a wedding in La Miserias."

She pauses and looks up at me, her voice cracking as she says the rest.

"The person who sent the tip says the police believe it's in retaliation for what happened last night to Ernesto Diaz."

25

La Miserias was located about an hour south of Culiacán.

They took two vehicles—Ramon and Carlos in the pickup, the PFM agents trailing them in the rental car. Ramon drove while Carlos sat in the passenger seat, his window down so he could smoke. It was early evening, the sun having just set, and they both should have been gone for the day. Carlos at home with his big screen TV and dog, Ramon at home with his wife and baby.

As if sensing Ramon's thoughts, Carlos asked, "How is your little girl doing?"

"She's good."

"Talking yet?"

"Just babbling."

Carlos took a final drag on his cigarette and flicked the butt out the window.

"Just wait until she says 'mama' and 'dada' for the first time. You'll never forget it."

Ramon smiled and checked the rearview mirror to make sure the PFM agents were still behind them.

He and Carlos had taken them to the motel earlier, then to Miguel Dominguez's apartment, and that was about it. Besides those two places and the building in which the bodies were found, they didn't have much else to go on. They had found a recent photo of Miguel and sent it around for officers to keep an eye out, but that was it. The PFM agents made their notes and said they were going to check into their hotel (they'd be staying for at least a couple days), when news had come across about the mass shooting in La Miserias. When they learned rumor had it Fernando Sanchez Morales had approved the shooting, the agents wanted to investigate the scene as well.

When they arrived at La Miserias, several police cars were already there, as were a number of ambulances.

There were crowds near the center of the town where the shooting took place. As they stepped out of the car they heard women crying.

Bodies were splayed in the town square. Men and women, even some children. Ramon had heard at least twenty bodies, but judging by the carnage, the number looked to be larger.

Carlos lit another cigarette, shaking his head as he muttered, "Jesus Christ."

The PFM agents stepped up next to them. Just like Ramon, both wore masks. Serrano nodded at the nearby buildings.

"We're going to look around."

The two agents walked away.

Ramon and Carlos watched them for a couple seconds before turning their attention back to the bodies.

Carlos said again, "Jesus Christ."

He pointed.

"Do you see her over there? They killed the bride."

Her wedding dress was stained with so much blood it had almost become black.

One of the officers noticed them and hurried over. Before he could even open his mouth, Carlos raised a finger.

"Let me guess. The people who did this were wearing masks so nobody knows who they were and nobody in town is about ready to speculate."

The officer's shoulders dropped as he nodded solemnly. "Yes."

Carlos said, "Can anybody at least say how many shooters there were?"

The officer shrugged.

"One person said six. Another said eight. Two pickup trucks tore into town while everybody was dancing in the square. The whole town was here."

The officer trailed off, shaking his head. He looked sick to his stomach even relating the events.

Ramon asked, "Does anybody remember from which direction the pickup trucks came?"

"I heard they came from both directions. One came down the street, the other came up. They stopped and men jumped down from the truck beds and opened fire. It lasted only a minute, and then the men jumped back into the truck beds and the trucks drove away."

Carlos glanced at Ramon to see if he had any further questions. Ramon shook his head. Carlos dismissed the officer saying that they would check the bodies soon. The officer nodded and returned to help the other officers as they attempted to keep everyone back. A few of the crying women kept trying to break past the officers to cling to their dead loved ones.

Carlos said, "There's no rhyme or reason here."

"What do you mean?"

"The people of this town aren't connected. They have no ties to the cartel. Most of them are farmers."

Carlos sighed, shaking his head.

"We both know who's responsible. Everybody in this town knows who's responsible."

He left it at that. He didn't need to say the rest. Fernando

Sanchez Morales was part of the Sinaloa Cartel. Not quite a drug lord yet—that would be a few more years off if he played his cards right—but he was powerful enough to pay off the right people to stay out of trouble. What had happened here this evening was just what they'd been told when the call first came in. Retribution for what had happened to Ernesto Diaz last night. And it wasn't because anybody in this town had any connection to what happened to Diaz, but because Morales no doubt decided there needed to be a consequence for what happened, so why not kill some innocent townspeople?

Ramon turned and stared off at the hill two miles away and the large house on top of the hill.

"He's probably watching us right now."

Carlos lit another cigarette, nodding.

"Probably."

"And there's not a goddamned thing we can do about it."

"No, there is not."

"Sometimes I hate my job."

"*Sometimes*?"

Carlos snorted smoke through his nose.

"Wait until you get to be my age. You'll hate every goddamned minute."

Ramon shook his head and turned his attention back to the town square and the crowd and the dead bodies. He started to say something else but froze.

Carlos said, "What's wrong?"

Ramon didn't blink as he stared ahead, not wanting to lose sight of her.

"Samantha Lu is here."

26

Twenty-eight.

That's the number of bodies littering the town square. At least, that's the number I'm able to count from where I stand in the crowd with Gabriela.

She has her phone out, snapping pictures, documenting the scene. My first impulse is to grab the phone from her hand, smash it on the ground, ask her what the hell she's thinking. But this is her job. Her purpose. The whole reason she's here. She didn't have to agree to let me tag along. That was her decision, and I respect the work she does.

A minute or two has passed, but it feels like an hour. It's night now, and there aren't that many lights around the town. The headlights of the police cars and ambulances mostly light the square. Around us women sob and murmur prayers. The few police officers are doing what they can to keep the relatives back, but many of them want to be close to their loved ones.

An old man stands near us. His shirt and pants are still fresh with blood, though it's clearly not his blood. Gabriela asks him what exactly happened. He doesn't answer at first, just stares at the bodies, but then he shrugs his old shoulders. In a raspy voice he says two pickup trucks came into town during the party and men got out with guns and started shooting. The man's voice cracks as he tells us one of the dead bodies is his granddaughter.

I close my eyes. Take a deep breath. Try to slow my heartbeat.

Beside me, Gabriela pauses in her discussion with the old man. She sucks air in between her teeth. The sharp noise catches my attention and I open my eyes and look at her.

At first I think she's looking right back at me. But no—she's staring past me. I glance over my shoulder, not sure what I'm supposed to be looking for, but then I see him.

Ramon is weaving through the crowd, heading our way.

I turn and look past Gabriela and see the older man, Carlos, heading our way in the opposite direction.

Which means our only way out is behind us, deeper into town.

Without hesitation, I grab Gabriela's arm and pull her toward the fringe of the crowd. For her credit she doesn't protest, just follows me as I step left and right, zigzagging us out of the crowd.

I spare a second to glance over my shoulder and determine that, yes, Ramon and Carlos are indeed coming for us. They're pushing through the crowd now, not even making any attempt of discretion.

We step past the few people lingering on the outskirts of the crowd and break for the closest alleyway.

We're halfway down the alleyway when I hear Ramon shout behind us, telling us to stop.

We're near the end of the alleyway when I hear Ramon threaten to shoot if we don't comply.

We turn the corner and there are two men standing in our way. They look official. Both wear masks just like Ramon. Each aims a gun at us. My own gun is in the waistband of my shorts.

It would take two seconds to reach for it, pull it out, but by then one of these men could easily shoot us in the narrow space.

Gabriela and I stop short. I raise my hands. Gabriela, after a stunned second, raises her own hands.

Ramon and Carlos catch up to us, Carlos breathing heavily.

Carlos says, "Jesus Christ. I'm out of fucking shape."

Ramon now has his own gun in hand. He approaches us carefully, keeping the gun aimed.

"Get up against the wall."

I ask, "Aren't you supposed to buy us dinner first?"

Ramon doesn't smile. Doesn't say anything. None of the men do.

Gabriela and I turn and place our hands against the cold brick wall.

Down at the end of the alleyway, an old woman with a cane watches us. Carlos yells at her to go away. The old woman doesn't move for several long seconds before she shuffles out of view.

Ramon steps up behind us.

"I need to search you both."

I say, "No, you don't."

"Yes, I do. At this moment I'm under the assumption you're armed. Is that assumption correct?"

"This is the worst vacation I've ever been on."

Ramon repeats himself: "Is that assumption correct?"

"I'm going to ask my travel agent for a refund."

I glance at Gabriela but she doesn't seem amused. She's staring straight at the wall, her lips moving quietly in what may be a silent prayer.

Ramon pats me down first. He finds the gun easily enough. He hands it to Carlos, then checks my front pockets. Pulls out my passport and the disposable phone and the few pesos I have left as well as the picture the prostitute outside that motel gave me.

Ramon unfolds the picture enough to glance at it in the dark alleyway.

"Who is this supposed to be?"

I say nothing.

Ramon hands the items to Carlos and then pats down Gabriela. He takes out her cell phone and her keys and some money.

"No identification. I guess that means I'll have to ask you who you are and what you're doing here, and I hope for your sake, you're honest."

Gabriela's lips pause. She stares straight ahead at the cold brick, considering it. Before she can answer, though, I speak.

"Don't tell him."

Ramon says, "We'll get to you later."

"Why not get to me now? You have questions, I have answers."

"As I said, we'll get to you later. There's more to you than we first thought."

Carlos has set our items down on the ground. He has his gun out, pointed at us.

"Enough of this bullshit. Ramon, cuff them."

Okay, this is definitely not heading in an ideal direction. Time to mix things up.

As Ramon grabs my left arm and starts to pull it back, I say, "Don't."

He pauses.

Staring at the cold brick wall, I say, "If you know what's good for you, give us back our stuff and we'll be on our way."

One of the government men snorts a laugh.

"Is that a threat?"

"No, this is a threat. If you don't give us back our stuff and let us be on our way, you all will have massive headaches in the morning."

For a moment, nobody moves. Then Ramon continues to pull back my left arm. As the plastic zip-tie touches my skin, I twist to the left, spinning into him, and with my right fist punch him in the face.

Stunned, Ramon lets go of my arm, stumbles back. He's still standing, though, so I wrap my left arm around his neck as I move to the right and launch myself in the air, my momentum enough to swing me around toward the two government men. My foot connects with only one of the men, right in the side of his face, but it's enough to send him stumbling into his partner. Both feet on the ground again, I release my grip on Ramon's neck and kick him in the back of the knees, sending him to the ground, and as he falls I somersault over him toward Carlos. Before he can fire off a round, I punch him once in the stomach and then push him straight back into the brick wall. The gun falls from his hand and I grab it midair, then turn and scramble to the government men who are trying to get back on their feet. I jump at the wall and use the momentum to perform a roundhouse kick at both of the men's faces. One of the men gets knocked out. The other manages to stay upright for another moment, just long enough for me to kick him straight in the chest. Behind me, Ramon jumps to his feet and I spin, throwing another roundhouse kick in his direction. He's expecting it, though, and ducks the kick. Before I try another kick, I remember I'm still holding a gun and aim it at Ramon.

"Get on your knees."

He stares at me and says, "You're not going to shoot me."

"Do you want to test that theory?"

Ramon's face is impassive.

"You shot those pimps outside Miguel Dominguez's apartment building, didn't you? We know it was you. What were you doing there?"

"Minding my own business."

Behind me, one of the government agents grunts as he tries to rise to his feet.

I spin and throw another kick at his face. This one sends him down and out.

I turn back to Ramon who hasn't moved.

"I said get down on your knees."

He slowly lowers himself down to the ground.

"Now pull your gun from its holster and toss it over here."

He pulls the gun from its holster and tosses it at my feet.

Keeping Carlos's gun aimed at him, I crouch down and grab the gun and fling it onto the roof of the closest building. I step back and unburden the two government men of their guns and fling those up on the roof as well.

I step close to Gabriela, nudge her with my elbow.

"Get our things."

She doesn't move at first, and I think maybe she's frozen with shock. But then she shakes it off and hurries over to where Carlos placed our items. She scrambles to pick up everything, but Carlos leans forward from where he is on the ground, trying to grab her. She shrieks and jumps back.

We don't have time for this, so I step forward and whack Ramon with the butt of the gun. He falls to the ground. Just like I told the men, they're all going to have massive headaches in the morning.

Hurrying over to Gabriela, I give Carlos a whack on the side of the head with the gun and then grab Gabriela's arm and pull her back down the alleyway.

"My ID and passport?"

She hands them to me as well as the disposable phone and says, "I didn't grab the photograph."

I shake my head, tell her not to worry about it. The ID and passport are the most important things. Not that either gives my actual name, but less documentation in the authorities' hands, the better.

We hurry across the street into another alleyway. The men will be giving chase in no time. We might manage to make it back to Gabriela's car, but I'm worried about getting into a chase on the main road.

We reach the end of the alleyway and I pause, glancing back the way we came. I can see two of them farther away, just shadows in the dark.

"Come on, let's go."

Despite lights on inside, the houses along here all stand still and quiet. Of course they do. I would imagine everybody in town is still at the square.

I pull Gabriela toward one of the nearest houses. It's only one story tall. There's a way to climb up to the roof from the outside. Not quite a ladder, but enough places to grip to climb up.

As quietly as I can, I motion for Gabriela to hurry and climb up to the roof. She does it faster that I thought she would, scaling it like a pro. I stuff the gun in the waistband of my shorts and climb up after her.

On the top of the roof there's just enough space to lie flat. I lie there with Gabriela and wait.

It doesn't take long.

Seconds later we can hear the heavy pounding of footsteps. Then the shouting of the men's voices as they speculate where we went. One of them—Carlos?—suggests searching the houses. The men apparently agree to this idea without question because then we hear front doors opening and closing. This goes on for several minutes, the men hastily searching each house, before a woman shouts.

"What are you doing to our homes? Get out! Get out of our homes!"

One of the government men tells the woman that they're searching for suspects.

The woman shouts, "Suspects for the killing that occurred here tonight?"

The government man doesn't answer.

The woman shouts, "Our town is in pain and you go through our *homes*? Get out! Get out! *Get out!*"

Other townspeople take up the chorus. They must have

heard her from the square and hurried over to find out what was wrong. Soon her voice is accompanied by a half-dozen more, then a dozen more.

"Get out! Get out! Get out!"

It becomes a chant. A chant of a town which just suffered a great loss. Ramon and Carlos and the government men aren't about to cause more grief. They relent and leave.

Minutes pass, and the townspeople below start to wander away, either back to their homes or back to the square to continue grieving. Gabriela is motionless beside me. The urge to glance over the edge of the roof, to check whether the coast is clear, is strong, but we remain where we are. We lie on our backs and stare up at the clear night sky.

Until, down on the street in front of the house, a woman speaks.

"You can come down now."

Gabriela tenses.

I turn my head and stare back at her, urge her with my eyes to remain quiet.

The woman on the street speaks again.

"They are gone. You are safe now. You can come down."

Is it a trick? Possibly. But after what just happened it doesn't feel like a trick. The townspeople ran our pursuers out of town. No chance it was all a ruse. Besides, the woman who just spoke, she sounds like the woman who had started yelling in the first place. The woman who started the chant for the men to get out.

I look at Gabriela once more. She looks terrified. I take a deep breath, roll over, and raise myself just enough to peek over the edge.

The old woman with the cane stares up at me. She motions at the empty street.

"Well, what are you waiting for?"

27

The old woman doesn't move as we climb down from the roof. She just watches, leaning on her cane. Occasionally she'll look up and down the street to ensure nobody is coming, but besides that she watches us with an almost bored expression. Then, once I've helped Gabriela to the ground, the old woman motions at us.

"Follow me."

She turns and starts shuffling down the street and only goes several paces before she realizes we're not following and turns back.

"Is there a problem?"

I survey the street to make sure it's empty as I step forward.

"Why should we come with you?"

The woman leans all her weight on the cane, pursuing her lips.

"I'm trying to help you."

"How so?"

"Did you not hear me tell those men to leave this town? Now they have left—I saw it with my own eyes—but there are other police still in town. They are already loading the bodies into trucks. I should be in the town square right now with everybody else mourning, but something tells me you two could use my help. So will you let me help you?"

I glance at Gabriela, who stands there uncertain, and I turn back to the woman and nod.

"Lead the way."

Because of the cane, the woman doesn't move very fast. She veers off the street at one point and takes us between houses to the next street, then between more houses to another street. I have Gabriela walk between us, keeping the gun in my hand just in case. At one point the old woman glances back, notices the gun, and chuckles.

Then we finally come to yet another house and the old woman opens the back door and motions us inside.

We enter a kitchen. The smell of food lingers, causing my stomach to growl.

The old woman lets the door close behind her as she walks past us through the kitchen and deeper into the house.

"You should be safe here. I don't imagine those men who chased you will come back, but if they do, I guess we will just have to run them off again."

She smiles at us, but then all at once her expression turns solemn. In the light it's easier now to see the scars on her face. From her forehead to her chin, they streak her face like chasms.

"My name is Yolanda. What are your names?"

Neither Gabriela nor I say anything.

Yolanda nods as if she understands the reason for our reticence. She motions us to sit on a couch as she lowers herself down onto a chair.

Gabriela and I sit on the couch. Neither one of us speaks.

A brown cat pads into the room. It pauses to look at us, then slinks over to the chair and jumps up onto Yolanda's lap.

Yolanda smiles down at the cat as she strokes its back.

"This is Dorado."

Still Gabriela and I don't speak. The house is silent, but we must not be too far away from the town square, because even inside we can hear the distant sobbing.

The silence in the house starts to become almost too unnerving, so I decide to break it.

"I'm sorry for what happened tonight."

The apology is more than just perfunctory. In many ways, I'm responsible for those dead twenty-eight people, not to mention the others who had been wounded and have since been taken to a hospital.

Yolanda stares down at the cat as she pets it.

"It is not the first time tragedy has befallen this town, and it will not be the last. Every time we are able to bounce back from it."

I ask, "Why is this town called La Miserias?"

Yolanda pauses to give me a sidelong glance.

"As I said, it is not the first time tragedy has befallen this town."

She leaves it at that for a long moment, petting the cat again, before she rests her head back on the seat and closes her eyes. For a moment I think she's going to fall asleep, but then her eyes snap open and she looks at us again.

"What did those men want with you?"

We say nothing.

Yolanda says, "I sent those men away. I am hiding you in my home. I think the least you can do is be honest with me."

I'm not sure what to say at first. I don't quite agree that the least we can do for this woman is be honest with her, but before I can even argue that point, Gabriela opens her mouth.

"We are journalists."

This clearly wasn't what the old woman was expecting to hear. She sets the cat aside as she leans forward in her seat.

"Is that right?"

Gabriela nods.

"We came here to write about what happened. One of the men recognized me and tried to catch us."

Yolanda's gaze flicks from Gabriela to me.

"I saw what you did to those men. Based on how quickly you moved, you do not strike me as a writer."

I say nothing.

Gabriela asks, "Is it true what they say happened?"

Yolanda says, "I suppose that depends on what they say happened."

"They say that Fernando Sanchez Morales wanted retribution for what happened to Ernesto Diaz last night."

Yolanda doesn't answer right away. The cat sits at her feet, watching us. Yolanda leans down and picks up the cat and places it back on her lap and starts petting it again. She seems lost in a trance before she blinks and slowly nods.

"That is what one of the men said before they opened fire. When men like those come to kill, they do so with a purpose more than just killing. They want to make a point. And they make sure their point is known."

I ask, "How can they get away with that?"

Yolanda smiles.

"You are not from around here, are you?"

She squints at me.

"You sound American. Are you American? If you are American, then I cannot imagine you write for any newspaper in this country."

I say nothing. Gabriela says nothing. Yolanda issues a heavy sigh and goes back to petting the cat.

"The cartels can do whatever it is they please, especially in towns like this one. We have no local law enforcement. We are just common people. We do not have much money, so politicians do not care about us. When President Cortez entered office last year, he promised to do something about the cartel violence. He ran on that platform. The cartels did everything they could to try to stop him—they even murdered his son and his son's family—but he still won."

Yolanda nods to herself, still petting the cat.

"Many years ago the people in towns like this stood up to the cartels. They called themselves *autodefensas*. They were tired of the cartels coming into their towns and doing whatever they pleased. They started to fight back."

I ask, "What happened?"

Gabriela answers.

"They were eventually disbanded. The movement became too large, too unruly. Some of the men started acting just as bad as the cartels. They would steal from the people. Some raped women. In some cases, cartel members even joined the groups so that they could be on the inside. Nobody knew who was in charge. The government needed to step in. They said that those who wanted to still fight against the cartels could do so but they would need to join the Army and register their weapons. Many of them did, while a few refused. Those were arrested."

I glance at Yolanda.

"Where did this happen?"

The old woman says, "It started in Michoacán. But a few similar groups popped up around the country in different states. There are more regular citizens than there are cartel members. But the cartel has a lot of money, and they have a lot of weapons, which makes it difficult for a town such as ours to fight back."

There's a silence. The only sounds are the continued sobbing out in the town square and the cat purring on Yolanda's lap.

The old woman watches me. For a moment, it feels like Gabriela isn't even in the room with us, that the cat isn't even there, and it's just Yolanda and myself.

The woman says, "I wonder when it will happen again."

"When what will happen again?"

"When Morales will feel the need to prove a point. When he will send more men to kill the people of this town. Tonight is not the first time it has happened, and it most certainly will not be the last. I wonder when it will happen again. I wonder … I wonder how many people will die next time."

28

I drive us back to the city.

Gabriela is too shaken to drive. At least, that's the impression I get. She doesn't say it so much as displays it with her actions. Her hand trembled when she gave me her keys, and when she slipped inside the car she slumped down in her seat and stared out her window and didn't say anything.

A half hour has passed since we left La Miserias and it's at least another half hour to go before we hit the city.

I clear my throat.

"How do you feel?"

Gabriela doesn't answer.

I let it go for another minute, just driving, trying to figure out what I can possibly say to the girl to get her to come around.

But then she shifts in her seat and looks at me.

"I don't think I can do this anymore."

Her voice is so soft I can barely hear it over the tires humming on the highway.

I say, "You don't think you can do what anymore?"

"Just … *this*."

She motions at the car's dashboard, as if that explains everything. Which in a way it does. I know exactly what she means, but I want to hear her say the words.

"What's this?"

She takes a heavy breath, staring hard at me now.

"You know exactly what I'm talking about. I thought I could do it—I'd done it for months already without any problems—but after tonight …"

She shakes her head as her voice fades away. She leans back in her seat, places her head against the headrest. Doesn't say anything else.

I check the rearview mirror once again to make sure we're not being followed.

"Earlier today teenagers with guns came at us. Do you not remember that happening?"

She issues a soft, desperate laugh.

"Of course I remember that happening. And that was scary, but this …"

She lifts her hand, wobbling it back and forth, as if the missing words will somehow appear in her palm. Then she drops the hand and sighs.

"Before it didn't seem real. I mean, I *know* it was real—I was right there when it happened, saw everything with my own eyes—but for some reason it just didn't feel real. But tonight … I thought those men were going to kill us."

She shakes her head suddenly, sitting up in her seat.

"No, I thought they were going to rape us before they killed us. And that … that realization somehow made it all the more real. All the more worse. Stupid teenagers with guns are one thing. But corrupt cops …"

She shakes her head again.

"I sound so weak, don't I?"

I don't answer at first. I'm not sure what to tell Gabriela. The fact is I don't know her very well. She seems tough, seems dedicated, but sometimes those things can be simple facades. The people who act the strongest are sometimes those who are the weakest. They hide behind bravado so long they soon start believing their own bullshit.

"Do you think Ramon and Carlos are corrupt?"

She shrugs, staring out her window.

"I don't know. Probably not. It's impossible to say who in law enforcement is corrupt. And maybe they wouldn't have raped us and killed us—maybe they would have just taken us to jail—but once the idea entered my mind ..."

She shakes her head again and turns to look at me.

"Do you think I should stop?"

"I have no clue. If you don't want to keep doing this, then stop doing it. It doesn't matter to me."

In the flash of headlights from a passing car I see her eyes tearing up.

She says, "Don't you ever get scared?"

"All the time."

"How do you deal with it?"

The question gives me pause.

"I'm not sure. The truth is, I've never thought about it much. I guess I just live my life day by day. I don't worry about next year. Or next month. Or even tomorrow."

"But don't you ... have dreams? Like to someday get married and have children?"

"Honestly? It's never really appealed to me."

"But haven't you ever been in love?"

I say nothing to this. Of course I've been in love. And just my luck, of course the guy I loved turned out to be one massive douche who faked his death along with my father and then came back, years later, to try to kill me.

My silence is enough to give Gabriela the hint. She slumps in her seat again and stares out her window. When she speaks next, her voice is just above a whisper.

"I've been in love too many times to count. It sounds silly, I know, and maybe it's because I'm so young. But every time I go out with a guy I instantly fall in love with him. It sounds pathetic, doesn't it? I don't come on too strong—that's not what I mean—but in my heart I instantly see myself living the rest of my life with whoever I'm out with at that moment. I think it's because I want to get married some day, have children, all of that. I want to move away from Culiacán. I want to move to the United States where it's safe. Where you can raise a family and not worry about getting killed in your sleep."

Gabriela falls silent, wiping the tears from her eyes.

I ask, "Do you have much interaction with the cops around Culiacán?"

"Not really. I know *of* them, but I don't know them."

"Do you know where Ramon lives?"

This makes her pause. She watches me in the dark for a very long time, studying the side of my face.

I say, "Relax. I'm not going to kill him."

"Then why are you asking where he lives?"

"After what happened tonight with Ramon and his partner and those government men, I want to assure Ramon that I'm not the enemy here."

"Ramon is *policía*, so his information won't be easy to find, but I'll email the publisher of *La Baliza*. Maybe he'll be able to track it down."

"Also see if he can find Ramon's phone number."

She nods, already typing away on her cell phone. After a long moment, she hits a final button and sets the phone in her lap.

"Done."

"Thanks. Now, about your story."

Her voice becomes all at once guarded.

"What about my story?"

"Are you going to write it?"

Gabriela hesitates a beat.

"I might."

"I think you should. And I think you should sleep on your decision to stop doing what you do. Like you said, if you don't do it, who else will?"

Gabriela leans back in her seat, stares out her window as she answers in a soft voice.

"I'll think about it."

Ten minutes later, just as we see the city lights ahead of us, Gabriela's cell phone dings.

I ask, "The publisher?"

She nods, reading the screen. Then she smiles at me.

"He found it."

29

Ramon winced at the touch of the rubbing alcohol.

His wife said, "Hold still. Don't be a baby."

"But it stings."

They were in the kitchen, just the two of them, his daughter already in her crib and sound asleep.

His wife took her time as she dabbed the cloth soaked with rubbing alcohol on the side of his head. That was where Samantha Lu—or whoever she was—had kicked him.

"Were you there?"

His wife didn't meet his eye as she asked the question.

He asked, "Was I where?"

She leaned back, inspecting the side of his face, and then tossed the cloth into the sink. Without a word she stood up and went to the sink and started washing her hands. Ramon watched her for a long moment, his beautiful wife, the woman he had known since school. As a nurse she spent her days dealing with people who needed their wounds stitched up, and now here she was at home doing it for her husband.

She rarely asked about his job. She had decided long ago

that she didn't want to know, that she didn't want to face this reality. But now she had asked if he was there, and of course he knew what she meant. Not at La Miserias—she already knew he had been there earlier tonight—but at that abandoned brick building with the three charred bodies.

"I was, yes."

She turned back to him, her face all at once pinched.

"What was it like?"

He had to actually think about it for a moment. Until then, he hadn't really had a chance to process it.

"It was terrible."

"But you've surely seen worse before, haven't you?"

He had. Of course he had. Being an investigator in Culiacán presented him with awful things on a daily basis. He'd seen children lying dead in the streets. A man who had been skinned alive. A woman's headless body propped up in the doorway of a church.

He took a deep breath, let it out slowly.

"This was different somehow."

She pulled out the chair across from him and sat down.

"What do you mean?"

"Just ... just the idea that it might be the work of the Devil"— Ramon shook his head—"I had a chill when I first saw the bodies."

"And it was really her?"

Ramon nodded.

"Yes. I mean, it has to be her. She would have been the only woman in that house before it was attacked. Her and the children. Besides, the call that came in said as much."

Her voice trembled as she asked the next question.

"He called?"

"Yes. He told the police where to find the bodies. I don't think anybody took it seriously. We've gotten crank calls like that before. People who say they know who the Devil is and want the reward or people confessing to be the Devil because they're crazy. But this … this was different."

"How is Geraldo taking it?"

"How would you think he's taking it? He came out to the site briefly, but that was it. I haven't seen him since."

His wife placed her hand to her mouth, shaking her head slowly. Her eyes turned glassy as she started to tear up.

"I'm so sorry for him."

"Yeah, me too. I don't expect he'll be in tomorrow. But maybe he will be. You know how those two didn't have the best relationship."

"Ramon, that doesn't matter. She was his daughter. So what if they hadn't spoken to each other in years? So what if they were estranged? She was his *daughter*."

He leaned forward and took her hands in his, squeezed them tight. Leaned forward even farther and kissed her on the lips.

"I know. I can't imagine what he's going through."

She wiped at her eyes as she stood up from the chair.

"I've had a long day. And I need to be there first thing in the morning. I should go to bed."

He helped her clean up the kitchen and then followed her to the bedroom. He paused and entered the nursery. His baby daughter was asleep in her crib. He studied her precious face for a moment before he turned and exited the room.

His wife was already undressing in the bedroom. He had barely walked in when the phone rang.

He frowned at his wife.

"Are you expecting a call?"

She shook her head.

"No. And even if it was work, they'd call my cell phone."

The phone rang again. It was the landline, and the only extension was in the kitchen.

His wife said, "Answer it before it wakes the baby."

He hurried out of the bedroom and down the hallway to the

kitchen. The phone was about to ring a fourth time when he snagged it off the wall and placed it to his ear.

"Yes?"

Samantha Lu asked, "How does your face feel?"

30

For a long moment there's silence, and I think Ramon has hung up the phone. But no—I can hear him on his end, breathing quietly. I'm tempted to ask another question when he speaks.

"What do you want?"

"We need to talk."

"About what?"

"About what happened tonight."

"I think it's pretty clear what happened. You assaulted law enforcement."

"Sorry about that. But to be fair, I did warn you guys."

"Who are you really?"

"I told you—I'm just a tourist."

"I initially bought your story about driving along the road and seeing the smoke. It seemed plausible that's how you ended up at the murder scene. Now, I know you were full of shit."

"How so?"

"I'm not going to waste my time going over everything that happened today. Why did you call me?"

"Because I want to make it clear I'm not your enemy."

This answer clearly isn't what he had expected, causing him to chuckle.

"You certainly have an interesting way of showing it."

"Again, Ramon, I am not the enemy. In fact, I'd like to think I could be your friend."

"What does that mean?"

"From what I can tell we both have the same objective."

He's quiet for a long moment, letting this sink in, before he clears his throat.

"Are you talking about the Devil?"

"Right now I want to find this guy just as much as you do. You seem like a straight shooter, Ramon. Which makes me think you play by the rules. You want to catch this guy, but you also need to follow the law. But me ... I don't give a shit about that."

Again he's quiet for a long moment before he speaks.

"Why were you at La Miserias tonight?"

"From what I heard the shooting was retribution for Ernesto Diaz's death."

The mere mention of Ernesto Diaz causes him to pause.

He says, "How do you know about Ernesto Diaz?"

"Word travels fast. Is it true?"

He's quiet for another beat, and then sighs.

"As far as we can tell, yes."

"Why?"

"What do you mean, why?"

"Why was the town targeted for retribution? They clearly had nothing to do with Diaz's death."

Ramon snorts a derisive laugh.

"Why is the sky blue? Why do bad things happen to good people? That's just the way it is. Fernando Morales is a bully. He likes to pick on people weaker than him. For some reason he felt Diaz's death needed payback, but he clearly didn't know who was responsible. So he took it out on the town. Why do you care, anyway?"

I don't answer. I'm picturing the town square. Those twenty-eight dead bodies. The bride's dress soaked dark with blood.

Ramon says, "What were you looking for earlier today?"

I blink, the question catching me off guard.

"What?"

"At the murder scene. After we had spoken. Before I told you you could leave. What were you looking for down on the beach?"

"I wasn't looking at anything."

"Whatever it is you were looking for, we will find it."

"I don't know what you're talking about. But just remember what I told you—I'm not the enemy."

"That still doesn't excuse what happened tonight."

"I guess it doesn't."

"If I or my partner see you again, we'll have no choice but to arrest you."

"Then let's hope you don't see me again. Good night, Ramon."

From where I am on the roof of the building across the street, I have a clear view of Ramon standing in his kitchen. He waits there for a moment, holding the phone away from his head like he isn't sure the conversation we just had was real. Then he sets the phone in the receiver and wanders out of view.

I stay on the roof for another couple minutes. Until all the lights go out in the house. Until it's clear that everybody is in bed asleep.

I stay there another half hour, watching the street, making sure nobody else is watching the house, before I decide it's time to head back to Gabriela's. I'm exhausted, but I'm not sure yet I want to sleep. With the smell of those three charred bodies still fresh in my memory, I'm worried about the nightmares that will come.

31

Just over one thousand kilometers south of Culiacán, in the southern region of Mexico known as Tierra Caliente, or the Hot Land, the morning sun had just begun to peek up over the horizon.

Horacio barely noticed. He kept his focus on the road illuminated by the SUV's headlights, though what lay before him could barely be called a proper road. None of it was paved, and much of it was bumpy. He followed the SUV ahead of him, every couple seconds checking the rearview mirror to make sure the third SUV was behind them. The three vehicles had been driving now for nearly an hour. And they would keep driving if need be, all the way out of Tierra Caliente, all the way past Michoacán. That was their task, what they had been ordered to do.

The man beside him kept his focus out his window. Surveying the hills and trees on his side of the vehicle. Just as the two men in the back watched out their windows for any sign of danger.

The two men in the back held AK-47s. So did the man beside Horacio.

Horacio, because he was driving, only had a pistol and knife holstered to his belt.

The men in the other SUVs were armed in much the same way. Just like Horacio, the drivers of those SUVs were also armed with pistols and knives.

The distance between each SUV was about three hundred yards.

Which meant Horacio had several seconds to react when an RPG hit the SUV ahead of him.

One second the SUV in front of him was just driving, the next second the tail end burst into flames, flipping the vehicle over onto its top.

The man beside Horacio shouted, "Watch out!"

Horacio's foot hovered for an instant over the brake pedal but didn't apply pressure. Instead, Horacio stomped on the gas and gripped the steering wheel tightly and swerved around the SUV in front of them, its bottom now in flames, and he was aware of one of the men in the back shouting something at him, and he was aware of the man beside him hefting the AK-47, but Horacio's focus was on getting them past the first SUV, and he swerved around it on the left-hand side, trying to give it as much breadth as he could, not wanting to drive entirely off the road, and his eyes darted everywhere, searching for their attacker, but the sun was barely up yet and the only light came from his headlights, and he spotted a figure off in the distance at the last second, a figure maybe two hundred yards away with an RPG launcher on its shoulder, and he shouted at the men in the SUV at the same moment the shadowy figure fired a second RPG.

"Hold on!"

He jerked the wheel as hard as he could, sending the SUV into a momentary tailspin. The RPG hit the SUV near the rear end. The sudden force was enough to send them careening off the dirt road into an embankment. Horacio tried to maintain control of the steering wheel, but the thing was completely out of his control, and a second later they hit the embankment at such an angle that it caused the SUV to tip over onto its side.

For a moment, there was complete silence, and then they heard another explosion, what was no doubt from the third SUV.

Horacio wasn't wearing a seatbelt and had fallen into the passenger when the SUV tipped onto its side. The passenger pushed at him violently, like Horacio was trying to strangle him. Horacio shouted at him to calm down, that they needed to take a moment to regroup, but the man wasn't having any of it. He even went so far as to punch Horacio in the face to make enough room to raise the AK-47 and send out several bursts at the SUV's front windshield. Then he was leaning into the shattered glass, breaking through it, and the two men in the back scrambled over the seats past Horacio, one of them shouting that the thing was going to blow up, and it was then Horacio smelled the smoke in the air and he smelled gasoline and glanced back to see the vehicle was still on fire.

He hurried out of the SUV, through the shattered windshield, following the three men who had left him to burn.

Two of the men raced up the embankment toward the road. One of the men was taller, and he was the first one killed when he crested the embankment.

Horacio heard a single gunshot and watched the tall man's head snap back as he fell to the ground.

The other man raised his rifle, fired off several rounds, but then two heavy rounds punched into his chest sending him somersaulting down the embankment back toward the SUV.

"Psst!"

The last remaining man motioned Horacio behind some nearby rocks for cover.

Horacio started toward the man when an intense pain shot up his leg.

He fell to the ground, grabbing for his wounded knee, just as he heard the echo of the gunshot.

The other man ducked behind the rock, waited several seconds, then peeked up.

A volley of bullets peppered the rock behind which the man hid. There was a beat of silence, and the man peeked up over the rock again.

Like the man who'd been racing up the embankment, his head snapped back when the shooter released a single round.

Horacio lay on the ground, looking toward the rocks, then toward the SUV that was still in flames.

He grabbed for the pistol holstered to his belt. He tried to climb to his feet to run, but the pain was too intense and sent him back down to the ground. He started crawling toward the rocks.

Up the embankment, several more gunshots tore through the early morning stillness. He heard shouting and then he heard more bullets and the shouting stopped.

Then, suddenly, besides the sound of the burning SUVs, there was silence.

Horacio paused. Was that it? Was it over?

He glanced up the embankment and saw the figure standing there. It held a rifle at its side. It didn't move for a long moment, but it was more than enough time for Horacio to raise his pistol.

The figure was quicker, squeezing off a single round.

Horacio's other leg screamed in pain as the bullet tore into his thigh.

He dropped the pistol and went to grab it again, conscious of the fact that the figure was making its way down the embankment. It wasn't even hurrying, knowing that it had time. All the time in the world.

Or no—that wasn't right. The figure was limping, favoring its left leg. Based on the blood soaking the pant leg, the figure had been shot.

Horacio's fingers grasped the pistol and he raised it again, but suddenly the figure was right there beside him. The figure bent down and tore the pistol from Horacio's grasp, tossed it toward the burning SUV.

The figure wore all camouflage. And a black mask. Only the eyes could be seen, though with the lack of light, Horacio could hardly see them.

It didn't matter, though. Horacio's gut told him this was the Devil. No doubt about it.

Horacio knew he was going to die, so he figured what the fuck, might as well go out in a blaze of glory.

"We tricked you, you son of a whore. You thought we were transporting them, but that was just what we wanted you to think."

The Devil said nothing. He leaned on his right leg while his left leg continued to bleed.

Horacio hawked a loogie to spit at the Devil.

"We outsmarted you, you piece of shit. You'll never get to them."

The Devil set his rifle aside on the ground and stepped close to Horacio.

Horacio said, "Get it over and kill me, motherfucker. I won't tell you shit."

The Devil reached for his belt, unsheathed a long knife.

"You think death is the end?"

There was something wrong with the Devil's voice. It sounded muffled, though it wasn't because of the mask. There was something internally wrong, like the man's lungs and vocal box had been damaged.

The Devil crouched down beside Horacio. He held up the knife, and slowly moved the blade so its tip touched the space between Horacio's eyes.

"There are some things worse than death."

Keeping the tip of the knife pressed against the space between Horacio's eyes, the Devil used his other hand to pull up the mask.

Horacio had been prepared for it, but the sight was still enough to make him cringe. Only it didn't manage to distract him from his true intention—which was reaching for his own knife sheathed to his belt.

With the Devil so close, Horacio jerked up and plunged the blade into the Devil's side.

The Devil grunted, fell to a knee. With his free hand, he punched Horacio in the face, then gripped the knife from Horacio's hand and flung it away. The Devil rose up, pressing his hand against the new wound.

Grinning, Horacio whispered, "I won't tell you where they are."

The Devil grunted again and crouched back down, carefully this time, pressing the tip of the blade even harder against the space between Horacio's eyes.

"Yes, you will."

32

I don't have any nightmares, but I don't sleep well either.

I spend the few remaining hours of night on Gabriela's bedroom floor. She's given me pillows and a blanket, and I lie there on my back staring at the ceiling. The gun is only inches away. If need be, I can grab it within seconds.

Sleep comes and goes, and in the morning when Gabriela stirs, I'm already wide-awake.

She sits up and looks down at me, frowning.

"Didn't you get any sleep?"

"Maybe an hour or two."

"You look exhausted."

"I am exhausted."

"Is it because you're on the floor? If you want, you can try to sleep in my bed."

"I'm okay."

I'm not, though, and it's obvious. It's been days since I got a full six hours of sleep. They say the body needs at least eight hours of sleep, and maybe that's true, but in my line of work, I'm lucky if I can get six consecutive hours.

Except I'm not in any line of work anymore. Those days are behind me. Now I'm ... well, just what the hell am I?

Gabriela takes a shower in the bathroom down the hall. I lie on the floor and stare at the ceiling, deciding what needs to be done next. When Gabriela enters the bedroom, wrapped in a towel, she tosses an extra towel at me.

"Are you going to shower?"

Oh yes.

Standing under the warm water beating on my skin, I'm half tempted to close my eyes and fall asleep. But I don't. I'm in and out, as fast as possible, and when I return to Gabriela's room she has some clothes waiting for me.

"We're about the same size. You're a little thinner than me, but I think these clothes will fit you."

I thank her for the thought but tell her I'll just wear the clothes from yesterday again.

She shakes her head.

"Absolutely not. They're filthy. And there's even some blood on them."

In the end I relent. Her jeans and T-shirt fit just fine, and once I'm dressed and have my hair dry, I head downstairs to find Gabriela has woken her grandmother from her grandmother's first-floor bedroom. She helps her grandmother into the kitchen. She pulls out a chair at the table and eases her grandmother down.

Her grandmother smiles at me, as if just seeing me for the first time.

"*Buenos días.*"

I smile and nod and repeat the same.

Gabriela drifts over to the refrigerator, glances back at me.

"Would you like breakfast? We normally only have protein shakes in the morning, but we have some eggs and bread if you'd like that."

"I'll have whatever you're having."

Gabriela pulls out the milk and sets it on the counter, then reaches up into a cabinet and pulls down three glasses. She unscrews the top off a plastic container and uses a plastic scoop to fill each glass with some protein powder, and she fills those glasses with milk and stirs them with a whisk. She hands the first glass to me, then takes the other glass over to her grandmother. Her grandmother smiles at her again, and there's an instant where confusion flashes in her eyes before she blinks it away. Gabriela puts a straw in the glass and holds the glass so her grandmother can drink.

I sip from my own glass, watching them.

Once Gabriela's grandmother finishes the remains of her protein shake, Gabriela rinses the glass out in the sink, sets it aside, and then turns back to her own shake. She drains the entire glass down in what seems like one nonstop gulp. She rinses out her glass, takes my empty glass and rinses it out too.

I say, "Now what?"

Gabriela glances at her grandmother, answering me with a low whisper.

"Now I need to bathe her. Probably change her diaper too. I'm sorry, but it's probably going to take a while."

I shake my head.

"No need to apologize. Take all the time you need. I think it's great what you do for her."

Gabriela shrugs and offers up a somber smile.

"She's the only family I have."

Gabriela's grandmother sits at the table, staring into the distance, like she doesn't even know we're there.

I ask, "Does anybody check in on her when you're not home?"

"I've hired a woman to check in on her for a couple hours each day. She helps clean the kitchen, do the laundry, that sort of thing."

"Have you given any thought about what I said last night?"

Gabriela pauses, thinking about it, and smiles again. Only this time the smile has more happiness.

"Of course I'm not going to quit. I knew what I was getting into when I started this. It's scary, but somebody needs to do it."

She pauses, looks at me again.

"What are you planning to do today?"

"I want to go back to La Miserias."

"Why?"

"I'm not sure yet."

"I can give you a ride there once I finish here."

"I'll find a ride."

Gabriela smiles.

"You mean steal a ride."

"Borrow would be a less sinister word."

"I'm happy to drive you, but first let me bathe my grandmother. It won't take too long, I promise."

33

Carlos was already at headquarters when Ramon arrived in the morning. Ramon found him at his desk, leaning back in his chair, studying a crumpled piece of paper.

Ramon said, "What's that?"

Carlos held up the crumbled item, and Ramon quickly realized it wasn't a piece of paper but a photograph.

Carlos said, "This was left behind by the two girls last night."

Ramon looked around the room at the other officers at their desks and in their cubicles. He motioned for Carlos to keep his voice down.

Carlos rolled his eyes, leaning forward in his chair to set the photograph on his desk.

"I'm pretty sure the Asian girl had it on her. I took it home with me last night."

Ramon stepped forward to give the photograph a good look. It was a young woman, barely in her twenties, wearing short shorts and a halter-top and heels. Long hair. A belly button ring.

Ramon grinned down at Carlos.

"I bet you did take it home last night, you old pervert."

Carlos gave him an annoyed look. He sighed, focusing again on the photograph.

"For the life of me I can't figure why she would have this on her. And why it was crumpled like this. This was exactly how she took it out of her pocket."

"What are you thinking?"

"Well, if she crumpled it herself, why keep it? Why not just throw it away?"

"Or?"

Carlos tilted his head back and forth, considering it.

"Or somebody else crumpled the photograph and it ended up in her possession. In which case the question is again, why keep it?"

Ramon stared down at the photograph. He wasn't thinking of the girl in the picture but of Samantha Lu, or whatever her name was. He wasn't sure yet whether or not he wanted to tell Carlos about her calling him last night.

Suddenly the large room took on a strange feel. Like everybody froze and held their breath at the same time. Even Carlos felt it. Frowning, the older man stood up from his chair, stared across the room, and whispered.

"Jesus Christ, he showed up."

Comandante Geraldo Espinoza had entered the room and was making his way toward his office. A few of the other officers approached him quietly, offering up their condolences, and Espinoza nodded soberly and thanked them for their kind words before moving past them. Finally, only steps away from his office, he paused and turned to address the entire room.

"I want to thank everybody for their thoughts and prayers. I truly appreciate it. And I know you're surprised to see me here. But ... I think we all mourn in our own ways. For me, I want to catch the bastard who did this to my daughter and those children. Understood?"

There was a round of nods across the room, a few murmured yes sirs, and that was it. Espinoza stood there for another moment, surveying the room, and then entered his office, closing the door behind him.

Carlos said, "He looks like he hasn't slept all night."

"I wouldn't blame him for not sleeping."

"I spoke to him on the phone earlier this morning. He didn't mention he would be in."

"Why did you call him?"

"I stayed up late last night doing some digging. I thought I'd found a connection between his daughter and Miguel Dominguez."

"What kind of connection?"

"To be honest, there wasn't much. They attended the same school. But for the area that isn't surprising. Maybe they were friends. Maybe they dated. Maybe they never even knew the other existed. I called Espinoza to see if the name rang a bell with him but he said it didn't."

Ramon grabbed the chair from the desk across from Carlos. He leaned close to his partner, lowering his voice.

"She called me last night."

"Who called you last night?"

"Samantha Lu. Or whatever her name is."

"You're joking."

"I'm not."

"How did she get your number?"

"I have no idea."

"What did she want?"

"She said she's not our enemy."

Carlos snorted at this, touching the side of his face where he'd been kicked last night.

"She has an interesting way of showing it."

"I know. I told her the same thing. She said she had no choice. That she and the other girl couldn't be detained."

"Did she say what she wants?"

"She wants to find the Devil just as much as we do."

Carlos's brow creased as he frowned.

"Why does she want to find the Devil?"

"I don't know. Maybe because she found the bodies. Or …"

"Or?"

"I'm not sure. But there's certainly more going on with her than we know about."

Carlos nodded and held up a finger.

"Speaking of which, have you checked out *La Baliza* lately?"

Ramon grimaced.

"You know I can't stand that website."

Carlos turned in his seat and moved his mouse to wake his computer. Within seconds he had a web browser up and had pulled up *La Baliza*. He scrolled down and pointed at one of the stories.

"See here? This story is about the bodies being found yesterday, and how Miguel Dominguez is a suspect. Christ, look here. They even have pictures of Dominguez's apartment."

Ramon tried to skim the text, but the pictures kept distracting him. One was of the Paraíso Motel, the other of Miguel Dominguez's apartment. On the surface the picture could have been of anybody's apartment, but Ramon had been there just yesterday. Had stood in the middle of the place. Smelled the dankness of the room. These pictures were legit.

Carlos said, "Remember our pimp friends from yesterday? They said they followed Samantha Lu to that building. The same building where the landlord was shot and killed and where those narco wannabes got beat up."

Ramon forced himself to look away from the computer screen. He fixed his eyes on Carlos.

"Are you saying this Samantha Lu writes for *La Baliza*?"

"My gut says she doesn't. But remember, when she came out of that building, she wasn't alone. She was with another girl, who I'm betting is the same girl she was with at La Miserias. Speaking of which, should we tell the boss about what happened last night?"

"You mean getting our asses kicked?"

Carlos touched the side of his face again.

"My wife's passed five years now. I can't quite use the excuse that she punched me last night. Yours doesn't look so bad, by the way."

Ramon just nodded. He didn't want to tell Carlos it was because his wife had touched it up with some of her makeup this morning. It was too embarrassing, though maybe not as embarrassing as being beaten up by a woman.

Before Ramon could say anything, Carlos's desk phone rang. Carlos answered it, listened for a couple seconds, then said they would be right down and replaced the phone in its cradle.

Ramon said, "What's up?"

"That was Jorge. He's ready for us."

Jorge was the medical examiner. He worked in the basement, examining the dead bodies that came in every day.

Carlos pushed his chair back and stood up.

"Ibarra and Serrano are downstairs waiting for us too. Let's hope they also want to act like last night didn't happen."

Ramon stood up and gestured for Carlos to go first.

"Age before beauty."

Carlos snorted as he started toward the elevators.

"Says the guy wearing makeup."

Down in the basement they found the two PFM agents already back in Jorge's lab. The bodies were laid out on three tables, covered with sheets. Still, the smell of the charred flesh lingered in the air.

Jorge said, "Now that you're all here, do you want me to show off my brilliance or just tell you my conclusion?"

Carlos said, "Which one do you think?"

Jorge beamed a bright smile.

"My brilliance, obviously."

He waited a beat, and when nobody laughed or even smiled, he sighed.

"Fine, I'll jump right to my conclusion. Something that may or may not be pertinent to the case."

Ramon asked, "Which is?"

"At this time there's no way for me to identify the bodies."

"Why?"

"Because I'm still waiting on the dental records, and without those, there's no way I can make a match. Besides, we're not even one hundred percent certain who the victims are."

Jorge held up a hand before anybody could interrupt.

"Yes, yes, I know we believe we know who the victims are, and that may very well be true, but without one hundred percent certainty I won't say one way or another. All I have right now is the woman's jewelry."

He gestured at a stainless-steel bowl on the counter behind them.

"One earring. That's it."

Carlos crossed his arms, impatient.

"And your conclusion?"

"Based on the fact that there was no smoke found in their lungs, their throats were cut before they were burned. All three of them."

This caused the PFM agents to trade glances. They didn't say anything, though, and just turned their attention back to Jorge.

Ramon said to the agents, "Anything you want to share?"

Ibarra shook his head.

"Not at the moment, no."

Carlos heaved a heavy sigh.

"We're all on the same team here, right? Don't leave us in the dark. If you have information to share, share it."

The two agents traded glances again. They stared at each

other for a long moment, communicating silently, and then Serrano nodded.

He said, "This is new."

Ramon said, "What's new?"

"The Devil cutting their throats before burning them. From what we've learned about the past murders, he ties them up, douses them in gasoline, and sets them on fire. They burn alive until they die."

Carlos drifted over to the counter and glanced inside the stainless-steel bowl at the single earring.

"So what does that tell you about these murders?"

Ibarra shrugged.

"We're not sure yet. We'll have to call headquarters and see what they think. One theory is that he had no choice but to cut their throats. That he was pressed for time."

Still smelling the charred flesh in the air, Ramon asked, "How long does it take for somebody to burn alive before they die?"

The agents glanced each other again, but this time it was clear they weren't trying to hide information. Instead, each was curious if the other knew the answer.

Ramon said, "Never mind. I don't think I want to know. Jorge, is there anything else?"

The medical examiner shook his head.

"Not unless you want to hear my brilliance."

Carlos was already headed out of the room.

"Not today, Jorge. You stay cool down here."

Ramon nodded his thanks to the medical examiner and hurried to keep up with Carlos. The two agents lingered behind.

As they stepped onto the elevator, Ramon said, "I feel like they're hiding something from us."

Carlos nodded, staring up at the elevator's ceiling.

"Probably."

"What do you think we should do now?"

"First, I want a cigarette. Then second, I think we need to find Miguel Dominguez."

"Do you think he's still alive?"

The elevator door opened, and Carlos stepped out, shaking his head.

"Not a chance."

34

La Miserias looks different.

Granted, it's daytime now, midmorning to be exact, so there's more of the town to see than there had been last night. Still, something about it feels off. Like it's not real. Like it's hollow. Which, of course, is to be expected after last night's massacre.

We walk down the main street leading to the square. The bodies are gone, but there are still people there, mostly old men. Some are sweeping up the debris. Others are laying down hay to cover the blood-spattered dirt.

Gabriela whispers, "What are we doing here?"

Good question. She'd asked it during our drive and I hadn't had a proper answer then. I still don't.

I motion her toward one of the side streets.

"Let's go this way."

A minute later we're standing outside Yolanda's house. Dorado, the chubby brown cat, peers out at us from the window.

I knock.

No answer.

I knock again.

Still no answer.

Dorado just watches us lazily from his perch on the windowsill inside.

I say, "Maybe we should try the back."

Before we can move, though, a young kid appears down the street. He doesn't look any older than ten years old. He reminds me of the kid who sold me those firecrackers, and for an instant I wonder what this kid might be peddling today. But he simply approaches us, his expression much too serious for a kid his age.

"Are you looking for Yolanda?"

We nod.

He says, "I know where she is."

We follow him between several different houses until we come to one packed with people.

The kid squeezes inside without a word, leaving us alone outside. The few people crowded in the doorway glance back at us. A minute passes, and then Yolanda appears. She gazes outside, frowning, and shuffles toward us, leaning heavily on her cane.

"You girls were the last two I expected to see today."

I say, "Is there somewhere we can talk?"

She gazes up and down the empty street.

"Why not here?"

"I'm sorry again about what happened last night."

"You came here to apologize?"

"No. I came here to ask you a question."

The old woman leans on her cane.

"And what is your question?"

"Last night you said you wondered when Morales will strike again. You said you wondered when more people will die. You said that it's a bloody cycle."

"Yes, I did say that. Is that your question?"

"No, my question is, do you want to break the cycle?"

In the sunlight the scars on her face are even more pronounced. She stares at me, studying my face.

"What are you saying?"

"You told me about the *autodefensas*, how they once stood up to the narcos. Why not stand up to them again?"

Yolanda closes her eyes and shakes her head slowly.

"As I told you, the *autodefensas* have been disbanded. They have become illegal. And besides, we are a small town. The weapons we have are simplistic. A few handguns, maybe, a few hunting rifles. The narcos have military weapons. How are we supposed to defend ourselves?"

One of the old men from the doorway has drifted outside to smoke. He's the same old man Gabriela had spoken to last night in the town square. He clears his throat and speaks in a low gravely voice.

"The boys have weapons."

Yolanda glances back to glare at him.

"Be quiet, Antonio."

I ask, "What boys?"

Antonio says, "The narcos. The ones here in town."

I look at Yolanda.

"You have narcos in town?"

Yolanda sighs.

"There are narcos in every town. Narcos need a place to live too. They aren't all rich like Fernando Morales."

"How many are there?"

Antonio answers.

"Two of them. Sometimes more. But two of them stay in the house on the edge of town. They're young, about your age. They came one day and kicked the family out of the house and have been there ever since."

I ask, "And they have weapons?"

The old man nods.

"I would guess so."

I look again at Yolanda.

"Are weapons the only thing stopping you from protecting yourselves from the narcos?"

Yolanda shakes her head again, this time sadly.

"You two should leave. Forget about this town and what happened here."

"Last night you told me about how towns like these once stood up to the narcos. You made it sound like this was something you wished happened again. Now, do you still feel that way?"

Before Yolanda can answer, Antonio grunts.

"I wish we did."

Yolanda shoots him another glare.

"Thankfully that is not a decision for you to make."

Antonio takes a final drag of his cigarette before dropping it on the ground.

"You are right, Yolanda. It is up to the town."

He motions at the crowded house behind him.

"Why don't we ask them?"

35

The house is small, and about thirty people are crowded inside. Some sit on the couch and chairs, others on the floor, while still others stand leaning against the wall. There are only a few middle-aged people, the youngest maybe in their thirties. Most are older, about fifty or sixty, and immediately I realize that these are the town elders.

Gabriela and I have interrupted a town meeting.

Whatever conversation the people inside were having dies once we enter the house. All eyes turn to us.

Someone asks, "Who are they?"

Before Yolanda can answer, Antonio clears his throat and addresses the group.

"It does not matter who they are. What matters is last night narcos came into our town—during a wedding, no less—and murdered our people."

Someone else says, "Yes, Antonio, and that is why we are meeting. To discuss the funerals."

Antonio growls at this.

"Fuck the funerals."

He pauses, and his shoulders drop, his angry expression going all at once somber.

"Obviously I do not mean that. The funerals are important. But what I want to talk about is the narcos who did this."

An uneasy silence fills the room. Many of the townspeople glance around at each other, but nobody responds.

Yolanda says, "Sit down, Antonio. You are being foolish."

He turns to her, his eyes starting to well with tears.

"My *granddaughter* died last night. The bullets did not even kill her right away. At least that would have been a mercy. They hit her in the stomach. I told her she would be okay while I did everything I could to try to stop the bleeding. But it was not okay. She died in my arms. My granddaughter *died.*"

Stunned silence. Everybody's focus is on Antonio.

The old man stands in the middle of the room, turning slowly to address each of the townspeople.

"We all lost somebody close to us last night. And it was not the first time. And it will not be the last time. And I am sick of it. I am *sick* of it!"

Spittle flies from his mouth. He wipes it and the tears in his eyes away but doesn't say anything else.

Somebody says, "We're all sick of it, Antonio. But what can we do?"

Somebody else says, "We can stand up to them."

Another person says, "No, we can't. If we stand up to them, that will only lead to more killing."

As if a switch is thrown, the townspeople all start talking at the same time. Some arguing that no matter what they do the cartel will keep sending more narcos to kill them. Others arguing that it had worked in the past, that the *autodefensas* were successful.

Somebody shouts, "But look what happened to the *autodefensas*! They're gone. The government won't allow it."

Somebody else counters, "That is because they were spread-

ing from town to town. There is nothing to stop us from protecting our own people."

Again the townspeople start talking over each other.

Gabriela and I stand off to the side. There's nothing for us
to say.

Finally somebody hollers for Yolanda to speak, and the
townspeople quiet.

Yolanda leans on her cane. She hasn't spoken this entire
time. She just stood there and listened and now it's her turn to
speak and I wonder what it is she'll say.

She surprises me.

"I think we owe it to the loved ones we lost last night—to
the loved ones we have lost before last night—to stand up for
ourselves. I think we owe it to our own children and grandchildren. They have learned to live in fear of the narcos. It has
become part of their life. But it does not have to be."

Many of the townspeople agree with Yolanda. Others don't.
They start arguing again, some saying that fighting back will
mean they'll all die, others countering that if they don't fight
back they'll eventually die anyway. After a while, Antonio raises
his voice again.

"I call for a vote."

This quiets the room.

Antonio says, "Let us vote on it. We are a small town, and
we are all friends, but clearly we all have different ideas on what
we should do. But something must be done, so let us vote."

Murmurs ripple through the room. Several people nod their
assent.

Yolanda says, "Before we vote, I do want to say one thing."

The crowd goes quiet again.

"Last night I felt just like Antonio does now. I wanted to
fight. I wanted vengeance for our loved ones. But this morning
when I looked in the mirror and saw my face I felt differently.
As my scars will attest, I am very familiar to the brutal ways

of the narcos. They can be heartless. They can be brutal. They feed on fear, and expect those who are not narcos to be scared of them at all times. I fear standing up to the narcos may cause more bloodshed. But I also fear *not* standing up to the narcos. Even if the end result is the narcos coming here to kill us all, at least we have finally stood for something. And so I will cast the first vote. I vote yes."

After that, things move quickly. Antonio votes next, then it goes around the room, and within a minute every townsperson in the living room has voted yes. Each and every one of them.

There's a heavy silence as the realization hits them of their decision. From some of their expressions, it's clear they're immediately questioning their vote.

That's when somebody asks, "Now what do we do?"

Somebody else answers, "We kick the narcos out of town."

A third person asks, "How do we do that?"

There's another silence, which I take as my cue to step forward and raise my hand.

"I can help with that."

36

Like Yolanda said, the only weapons in town are a few hunting rifles and handguns. There are over two dozen of them, yes, but none of the weapons look new. None of the people who own those weapons look equipped to handle them very well. The rest of the townspeople gather up what weapons they can find: shovels, bats, metal pipes. Once word gets out about the vote, everybody in town wants to contribute.

The house in question—the one the narcos took over a year ago, kicking out the family who had lived there and threatening their lives if they tried to take the house back—sat near the edge of the town. Half of the people circle around toward the back, while the other half fans out in front of the house. There are over fifty people now—all ages and sizes—and they're determined, which is good, because it's clear many of them are scared. They know going up against the narcos is dangerous—many of them lost loved ones last night, after all—but they don't want to stand idly by anymore.

As much as I want to take the lead, this isn't my town. I'm

just a visitor. I said as much to Yolanda and Antonio, both who agreed, and because Antonio is a bit stronger on his feet, he's the one who knocks on the front door.

For a solid minute nothing happens. Complete silence in the house. I had asked before if there was a chance the narcos were gone, especially after what happened last night, but their cars were pointed out to me and I was told that they often slept late through the morning.

Antonio knocks again, this time banging his old, wrinkled fist against the door.

Twenty seconds later, the door opens and one of the narcos peers out. He's young, in his mid-twenties, and he's shirtless. The only thing he has on is his jeans, which are too large for him and hang low off his hip, exposing his boxer shorts. Tattoos pepper his arms and chest. He's holding a gun in his right hand while he wipes the sleep away with his left hand, so for a second or two he doesn't see everybody in the street, he only focuses on Antonio and the gun in Antonio's hand.

"What do you want, you old fuck?"

He pauses then, realizing that Antonio isn't alone. His eyes widen just a bit. Clearly this wasn't what he'd expected when he opened the door. Fear flashes in his face, but it's just for an instant, the narco needing to show no fear no matter how scared he might be.

Antonio says, "We want you to leave."

The narco simply shakes his head.

"Fuck you."

He goes to shut the door, but Antonio manages to press his weight against the door before it closes.

The narco raises the gun at Antonio.

"Get the fuck back, old man."

I finally decide, all right, enough is enough.

I step forward, swinging a gun at my side.

"Hey, asshole."

The narco's eyes shift toward me. For an instant, confusion fills his face. Clearly I'm not one of the townspeople.

I ask, "If you wanna play, why not play with me?"

The narco sneers.

"What do you think you're going to do?"

"Kick your ass."

I glance at Antonio, still pressed against the door.

"Antonio, step away from the door."

The narco grins, mimics me.

"Yeah, *Antonio*, step away from the door."

Antonio glares back at the narco.

"We want you out of our town!"

The narco just laughs. Then he glances back inside the house, nods once, and grins at me again.

"Okay, *puta*, you want to play, let's play."

He opens the door, and there are two other narcos standing there. They're about the same age, the same height and built, one shirtless, the other wearing a T-shirt. Both are armed. One of them has a gun, the other a Heckler & Koch MP5 submachine gun.

As the narco with the MP5 presents the most danger right now, he's the one I target first.

I look straight at him.

"Raise that thing and you're never going to walk right again."

The narco with the MP5 grins, clearly amused. The moment the barrel starts to lift, I shift my own gun just a bit and squeeze the trigger.

My bullet shatters his left kneecap.

The narco screams as he falls, dropping the MP5 to the floor. Both of his friends focus on him for an instant, shocked and confused, and I use the distraction to sprint forward and kick the first narco straight in the chest. He tumbles back, tripping over his own legs and falling to the floor. I turn to the last standing narco and plant a roundhouse kick right to his face.

It doesn't drop him, though, just stuns him, causing him to stumble, and then he's turning toward me, raising his gun, so I shoot him in the foot and he screams just like his friend as he falls to the floor.

The narco who first opened the door tries to scramble back up to his feet. Before he can get too far, I step over and kick him right in the face. He falls back, groaning, and starts to raise his gun at me.

I aim my own gun at him.

"Go ahead and try it."

The narco pauses. He doesn't keep raising the gun, but he doesn't lower it either. He just sits there on the floor for a couple seconds, glaring back at me, and then the groans of his friends catch his attention and he glances at them before grunting his displeasure and setting the gun aside.

I say, "Now here's what you three assholes are going to do. You're going to get in your cars and you're going to get the fuck out of this town and you're never going to come back."

The narco says, "But our stuff—"

I cut him off.

"Fuck your stuff. Did you let the family who you kicked out of here take their stuff with them?"

He shrugs.

"We let them take some of their stuff."

"Well, then you guys are much more generous than I am. You're lucky we're letting you keep your piece of shit cars."

I step back and motion with my gun at the door.

"Now get the fuck out of here before I change my mind and shoot you all in the head."

The first narco slowly climbs to his feet. He wisely doesn't reach for his gun. He glares at me again for just a beat, and then he starts to help his friends up from the floor.

It takes several minutes—first the narco shot in the foot being helped outside by his friend, then the narco shot in the knee—but pretty soon they're loaded up in just one car because only one of them is able to drive. For their credit, the townspeople stand their ground. They watch the narcos get in the car without a word, and they don't make a sound as the car quickly accelerates down the dirt road. Once it's clear the narcos are gone, though, everybody starts cheering.

I glance over at Gabriela for the first time. She has her phone out, taking pictures. We discussed this earlier, how she wasn't to take any pictures of me, and I'll have to check her phone later to make sure she kept that promise. As it is, she might have a pretty good story on her hands.

As a few of the townspeople hurry inside to collect the weapons and to search the house, Yolanda shuffles over to me. She leans heavily on her cane as she stares at me with renewed interest.

"Who are you exactly?"

"I'm nobody."

Antonio drifts over, a huge smile on his face.

"Is that it? Do you think it's over?"

I turn to glance at Fernando Sanchez Morales's large house on the hill a mile away. I shake my head and answer as bluntly as possible.

"Not even close."

37

Fernando Sanchez Morales disconnected the call, set the cell phone aside, and then leaned forward, placing his head in his hands. He hadn't slept much in the past couple days and it was starting to catch up with him. Or no—days wasn't right. It was more like months. Over a year since he'd started having restless nights. And it didn't help that last night Araceli had locked him out of their bedroom.

Jose Luis said, "How bad is it?"

Fernando ran his fingers through his hair and looked up at his right-hand man.

"Very bad. They had a decoy convoy running through the Hot Lands this morning when it was attacked. Everybody was killed."

Jose Luis frowned.

"Decoy convoy?"

"They tried to trap him. They put the word out that they were transporting her and the children, and they drove around, hoping that he would attack. Which he did. Three fucking SUVs, all of them loaded with armed men. It's unreal."

"And then?"

Fernando released a heavy sigh, shaking his head slowly.

"Then he managed to track down where they were hiding her and the children. They think he tortured one of the men from the convoy for the information."

"He took them, didn't he."

Jose Luis didn't bother making it a question.

Fernando nodded.

"Yes, he took them. Killed the five men they had guarding them. As of right now, they don't know where he's taken them."

Jose Luis started to say something but paused.

Fernando said, "Go ahead and say it."

Jose Luis hesitated again before he swallowed and blurted it out.

"You're the only one left."

Fernando glared back at his right-hand man. It wasn't anything Jose Luis had done that suddenly raised his ire, but simply the realization that it was true. He was the only one left. Or wait—not him so much as his wife and son.

Fernando leaned back in his chair, tipping his face up to stare at the ceiling. Above them was the master bedroom, with Araceli and Ignacio locked somewhere inside. The last interaction Fernando had with them did not go well. He'd grabbed Araceli's hair, had scared his son to the point that Ignacio had looked at him like he was a monster. God forbid, if something were to happen to them, he didn't want that to be their last memory of him.

Only no, he wasn't going to let that happen. He wasn't like the others. They had been stupid. Careless. Reckless to an extent. They hadn't had what it took to keep their families safe. But he did. After all, his wife and son were still alive, weren't they? The Devil hadn't managed to get them yet. What was to say he would manage to get them at all?

Jose Luis said, "Maybe you should take them out of the country."

Fernando thought about it for a moment, then shook his head.

"No. I'm not going to show fear like that."

Jose Luis's face tensed. It was clear his right-hand man didn't approve of this line of thinking. But that didn't matter to Fernando. There was a reason he was at the head of the family. There was a reason he had gotten this far. He knew when to take risks and he knew when to play it safe. He also knew, above all else, to never show fear. And it wasn't just for the Devil's benefit. It was for the benefit of the other cartels. He would be the last man standing. The one who hadn't lost his wife and son to the Devil.

Fernando pushed back from the table and stood up.

"Get more men to patrol the perimeter. I want this place guarded to the hilt."

Jose Luis nodded and watched his boss start out of the room.

"Where are you going now?"

"Up to see my wife and son. Now do as I say."

Seconds later he was upstairs and standing in front of the master bedroom door. Two of the bodyguards sat outside farther down the hallway. Fernando gave them a look, and they stood and shuffled downstairs to give him privacy.

Fernando tried the doorknob. It was locked, just as he had expected. He knocked quietly and whispered to the door.

"Araceli."

No answer.

He knocked again, a bit louder now.

"Araceli, open the door."

No answer, though he heard movement somewhere in the bedroom. He thought he sensed her standing right on the other side of the door.

"Araceli, I'm sorry about yesterday. It was wrong of me. But sometimes I feel you don't understand how serious this situation is. Just this morning, the Escalante family was attacked.

A whole convoy was taken out. And Escalante's wife and children—"

He paused there, not bothering to say the rest. Besides, he had a feeling he didn't need to say the rest. Araceli was a smart woman. She could fill in the blanks.

A couple seconds passed, and then he heard the soft click of the bolt turning.

The door opened just a bit, and Araceli peeked out at him. "They're dead?"

Fernando nodded, though he didn't know for certain whether or not they were dead. If they weren't dead by now, they would be soon.

"Yes. He killed over a dozen men to get to them. He'll stop at nothing. That's why it's so important that you and Ignacio stay in this house. It's for your protection. Do you understand me?"

Araceli didn't open the door any farther. She just stood there, staring out at him, and nodded.

Fernando said, "Can I come in?"

She seemed to think about it for a long moment, and then nodded again and stepped back, opening the door even wider.

Fernando stepped inside. He saw Ignacio lying on the bed, hiding under the covers.

"Ignacio, look at me."

Saying it in his soothing voice, the kind that promised he was not the monster his son had seen yesterday.

The covers shifted, and his son peeked up at him.

Fernando smiled and motioned Ignacio toward him.

"Come give me a hug."

His son didn't move at first, just stared at him from the bed. Then slowly he crawled out of the bed and made his way over to his father.

Fernando kneeled down to hug his son first, then stood to embrace his wife. He hated how he sometimes acted with them, but sometimes anger came to him too easily. Something simple could set him off, and when it was around his men that was one thing, but not around his wife and son.

In the hallway there were footsteps, and Jose Luis cleared his throat.

"Sir? I need to see you immediately."

Fernando held his wife an extra couple of seconds. He smelled her hair, then kissed her on the forehead before he stepped away.

"I'll be back soon. Okay?"

She nodded, her eyes starting to fill with tears.

Fernando left the bedroom to find Jose Luis and the two bodyguards in the hallway.

"What is it?"

Jose Luis said, "There's something you need to see."

The bodyguards stayed behind as Jose Luis led him down the steps and then out toward the front of the house. A car was parked there. Three men sat inside.

Jose Luis filled him in as they approached the car.

"They're our men from La Miserias. They drove up to the gate minutes ago. Two of them are badly injured. Both need medical attention, but the driver knew better than to take them to a hospital. He thought one of our doctors might be able to help."

"What happened?"

They had reached the car. Two of the men inside were writhing in pain. Both appeared to be clutching their legs. Fernando stepped even closer and saw that they'd been shot.

The driver said, his voice tremulous, "Can I get out of the car now?"

Fernando leaned down to look at the driver.

"What happened?"

The driver shook his head quickly, as if he was in shock.

"They kicked us out."

"Who?"

"The town."

"What do you mean, the town?"

"I mean the *town*. They fucking kicked us out. Said that if we came back they'd kill us. Now what about a doctor? These guys need help."

Fernando stepped back from the car. He turned first to stare toward La Miserias. Then he turned back to Jose Luis.

"How many men did you call to protect the perimeter?"

"Ten additional men are coming. They should be here within a half hour."

Fernando nodded, calculating the number in his head. The men who were already guarding the house and the additional men and how many more men they would need.

"See if you can get ten more."

Jose Luis stared at him while the driver from the car kept asking for help.

"May I ask why?"

Fernando felt that anger bubbling inside him. Usually it spiked in situations like these, but this was a low boil. He knew that eventually it would explode, but he needed to wait for it to happen at the right time.

"You know exactly why. Get the additional men here as soon as possible. The people in that town thought yesterday was bad? They haven't even begun to understand true misery."

38

Pork sizzles in the frying pan.

The sound alone makes my stomach grumble with pleasure.

Yolanda stands over the stove with a pair of tongs, turning each cubed piece of pork over so that all sides become browned. She already has the spices set aside, ready to add when the time is right.

Gabriela and I stand in the kitchen watching her. We offered to help, but she kept waving us away, saying that she was fine, despite the fact she moves slowly around the kitchen with her cane.

Dorado sits in the doorway, his tail flicking back and forth, watching patiently.

It's been two hours since we kicked the narcos out of town. Two hours since the realization of what the townspeople had done began to sink in. I could tell from some of their faces that a few were already beginning to regret it, but others hadn't. They'd looked proud. Relieved. Triumphant.

At the same time, they knew that this wasn't the end of it. That eventually more narcos would come, seeking revenge.

The townspeople needed to work on burying their loved ones from yesterday, but at the same time they needed to ensure that the town remained safe. So while a few worked on burial plans, the others were waiting with every weapon they had. We'd found several guns and rifles the narcos had stashed in their house, but it wasn't an arsenal. There was a chance that when more narcos came, the townspeople would be out-gunned and outnumbered. They acknowledged this, and they still wanted to fight.

As Yolanda browns the pork, she glances at us over her shoulder.

"How do you two know each other?"

Gabriela and I trade glances. We stare at each other for a long moment, and then I shrug.

"It's a long story."

Yolanda laughs, gestures at the stove.

"We have time."

Neither one of us speaks.

Yolanda chuckles to herself, shaking her head as she keeps browning the pork.

"You can keep your secrets. Gabriela, are you really a jour-nalist?"

"Yes."

"Who do you write for?"

Gabriela hesitates, then says, "*La Baliza.*"

"That is noble work, I imagine. Also dangerous. What do your parents think of it?"

"They're dead."

Yolanda sighs, shaking her head.

"Much too young. Much, much too young."

She peers at me.

"What about your parents?"

"I'd rather not talk about my parents."

Yolanda nods, focusing again on the frying pan.

"Very well. Then we will not talk about anything. We will stay silent here in the kitchen while our food cooks."

Dorado moves from his spot in the doorway. He slinks over to me and starts rubbing his face up against my leg. When I don't give him any attention, he drifts over to Gabriela, who bends down and strokes his back.

I ask Yolanda, "What about you?"

She doesn't bother to look back at me when she answers.

"What about me?"

"Tell us about your family."

She stares down at the frying pan, moving the cubes of pork around as they sizzle.

"My parents, as you can imagine, have long since left this earth. As for children ... I only ever had one child. A son. He grew up a good boy. Always listened. Always followed the rules. He was ambitious. He wanted to go to Mexico City and become a lawyer. I never understood why he wanted to become a lawyer. One day I asked him, and he said it was because lawyers made a lot of money. He said that was his goal—to make a lot of money. He always told me that one day he would make enough money so that he could buy me a place to live along the ocean. He was a sweet boy who meant well, but ..."

She lets it hang there and doesn't complete the thought.

I say, "Was a sweet boy. Does that mean he passed away too?"

"Yes, but not in the way you might think. All his talk about becoming a lawyer was when he was just a boy. My son meant well, but he was not smart. At least not smart enough to become a lawyer. To get into the right schools. I think he realized this as he got older. When he became a teenager, he realized that if he wanted to make money, he would need to find something else to do. He did not want to become a farmer and work in the fields all day. He did not want to leave me by myself either, so he decided to stay in town, but ..."

She pauses again, turning to look at us.

"Fernando Sanchez Morales did not always own that house up on the hill. His father lived there before him. His father also worked for the cartel, but he wasn't so awful."

Another pause. Yolanda shakes her head again, wipes at her eyes with the back of her hand.

"I know that sounds strange, but he was good to the people here. Morales would never have allowed those narcos to terrorize the town. He understood that towns like ours were just part of life. We were here to stay. When he became older, I worried something might happen to him. I worried somebody worse would take his place. As they say, better the devil you know than the devil you do not. I suppose Fernando could be even worse than he is, but he is bad. He is ruthless. And he was just a boy at the time, too, and my son knew this, and somehow he managed to meet Fernando somewhere and convinced Fernando to let him work for the cartel."

"Your son was a narco."

The old woman nods. The cubes of pork keep sizzling in the pan. They've been on much too long, and Yolanda suddenly realizes this. She takes the pan off the stove, turns to a large bowl, and drops them in.

"As I told you, my son was not very smart. He thought being a narco would pay a lot of money. And yes, it did bring him more money than he would have gotten working the fields, but it was dangerous work too. I told him that. I pleaded with him. Begged him. He knew how I felt about the narcos, especially after what they did to me. But he did not care."

"What happened to him?"

Yolanda covers the pork. She grabs another frying pan, sets it over the stove, and begins sautéing the onions.

"I do not know. I finally had enough. I told him that if he wanted to continue living in this house—if he wanted to continue being my son—then he needed to quit being a narco. He left that night, and I never saw him again."

"How long ago was this?"

She pauses for a beat, thinking about it. Then she shrugs, shakes her head, as she keeps moving the onions around in the frying pan.

"I cannot remember. It has been at least thirty years. Maybe thirty-five years."

"Maybe he's still out there somewhere. Maybe he's just been saving enough money to buy you that place by the ocean."

Yolanda wipes the tears from her eyes with the back of her hand again.

"No, he is dead. He has been dead for some time now. A mother knows. She feels it."

Before I can say anything to this, the front door bangs open.

My gun has been in my right hand this entire time. I raise it as I turn toward the front of the house, ready to shoot whoever's burst inside, but it's the boy from earlier, who had found me and Gabriela standing outside and took us to the town meeting.

He stops short when he sees the gun, his eyes widening. He's breathing fast, like he just sprinted a mile, and his face is flush from the exertion.

I lower the gun to my side.

"What's wrong?"

He pauses to catch his breath and blurts out the two words I've been waiting to hear since the moment the townspeople agreed to kick out the narcos.

"They're coming."

39

They come in three vehicles—two pickup trucks and an SUV.

The SUV is sandwiched between the two pickup trucks as they tear into town down the unpaved main road toward the square.

That's where I'm waiting, right in the middle of the road, the gun held loosely at my side.

The first pickup swerves and skids to a stop. Several men are crowded in the back cab, all of them armed with rifles, and the moment the pickup stops, they jump down and aim their rifles at me.

I don't move. I don't raise the gun. I just stand there and wait for the other two vehicles to stop, for the men in the cab of the second pickup to jump out and aim their rifles at me too.

I barely glance at them. I keep my focus on the SUV. It just sits there for several long seconds before the passenger side door opens and Fernando Sanchez Morales steps out.

At least, I assume it's Morales. He's dressed nicer than all the rest of the men, in slacks and a button-down shirt with the sleeves rolled up. His sunglasses look designer, not the cheap ones the rest of the men wear. He holds a gun at his side but doesn't aim it at me as he slams the door shut and starts to wander out into the middle of the road, scanning the empty square.

I say, "Stop right there."

He pauses a beat, clearly surprised by my forceful tone. But then he shakes it off and keeps advancing. He takes his time, a simple stroll, walking past his men who stand motionless with their rifles trained on me.

"Where is everybody?"

I don't answer. Besides the rumblings of the vehicles' engines, the square is quiet.

Morales asks, "Are they hiding in their homes?"

I say nothing.

He pauses again, now maybe thirty paces away from me. He takes my measure, apparently finds me wanting, and shakes his head dismissively.

"Who the fuck are you, anyway?"

I say nothing.

He takes another step toward me.

"Are you the one who ran off my boys?"

I keep my mouth shut.

His face flushes. His teeth even clench as he growls at me.

"Answer me, *puta*."

I mimic an overdramatic yawn.

Morales sneers.

"Fuck this."

He starts to raise his gun.

I say, "I wouldn't do that if I were you."

This causes him to pause again. But it's only for an instant, and then he keeps raising the gun until it's aimed right at my face.

That's when the rest of the townspeople show themselves.

First the men on the rooftops rise up and aim their rifles

down into the square. There are six of them, each with AK-47s, and they're spread out around the square so that the narcos are surrounded.

Then the other townspeople drift into the square. Some of them are carrying bats and metal rods. Many others carry guns.

I say, "Maybe you didn't get the message, but your boys were asked to leave and never come back. That means their asshole friends too."

I pause, squinting at Morales.

"That especially means you."

The man's face burns. He's visibly shaking, doing everything he can to hold in his rage. Because he knows that if he lets it out, things are going to get worse.

I say, "You're Fernando Sanchez Morales, aren't you?"

He says nothing.

"From what I hear, your father was a reasonable man. I mean, as reasonable as somebody who works for the cartel can be. But at least he didn't fuck with townspeople. He let them be. Let them go about their lives."

Behind Morales, the narcos haven't moved. They're still aiming their rifles at me, but they're looking around the square, especially up at the rooftops where the men are aiming their own rifles down at them.

"In case you didn't notice, Fernando, you and your men are in what's called a kill box. Are those men up on the rooftops skilled marksmen? No, obviously they aren't. But from where they're positioned, all they need to do is shoot and they're likely to hit somebody. Somebody like you."

He says nothing.

"Speaking of which, some of those AK-47s are courtesy of your men. Which is kind of funny, if you think about it."

I let it hang there, and it's enough for him to finally break his silence.

"What's funny?"

"That you and your men might get killed by the same guns your boys had hidden in their house."

Morales says nothing.

I say, "You and your men have less chance of walking away from this than the people of this town do. Is that something you want to risk?"

He says nothing, though his gun starts to dip, slowly, until it's back hanging at his side.

I say, "Why did your men come here last night and kill those people?"

He shakes his head.

"I have no idea what you're talking about."

Part of me wants to force him to admit he was the one who ordered those men to come here last night, but another part—a more rational part—knows that now is not the time.

"You and your men might be able to kill me and a few other of the townspeople right now, but many of your men are going to die too. I know you probably don't give a shit about them, but here's the thing, Fernando. You will die too. I know you probably don't believe me, but I promise you, that if you want to start something here, you will die."

Morales doesn't answer, just stands there seething.

"You don't own this town. You don't own these people. They just want to live their lives. Are you going to let them live their lives?"

He says nothing, keeps glaring back at me. Finally he glances over his shoulder at his men, then glances back at me.

"It's not going to happen today, but one of these days, I am going to kill you."

He's still seething, but he knows he has no choice. At least, not if he wants to make it back to the hill alive.

Fernando Sanchez Morales starts walking backward, slowly, toward his men.

"Soon, *puta*."

I give him a smile.

"Can't wait."

He glares at me for another moment and then turns and motions his men to disperse. They're leery, still watching the rooftops, but they start back toward their respective pickup trucks. It takes a minute before they're all loaded in the back of the cabs.

Morales takes his time walking back to the SUV. He pauses before he climbs inside, just long enough to glare back at me one last time.

Without a word he gets into the SUV, and almost immediately the driver pulls a slow U-turn to take them back down the unpaved road they came in on, the two pickup trucks following close behind.

I don't move—the entire town doesn't move—until the three vehicles are far enough away that we can't hear their engines anymore.

That's when the town starts cheering. Just like last time, they whoop and holler and act like it's New Year's Eve. When the cheering dies down, I shout so everybody can hear me.

"Remember, don't get too excited. They will come back. You need to decide who will keep watch. Make shifts. All day, all night."

Everybody nods in agreement, says they understand. A few even thank me, tell me that I'm a hero.

I want to tell them I'm no hero, but I don't want to ruin their good spirit. So after a couple moments, forcing a smile, I turn and start toward Yolanda's house.

Gabriela is waiting for me around the corner. Her eyes are wide with excitement.

"That was amazing! Weren't you scared?"

"Not really. It's not the first time I've been in a situation like that."

"But you could have died."

"Yeah, well, that's what happens when you have a gun aimed at your face. That's why I just always expect I will die. That way I'm not scared."

She stares at me, stunned, and then frowns as she reaches for her pocket.

I ask, "What is it?"

Gabriela pulls out her cell phone.

"A message just came in."

She stares at the screen for a moment, and then her eyes go wide again.

"Holy shit, they found him."

"Who?"

"Miguel Dominguez."

"Is he alive?"

She scans whatever message came through and shakes her head.

"No, they only found his body. But I know where it is. Shit, I need to go there right now."

I glance back toward the square and the few townspeople milling about.

"After what just happened, I should stay here."

"I shouldn't be long. Maybe by the time I get there the investigators will be there. I'll tell Ramon you said hi."

"That's probably not a good idea. Look, Gabriela, you need to be careful."

"I know."

I hand her the gun.

"Take this."

She stares down at the gun for a long moment.

I say, "You've fired a gun before, right?"

"Of course."

But the way she says it, she doesn't sound very convincing.

"See this thing here on the side? That's the safety. Just take it off like this and then point and squeeze the trigger."

She nods and takes the gun from me.

"I'll be fine. I won't have to use it."

"Let's hope not. Now, I want to get back to Yolanda's before the food gets any colder than it already is."

40

Ramon stared into the barrel and thought of a jigsaw puzzle.

Years ago, a foot had been found by children playing in a field. The foot was bare and severed at the ankle. They had searched the area but found no other body parts. Then, a week later, an arm was found across town. A week after that, a leg. Little by little, a body had begun to emerge from all the missing pieces until finally the last piece, the victim's head, was found on the doorstep of the police station. At that point they were able to establish who the victim was—a shopkeeper who had gone missing the previous month—but it was unclear what sin the man had committed to deserve such a vicious and elaborate death.

They had never figured out who murdered the shopkeeper, which wasn't rare in their line of business. They were crime scene investigators, yes, and they were pretty good at their jobs, but they didn't have the resources they needed to follow up on leads. Still, following those body parts week after week had stuck with Ramon ever since, and now as he stared into the barrel, he was reminded of how disgusted he was at the world then, and how he had been disgusted at the world ever since.

Miguel Dominguez had been cut up in pieces much the same way as that shopkeeper years ago. Only the killer had been kind enough not to disperse his body parts all over the city. At least, it didn't appear that way from where Ramon stood. Everything was in the barrel—Miguel's feet and legs and torso and arms and hands. His head was at the very top of the heap, staring up at the cloudless sky.

Carlos said, "I have a hunch our friend here pissed somebody off."

Ibarra and Serrano stood around the barrel with them. A few other officers sealed off the area the best they could. They were in an alleyway, and crowds had begun to form on both ends.

Carlos stepped back and looked at Ramon. When he realized Ramon was still staring into the barrel, he reached out and snapped his fingers in front of his face.

"Hey."

Ramon blinked, looked at his partner.

"What?"

"You look pale. You're not getting soft on me, are you?"

Ramon shook his head, focusing again on the barrel.

"I'm just thinking about that shopkeeper from a couple years back."

"Oh yeah. Whoever did that was one sick fuck. Hell, whoever did *this* is one sick fuck. Maybe it's the same person."

Carlos chuckled at his own joke and then went quiet. He squinted at the two PFM agents.

"What do you two think?"

Serrano said, "Doesn't add up."

"How so?"

"Call it a gut feeling."

Carlos snorted.

"My gut is telling me this guy pissed off the wrong person."

Ramon murmured, "You said that already."

"Well, I think it bears repeating. From what we can tell, Miguel wasn't a drug dealer. He worked at that shitty motel and made shitty money and lived in a shitty apartment. Not the kind of person somebody would want to cut up and stuff in a barrel."

Ibarra pulled his cell phone from his pocket and turned away as he placed it to his ear.

The other men didn't say anything while the agent spoke quietly on the phone. They stared down at the pieces of Miguel Dominguez's body. Right now they couldn't do much until the barrel was transported to headquarters so that Jorge could start his work. Though at this point Ramon didn't know what more Jorge would be able to tell them except maybe what kind of blade was used to sever the body parts. There was the possibility the can was covered in prints, but it was a good assumption none of those prints would belong to the killer.

Ibarra turned back to them as he disconnected his call.

He said to Serrano, "We need to leave."

Serrano said, "Where?"

"Pátzcuaro."

Pátzcuaro was a town located in Michoacán.

Carlos said, "What's in Pátzcuaro?"

The agents traded a quick glance before Ibarra cleared his throat.

"Earlier this morning the Devil attacked a convoy. They had been working as a decoy to lure him out with the idea they were transporting the wife and children. One of the men was missing, from what we understand, and it's believed the Devil tortured him for information."

Ramon said, "What kind of information?"

"The whereabouts of the wife and children."

"How do you know?"

"Because their bodies were just found."

There was a brief silence as the men digested this new information, and then Carlos shook his head.

"Wait a minute. Pátzcuaro has to be at least one thousand kilometers from here."

The agents said nothing.

Carlos said, "Just to be clear, do either of you think this man was killed by the Devil?"

The agents said nothing.

Carlos said, "You guys have been a lot of help, you know that?"

Serrano said, "We need to head out. Send us updates as they come in."

The PFM agents left them and hurried up the alleyway toward where they'd parked their car.

Carlos watched them and muttered, "Assholes."

He and Ramon stayed motionless for a long time, both staring down at the body in the barrel.

Carlos lit a cigarette and shook his head.

"Who in the hell did you piss off, Miguel?"

41

Dorado sits perched on Yolanda's lap, staring at me.

I sit on the couch across from Yolanda, staring back at the cat.

It's late in the day now, the sun already starting to fade, and the narcos haven't made another attempt to enter the town. So we've been waiting here in the house, Yolanda and I, and as I don't feel much like talking, we've mostly just been sitting in silence.

"Would your parents be proud of you?"

The old woman's question catches me off guard. I glance up at her, breaking my staring contest with Dorado.

"What kind of question is that?"

Dorado, triumphant with his staring contest win, hops off Yolanda's lap and scurries out of the room into the kitchen.

Yolanda says, "A simple question. Would your parents be proud of you?"

This gives me pause. Truth is, I've never really thought about it. Or, well, if I had thought about it, I didn't care much. But is that true? Screw this—I decide to throw the question back at the old woman.

"Were you proud of your son?"

Maybe it's the way I say it—a little too glib—but something changes in her face. It's clear I've hit a nerve.

I sigh, leaning forward on the couch.

"I'm sorry. I didn't mean that."

She watches me for a long moment, then shakes her head.

"No, I deserved it. I was making you uncomfortable, so you decided to make me uncomfortable."

Neither one of us says anything for a long time.

Dorado reenters the room. He stands there for a couple seconds, looking toward Yolanda and then toward me, before lying down on the carpet to stretch.

Yolanda says, "They will come back, won't they?"

"I don't know."

She holds her gaze steady with mine.

"Yes, you do."

"Fine. Yes, they will come back. When, I have no idea, but you said it yourself, Fernando isn't like his father. He's more vicious. He won't be able to let go what happened today."

Again, neither one of us says anything for a long time. We watch the cat, stretching on the carpet, until he rolls over onto his feet and pads over to Yolanda. He sits in front of her and meows.

She leans forward.

"Are you hungry?"

Another meow.

"You ate a half hour ago. You do not need anymore. What you do need is to lose some weight."

The cat meows a third time, like a protest, and then scurries back into the kitchen.

I say, "My mother doesn't know what it is I do."

Yolanda looks like she was about to push herself out of her chair to follow Dorado into the kitchen. Clearly, she's ready to give in to the cat. But she pauses and glances up at me.

"And what is it that you do?"

"I can't tell you. But I recently walked away from my job. And my mother, she never knew what it was I really did. The same with my father. She's been lied to for the better part of half her life. Or no—not lied to. It was never something intentionally devious. Just her ... ignorance was meant to keep her safe."

I shake my head again.

"Never mind. I feel like I'm rambling. I don't even know why I'm telling you this. But my mother ... I think she always wanted something better for me. And she's always been disappointed that I didn't turn out differently. Or at least the way she thinks I should have turned out. Except the truth is she has no idea what I've done. All the people I've killed. I should be ashamed about it, I guess, but all those people were bad people. And to keep my mother safe, she'll never be able to know the truth. She'll always ... be disappointed in me."

Silence again. After a couple moments, Yolanda looks like she's going to say something, but that's when the front door opens.

I reach for my gun as I stand and turn toward the door.

The boy from earlier hurries inside, a cell phone swinging in his hand.

Yolanda asks, "What's wrong?"

The boy pauses to catch his breath. Then he holds up the phone, its screen facing us.

"*La Baliza*. This was posted ... a couple minutes ... ago."

The boy steps forward and hands me the phone. The webpage is centered on a video. The headline reads JOURNALIST WHORE.

A dark foreboding tinge in my stomach, I press the play button.

At first the video is shaky, so it's unclear what's going on, but soon the camera steadies and focuses on a girl kneeling on the ground. A cinderblock wall is behind her. The girl's been stripped of her clothes and is completely naked, making it easy to see the bruises that have already been inflicted on her body. Her hands are tied behind her back, and tape covers her mouth.

Somebody behind the camera—maybe the cameraman himself—tells her to look up.

Gabriela looks up.

For an instant, she looks defiant. There are tears in her eyes, and her face is bruised and bloody, strands of bloody hair clinging to her face, but the defiance that flashes in her eyes gives me hope, if only for an instant. Because then, a second later, that defiance blinks out and is replaced by fear.

Yolanda is on her feet now, and with the help of her cane, she shuffles over to where I'm standing, frozen. The moment she sees what's on the cell phone's screen, she murmurs a quick prayer.

She says, "Turn it off. Do not give them what they want."

But I can't turn it off. I can't stop watching. This may be what the narcos want—after all, who else would post what is most certainly a snuff film—but I can't look away.

I hear myself say something, but the voice doesn't sound like my own.

"I need a car."

Yolanda says, "What?"

"I need a car."

Yolanda tells the boy to hurry out and find somebody who will loan me a car. The boy turns and sprints out of the house.

I keep staring at the screen.

Two men step into view, both of them masked. They have tools, and they use those tools like they've used them many times before.

I don't stop watching. I can't look away.

Because of the tape covering Gabriela's mouth, her screams are muffled, but they still cause a chill to race down my spine.

Yolanda is still in the room with me—I can sense her there—but it's the cell phone I keep watching, because the men take their time. They take turns. And Gabriela, despite the tape over her mouth, screams and cries and then screams some more.

How much time has passed since the video started is hard to say—five minutes, maybe, ten minutes—but at one point Yolanda's voice drifts in and snaps me out of my fugue state.

"A car is waiting outside."

But I don't react. I keep watching—the men leaning over Gabriela with their tools, twisting and tearing and rending flesh—until Yolanda grabs the cell phone and rips it from my grip.

I stare into space for an instant—into the void where the screen was just moments ago, so many thousands of pixels working to show Gabriela being tortured—and then I blink and turn my head to look at Yolanda.

She stares hard at me, the cell phone clutched to her chest, and says one word.

"Go."

42

I park three blocks away from the house, what feels like a safe distance, though for an instant I second-guess myself because adrenaline is still surging through my veins. I take a moment to try to calm myself, to simply breathe, and I'm surprised I managed to make it all this way without getting pulled over. I must have been doing at least one hundred miles per hour at some points, and now I'm here, three blocks away from Gabriela's house.

I shut off the engine and open my door. I don't get out at first, scanning the empty street. With the door open, I can hear the sounds of the city, but nothing strikes me as off.

Gun in hand, I step out of the car and quietly shut the door and start down the block.

A minute later I'm standing on the street outside Gabriela's house. The garage door is closed, but the gate has been forced open.

In the back of my mind I know this might be a trap. Narcos could be inside, just waiting for me to finally show myself. A few could even be positioned on rooftops right now, rifle sights leveled on my head.

I look up and down the street one last time before pushing the gate open and entering the yard.

I slip a penlight from my pocket as I approach the front door. Shine the light at the door and, yes, it has been forced open too, the lock smashed. The door has been pushed closed, so anybody from the street would think nothing of it.

Part of me knows that I need to be careful right now—those narcos could be right inside, holding their breaths with anticipation as they aim their AK-47s at the door—but at this moment I'm not thinking straight. It's reckless, I know, but I can't help it. I don't open the door quietly but instead kick it open and charge inside, my gun raised, the penlight sweeping back and forth searching for any movement.

Nothing.

The living room is empty.

Except, well, not quite.

Gabriela's grandmother sits in her chair in the corner. Her head is down, like she's dozed off, only I know she's not sleeping.

The front of her shirt is dark with blood.

I quickly approach and duck down, shining the penlight at her face. The bastards sliced her throat. All things considered, it's a small mercy.

It doesn't take long to search the rest of the house. The place has been ransacked, but there's nothing to find on either floor.

In Gabriela's room, the computer on her desk has been destroyed. I'm not sure what the thinking was behind that, but obviously they had used her computer to upload the video to *La Baliza* and then they had—

Wait.

Why come back here to upload the video on her computer? That seems like too much work. Like too much chance of getting caught. Unless …

"Shit."

I whisper it and then rush out of the room, down the stairs, through the house toward the door that leads into the garage.

The smell hits me almost instantaneously. It's not a stench, not yet, but it's certainly ripe. After all, it couldn't have been more than two hours since those men were here. The body, in many respects, is still fresh.

I don't bother with the penlight. I flick on the switch just inside the door and the single bulb in the ceiling blinks to life.

I didn't recognize the cinderblock wall of the garage in the video, but maybe that's because my focus was on something else. But this is where they did it. Where they stripped her naked and bound her wrists and ankles and slapped tape over her mouth and forced her on her knees so that they could record. Everything those two masked men did happened right here, just feet away from where Gabriela's grandmother sat dead in her chair with her face tilted down like she was taking a nap.

The men didn't bother cleaning up their crime. They even left the tools behind—the tools, I now realize, which were already in this garage. A cabinet in the corner has been busted open, and that's where the men found the screwdrivers and hammers and saw. Those tools now lie bloodied on the floor around the pieces left of Gabriela.

I don't know how long I stand there staring, the gun gripped tightly at my side. Blood is screaming in my ears, and my heart is going so fast it slams against my ribcage, and it takes everything I have at that moment not to shout and scream and cry out my frustration.

Then I blink, and I'm able to move again.

I turn and flick off the light and close the door and make my way back outside the house.

Narcos aren't waiting for me on the street. Neither are the police. The street is empty.

I keep the gun at my side as I head toward where I parked the car three blocks away. After the first block, I slip the disposable phone from my pocket and punch in the number I had memorized a week before. I place the phone to my ear and I listen to it ring and then I listen to the prerecorded message for Scout Dry Cleaners, and when the beep sounds, I tell Atticus to call me ASAP.

He calls back a minute later. By that point I'm in the car and driving back through the streets toward the highway.

"I need two things, Atticus."

He says, "It's nice to talk to you too, Holly."

This causes me to clench my teeth. I want to tear into him, tell him not to fucking start with me, but instead I relay today's events as quickly as possible so that he'll understand what's just happened.

He's quiet for a long moment, and then he clears his throat.

"I'm sorry, Holly. What do you need?"

I tell him the first thing. I know it's a long shot, but I figure if anybody has the resources to do it—or can find somebody who does—it's Atticus.

He says, "It's not going to be easy, but I'll see what I can do. What's the other thing you need?"

"Nova."

Part III

THE DEVIL

43

At just past two o'clock in the afternoon, Nova Bartkowski steps through one of the exits of Guadalajara International Airport. He's dressed nicer than I expected—khakis and a dress shirt—and he has a luggage bag strapped over his shoulder. Sunglasses cover his face, so I can't tell if he sees me at first. I'm standing across the drop-off area by the first terminal. I stand there, waiting, until Nova has time to scan the people and the cars and then he nods briefly and crosses over to me.

I say, "Welcome to Mexico."

He tilts his head down to look at me over the rims of the sunglasses, but he doesn't say anything.

"What?"

"Nothing. Wanted to make sure it was you. Feels like a long time since I saw you last."

In reality it's been one week since we parted ways. I had just killed Javier Diaz and his men in the elevator of my apartment building. Nova had shown up to help clean up the mess. And then that was it. One week, but yet it did feel like a long time.

He says, "Atticus told me you were in Culiacán."

"That's right."

"So then why did I just fly into Guadalajara?"

"How much did Atticus tell you?"

"He said that you needed my help. Something about a serial killer."

"That's part of it, yeah."

He raises an eyebrow.

"There's more?"

I grin and motion for him to follow me toward the car.

"Of course, Nova. There's always more. By the way, what's in the bag?"

"Just some clothes. Also your new passport and identification."

"Seriously?"

"Yeah. James gave it to me. I mean, I *think* it's your new passport and identification. I'm not fluent in Sign Language."

James is Atticus's assistant—at least, that's how I've come to think of him—and he's deaf.

"When did you see James?"

"He met me at the airport before I flew out. You know I came in on a private jet, right?"

"Atticus said that was the plan. Was it nice?"

"Is the Pope Catholic?"

We reach the car—the same car I'd driven the previous night to Gabriela's—and pop the truck for Nova to put in his bag. There's a blanket in the trunk, and I shift it to reveal the two handguns hiding beneath.

Nova says, "Thank God. I was starting to feel naked without a piece on me."

He sets the bag in the trunk and grabs one of the guns and stuffs it in the back waistband of his khakis. Then he zips open the bag, rummages inside, and pulls out a Holy Bible.

"Here you go."

I take the Bible and say, "Um, thanks?"

"The passport and ID are stitched in the front and back flaps."

I'm tempted to tear the book apart, eager to learn the name of my new identity, but that will have to wait. I toss the Bible in the trunk and slam the lid shut and offer the keys to Nova.

"Mind driving?"

"I don't even know where we're going."

"I'll give you directions. But I'm just going to warn you—I may drift off to sleep."

He tilts his head down to look at me again over the rims of the sunglasses.

"When was the last time you had a full night's sleep?"

"Maybe a week? I'm not sure."

"Jesus Christ, Holly."

I pause to give him a closer look.

"What happened to you?"

"What do you mean?"

"When I called Atticus and told him I needed your help, he said you were in the middle of something."

Nova says nothing.

"Where did you fly out of, anyway?"

"Monterey."

"You were in *California*?"

"Why do you sound shocked?"

"Because a week ago you were in D.C."

"Yeah, and you were in D.C. a week ago too. Now you're in Mexico. What's your point?"

"Nothing. What took you out to California?"

"A road trip."

"You're joking."

"What—I'm not allowed to go on a road trip?"

"You never struck me as the road trip type, is all."

"Yeah, well, something tells me we're about to go on a road trip of our own. How far are we going?"

"Three hours from here, give or take."

"What's there?"

"Hopefully some answers."

"Holly?"

"Yeah."

"Don't be vague. I've had a long couple of days, as I'm sure you have. I'm tired and I'm cranky and I want to know why I'm here."

I toss him the keys.

"Then let's go. You drive, and I'll try not to doze off while I tell you just what kind of shitstorm I've created this time."

44

We take the highway north all the way up to Colotlán, and as we drive, I tell Nova everything.

I tell him about the raid on Ernesto Diaz's house and finding the woman and children hiding in the closet. I tell him about taking the woman and the children up the coast where I left them by that abandoned brick building, and then returning later to find dark smoke pouring out the door and the three charred bodies inside. I tell him about meeting Gabriela and I tell him about La Miserias and Fernando Sanchez Morales. Finally I tell him about the snuff film uploaded to *La Baliza* for the whole country to see.

Nova says, "Jesus Christ."

I say nothing.

He says, "It's not your fault, Holly."

I say nothing.

He glances at me to see if I'm still there. I tilt my face to look back at him.

He says, "I'm serious. I know how your mind works."

"Oh really. And how does my mind work?"

"You left the woman and the children at that abandoned building. Where this Devil character apparently showed up and burned them alive. And because of that, you feel responsible. Like you, I don't know, took them to their deaths."

I say nothing.

"And then there's the town you told me about. How the narcos came in and killed the people at the wedding. The way you put it, the killings were retribution for Ernesto Diaz's murder. Which, of course, you carried out. So again, you feel responsible for all those people getting killed."

I say nothing.

"And then there's your friend Gabriela and her grandmother. Shit, Holly, do I really need to keep going?"

When I tilt my face this time, I glare back at him.

Nova just shakes his head and says, "You can't blame yourself. I mean, hell, of course you *can* blame yourself, but you shouldn't."

"Why?"

"What do you mean, why?"

"Why shouldn't I blame myself?"

"Because it's a waste of time. It's not productive. You did the same thing when Scooter died."

I close my eyes and shake my head, not wanting to think about the other member of our team who had died less than a month ago.

"Don't."

"People die all the time, Holly. Shit happens all the time. That's just the way it is."

I say nothing, staring out my window now and watching the passing scenery.

Nova doesn't say anything either. At least not for a couple of minutes, and then he asks a question.

"How old?"

I blink and frown at him.

"What?"

"You said those gangbangers who came to kill you at the apartment building—the ones the pimps sent—that when you realized they weren't even eighteen you decided not to kill them. Okay, so how old would they have to be for you to place a bullet in their heads?"

I slump back down in my seat, my head against the headrest, and stare out my window again.

"What does it matter?"

"I'm curious."

"They were kids, Nova. I don't kill kids."

"No, they were teenagers. At least they sounded like teenagers based on what you told me."

"Kids, teenagers—what does it matter?"

"Eighteen is considered the age somebody becomes an adult, right?"

I sigh but say nothing, just keep watching the scrolling scenery.

Nova says, "If this Devil guy were murdering the leaders of the cartels instead of their families, would you be as gung-ho in trying to stop him?"

I sigh again and roll my eyes at Nova.

"That's a stupid question."

"No, I think it's a valid question. Just as valid as how old somebody needs to be before you'll consider killing them. Christ, Holly, you said those two gangbangers had guns and were planning to kill you."

"They were just kids, Nova. Amateurs. There wasn't a moment I feared for my life."

"Even amateurs get lucky sometimes."

"Fine, what do you want me to say? Yes, of course it matters that this guy is murdering the wives and children of cartel families. That doesn't sit right with me. Does it sit right with you?"

"Of course it doesn't. But let me ask you this. If you could go back in time and kill Hitler when he was a baby, would you do it?"

I roll my eyes again and say, "Are you fucking kidding me?"

"Answer the question."

"It's a stupid question."

"Is it, though? Almost six million Jews died in the Holocaust. You take Hitler out when he was a baby, maybe those six million Jews don't die."

"Or maybe somebody else takes his place and causes the Holocaust. Maybe even more Jews die. Did you ever think of that?"

He tilts his head back and forth, considering it.

"That's certainly one interesting theory."

"Nova, what's the point of this?"

"Honestly? Just killing time. We've got another hour to go until we get to this town you want us to go to. Speaking of which, you told me about everything leading up to this point, but you failed to mention where we're headed and why."

"You know how I told you the men who killed Gabriela had uploaded the video to that website?"

"Yeah. It's still not up, is it?"

"No. It was taken down within hours. But before it was taken down, I told Atticus I wanted to find out who runs the website."

"Why?"

"The way Gabriela put it, *La Baliza* was the first to report on the Devil's killings. They didn't call him the Devil at the time—some other newspaper came up with the name—but they made sure to get the story out there."

"And?"

"And after Gabriela had uploaded her story about the three dead bodies in that building, the publisher emailed her saying he was taking out any reference to the Devil as there was no direct evidence identifying him."

"Okay, but what if this guy was just being careful? You know, journalists are supposed to make sure they get their facts straight before they publish. They're not supposed to speculate, even if it is for an online blog."

"Maybe. But something tells me the guy who runs the website knows more than he's letting on."

"What something?"

"Just a gut feeling."

Nova shakes his head and says, "You're kidding, right?"

I don't answer.

He says, "Wait a minute. You said your friend used that Tor browser to hide her identity online. The guy who ran the website did the same. If that's the case, how was Atticus able to track a location?"

Staring out my window again, I say, "The guy slipped up."

"What do you mean?"

"I told you, he took the video off the website. When he did, he must have done it in a hurry. Maybe he didn't use the same browser he always used. I don't know. But Atticus said he managed to find a source and traced it to Colotlán."

"Was he able to establish an exact location?"

"He did. And it's a strange location."

"How so?"

"It's a church."

45

The church in question is much larger than I had imagined it would be. It's several stories tall with two gothic towers reaching into the sky and stands in the middle of town.

Nova and I stand across the street. It's just past five o'clock and around us the town is mostly quiet. A few people walking here and there. A few cars driving past. No narcos in sight. No police, either.

Nova says, "This is the one, huh?"

"Yep."

"Maybe Atticus got it wrong."

"Maybe. Only one way to find out."

We cross the street and enter through the ornate doors into the church. The cathedral has a high ceiling and our footsteps echo through the mostly empty space as we advance toward the front.

Only an old woman sits in one of the pews, her head bent in prayer. At least, I assume she's praying. For an instant, the image of Gabriela's grandmother flashes in my mind, and I wonder if this old woman's throat has also been sliced open.

The old woman shifts in the pew as she grips onto her rosary, running the beads through her fingers.

Nova whispers, "This doesn't feel right."

I say nothing as we keep quietly walking down the aisle toward the front of the church. There are several confessionals off to the side. I wonder if anybody's in them.

As we near the front, a priest appears from a doorway in the corner. He's in his forties with gray close-cropped hair. For a moment he looks guarded. But when he sees us, he adjusts the glasses on his face and smiles.

"*Buenas tardes.*"

I smile and ask, "Do you speak English?"

The priest nods as he approaches us. There's something strange about the way he walks, something that probably nobody else would catch. It's there for only a second or two, and then he's standing right in front of us.

"Welcome. How can I help you?"

"My boyfriend and I are on vacation. When we saw this gorgeous church we wanted to stop in."

The priest beams with pride.

"It certainly is gorgeous, yes."

"Can we have a tour?"

The smile starts to fade.

"No, I am afraid that is not possible right now."

"Are you the only one here?"

Now the priest's brow furrows as he begins to frown.

"I do not understand the question."

I glance around the vast cathedral, spot the old woman again, and turn back to the priest. I lean toward him, lower my voice.

"May I confess to you?"

He says, "Are you Catholic?"

"Lapsed. But I'm hoping to start over again."

This isn't true on either account, but what the priest doesn't know won't hurt him.

He stands there for a long moment, clearly conflicted about something. He keeps glancing past us toward the church entrance, as if he expects somebody to walk through at any moment.

I say, "Please, Father …"

He blinks, looks back at me.

"Crisanto."

"Please, Father Crisanto. I did something terrible recently and I need to confess."

Nova hasn't moved from my side this entire time. Clearly he isn't sure where I'm heading with this, but he doesn't question it.

Father Crisanto stands there for another long moment, still conflicted, before he forces a smile and says of course and motions toward the confessionals.

Before I follow him, I turn back to Nova and whisper into his ear.

"See if you can get the old woman to leave. This may not turn out well."

He frowns at me for a second, but then he says, "Sure thing, babe."

I turn toward the confessionals before Nova can say anything else. Father Crisanto has already entered and closed his door.

As somebody who's never been in a confessional before, I'm not sure of the exact rules, but I figure I can wing it.

I enter and kneel in front of a square panel. It smells stale in the cramped space. Which I guess is to be expected. This is where people come to confess their sins and ask for forgiveness. A whiff of desperation and regret fills the air.

The partition between us slides open, revealing a mesh screen. Father Crisanto on the other side, waiting for me to begin.

Because I've seen my fair share of confessions on TV, I say,

"Bless me, Father, for I have sinned. It has been several years since my last confession."

Father Crisanto doesn't say anything, just waits.

"I recently hurt someone close to me. Someone who I did not know very long but whom I considered a friend."

Silence.

"She took me in when she didn't have to. She gave me a place to stay. She was a good person. A strong person. A person who took care of her grandmother ever since her parents died."

More silence.

"She wrote for a news hub. She wrote anonymously to protect herself from the cartels and from the corrupt police. She knew what she was doing was dangerous, but she did it anyway."

Even more silence.

"Because of what she wrote about, there was a bounty on her head. I guess there are bounties on the heads of everybody who writes for that website, but I knew there was a bounty on her head because I was paid handsomely when I told the cartel about her."

Father Crisanto hasn't moved at all this entire time.

"Because I am greedy I sold my friend out. I told the cartel who she was and where to find her, and they captured her. And they ... they tortured her before they killed her. They filmed all of it, and they uploaded that film to the website, and then—"

Before I can finish, Father Crisanto suddenly shifts from his silent resting place. There's a familiar click, and then he's up and out of the booth and is tearing open my curtain, and for an instant I can see the fury in his face, the pure rage, and he has a gun in his hand and starts to raise the barrel toward my face.

But in the priest's sudden rage, he momentarily forgets about Nova—who steps into view and places the barrel of his own gun against the back of Father Crisanto's head.

Nova says, "I've done many horrible things in my life, but I've never killed a priest and would prefer not to kill one today."

Father Crisanto freezes. He keeps glaring back at me, but then little by little the rage starts to fade from his face. He takes a deep breath, and his shoulders drop in defeat.

I say, "I had nothing to do with Gabriela's death, but I wanted to be sure you were the right person. You cared deeply about her, didn't you?"

"I care deeply about all my writers. How did you know where to find me?"

I don't answer the priest. Instead, I say, "Nova, I think you can give Father Crisanto space now."

Nova steps back, slowly lowering the gun to his side.

I stand up and exit the confessional.

"You don't normally carry a gun on you, do you?"

The priest shakes his head slowly, as if he's ashamed, but says nothing.

"I could tell when you approached us. By the way you walked. You're not comfortable having it on you. It digs into your back, doesn't it?"

The priest nods. He takes a moment to glance around the cathedral and notices the old woman is gone.

"Where did Dolores go?"

Nova says, "She took off right after she spotted my gun."

Father Crisanto sighs and then turns back to me.

"Did you really know Gabriela?"

"I did. I was with her the past two days before she was murdered."

He frowns at this, and then a certain understanding enters his eyes.

"You were the one who found the bodies, weren't you?"

"That's right. And that's why we're here. We're hoping you can give us some information."

"About what?"

"The Devil."

46

Father Crisanto lowers himself down into one of the pews with a heavy sigh. He stares up toward the front of the church at the large crucifix hanging on the wall. He takes his glasses off, rubs his eyes, replaces the glasses, and then looks at me.

"What do you want to know?"

"Who is he?"

Father Crisanto laughs.

"That's a long story."

I gesture at the empty cathedral.

"We have time."

Father Crisanto shakes his head and says, "Who are you, anyway? You were the one who found the bodies, yes? But you are no tourist. You or your boyfriend."

"For starters, he's not my boyfriend. And as to whether or not I'm actually a tourist, what does it matter?"

Father Crisanto squints at me, studying my face.

"Why were you there?"

"I just happened to be driving past."

He shakes his head again.

"No, you were there for another reason. Why?"

"It doesn't matter why, Father. What matters is the Devil killed that woman and the children. He—"

Father Crisanto cuts me off.

"He didn't."

"What?"

"He didn't kill the woman and children."

"How do you know?"

Looking uncomfortable again, Father Crisanto only shrugs.

I decide to try a different approach.

"Gabriela put in her story that the murders were done by the Devil. But then you took it out. You told her that there was no solid evidence that the Devil actually committed the murders, and until there was, you weren't going to speculate."

Father Crisanto takes his glasses off to rub his eyes again.

"Is that your question?"

"No, my question is why?"

Father Crisanto is silent for several long seconds. I think maybe he won't answer me at all, but then he issues another heavy sigh.

"He didn't do it because they weren't on the list."

"What list?"

"The list that—"

But Father Crisanto cuts himself off, shakes his head.

I lean forward and say as quietly and calmly as I can, "We're not here to hurt you, Father. We're just trying to get some answers. We want to know what's going on. If the Devil didn't kill the woman and children, then I want to know who did. But first I need to understand who the Devil is and why he's doing what he's doing. Tell me about this list."

Again, Father Crisanto doesn't look like he's going to answer me. He just sits there, his shoulders slumped forward, staring at the front of the church.

I glance at Nova, who's standing several paces away, keeping an eye on the entrance in case somebody enters. He looks at me and shrugs. I shrug back, and I'm about to try another approach when the priest speaks.

"Are you familiar with President Cortez?"

"No."

"He was elected just over a year now. The campaign against him was very nasty. President Cortez ran on a platform to do whatever it took to stop the cartels. As you can imagine, the cartels did not like this. They issued many death threats. One time they even tried to kill him, but the bullet only grazed his arm. After that, his popularity soared. It was clear then he would be elected the next president. So the cartels attempted one final pushback against Cortez. Something that they were certain would break the man and cause him to drop out of the race."

Father Crisanto pauses again.

"Cortez had a son named Alejandro. He was a lieutenant in the Mexican Army. Some believed he would one day lead the army. He was Cortez's only son, his pride and joy. Alejandro had a wife and two children of his own, a young boy and girl. Cortez loved his grandchildren very much. Anybody who knew the man knew that. Anybody who met the man would probably guess—"

Father Crisanto breaks off midsentence, shaking his head.

I say, "The cartels went after his grandchildren, didn't they?"

Father Crisanto nods.

"Yes, but not just his grandchildren. They went after the entire family."

"What did the cartels do?"

This was what cartels did, Father Crisanto says:

They sent *sicarios*, or hired killers, to take out Cortez's son and his family. They raided Alejandro's house one night. They stormed inside and put a gun to Alejandro's wife's head to force Alejandro to do as they said. But still Alejandro tried to fight them. For his trouble, one of the *sicarios* took out a knife and cut off Alejandro's wife's little finger. Her strangled cries echoed throughout the house. After that, Alejandro agreed to surrender.

They tied him to a chair. They brought his wife in and stood her in front of him, completely naked. And then they proceeded to rape her. The men took turns. After that, they brought in Alejandro's daughter, who was no older than ten years old. They raped her too. Finally, they brought in Alejandro's young son and raped him as well.

After the men were done, they tied Alejandro's wife and children to chairs and doused them with gasoline. They doused Alejandro, too.

The gasoline had dripped from each person, making a trail, so when one of the *sicarios* lit a match and threw it at Alejandro's wife, the fire began to fan out toward Alejandro and the children.

Father Crisanto pauses, shaking his head again. He's told the story so far in a stunted, toneless voice. Merely relaying events. Doing everything he could not to think about those events too much.

To nudge the priest along, I ask, "When did Cortez learn that everyone died?"

Father Crisanto takes a deep breath.

"The next morning word finally got to Cortez about what happened. He rushed to his son's house to see for himself. They were still in the room, their charred bodies still propped up on those chairs. The two children, the two adults. To Cortez and anybody else, it looked as if his son and his family had burned to death."

I glance at Nova and frown before I turn back to Father Crisanto.

"What do you mean, it *looked* as if his son and his family had burned to death?"

"Because"—Father Crisanto looks at me as if for the first time—"Alejandro survived."

47

When the *sicarios* broke into the house, Alejandro knew his family was going to die. It was not something he wanted to believe—or wanted to accept—but deep down in his heart he knew it was true. That was why he fought them at first. Did everything he could to give his family a chance. But once they cut off his wife's finger, once they rounded up the children and put guns to their heads, Alejandro knew he had no choice but to surrender.

Had he known just what the *sicarios* intended to do, he may have tried to kill his wife and children himself just to spare them.

After the men had beaten and raped his family, gasoline was poured on them, the scent so pungent it caused his muscles to tense. The next thing he knew his family was on fire, just like that, first his wife was in flames, then his children, and then the flames came for him.

The *sicarios* stood watching for maybe a minute before they left.

By that point, Alejandro was also burning. His legs completely on fire, the flames working their way up his body toward his face. He had been working at the ropes binding his wrists this entire time, trying to loosen them as much as possible without the *sicarios* noticing, so once the fire began to consume his hands, the rope became weak enough to break apart.

His entire body now on fire—the flames burning off patches of skin while parts of his clothes melted and fused to his body—he ripped his ankles free and fell to the floor, rolling back and forth to extinguish the flames. Then he slowly climbed to his feet and stood there for a moment, watching his wife and children still burning alive. They had been set on fire first, and he knew there was no saving them. The only thing he could do now was put them out of their misery.

Alejandro hurried out of the room into his office. He grabbed the lockbox out of his desk, managed to punch in the right combination, and extracted the already loaded pistol.

When Alejandro returned, his wife was no longer bucking in her chair. Neither was his daughter. His son had gone completely motionless, and Alejandro knew that he was probably already dead.

Cursing the *sicarios* and God and everything else that was holy and unholy in the world, he fired a bullet into each of their heads—his wife, his daughter, his son—and then he fell to his knees, most of his nerve endings already exposed, his entire body feeling more pain than it had ever felt a day in his life.

Outside, one of the *sicarios* had heard the shots. That *sicario* hurried back inside while the others prepared to leave. The *sicario* raced into the room, his weapon raised, not sure what to expect. He most certainly had not expected to find Alejandro standing there in the burning room, waiting for him.

Alejandro shot the *sicario* in the head.

He set the gun aside and grabbed the *sicario* and dragged him over to the chair they had tied him to. He propped the *sicario* in the chair he'd occupied and then quickly hurried over and grabbed his gun and ran for the closest exit.

Alejandro forced himself to work through the pain. The *sicarios* had done this to his family, and he was going to be damned if he let them get away with it.

He found the two remaining *sicarios* outside in an SUV. They saw him coming but thought he was the third *sicario*. They didn't recognize him for what he was until he was only feet away, and by that point Alejandro fired two shots into one of them and then used the butt of the pistol to smack the other across the face before he could raise his own weapon. When he was certain the driver was unconscious, Alejandro climbed into the SUV, pushing the man aside, and sped away.

Father Crisanto pauses again. As before, his voice has been stunted and toneless, though the more he went on, the easier it was for him to tell the story.

I ask, "How do you know all of this?"

Father Crisanto offers up a somber smile.

"I grew up with Alejandro. We were best friends. We entered the army together. I served only a year before I realized it was not for me. I told God I understood what he wanted for me and left the army to become a priest. I had kept in touch with Alejandro ever since."

Father Crisanto pauses again, and sighs.

"He showed up to my home one night. When I opened the door, I thought it was a monster. His face ... it was unrecognizable. I wanted to take him to the hospital, but he refused. I didn't understand why at first, but once he told me what had happened, I understood his plan. He asked me to help him, and I told him that I would."

They had tied up the remaining *sicario* and left him for several days. Didn't feed him, didn't give him any water. Didn't even let him use the bathroom. During that time, Father Crisanto treated Alejandro the best he could with the supplies he found at the store. What Alejandro needed was professional medical care, but he refused. He told Father Crisanto that as far as he was concerned the world should think he was dead. It was even broadcast on the news that Alejandro and his family had died (the *sicario*'s body had been burned so badly everybody believed it was really Alejandro). His father made a statement. The election was days away. His lead in the polls increased even more.

When Alejandro felt well enough, he met with the remaining *sicario*. By then the man was barely conscious. Alejandro fed him a little food, gave him a little water, just enough to help him focus, and then he started the questions. At first the *sicario* refused to answer any of the questions, and that was when Alejandro became physical.

Father Crisanto now shakes his head and says, "I don't like to think about what was done to that man. Especially as a servant of God, I know what Alejandro did was wrong, but … the man deserved it."

"What did Alejandro learn?"

"He learned that certain families within each cartel had come together to discuss his father and how they were going to keep him from becoming president. He learned the names of each of the men who were at the meeting, especially the man who initially came up with the idea. After he had learned everything there was to know, Alejandro killed the *sicario* and buried him out in the mountains. When he returned, he told me what he planned to do. I told him that he shouldn't. I pleaded with him. I begged him because I knew it would damn his soul if he went through with what he intended. But Alejandro … he no longer cared about such things. He only had one focus, and that was to avenge his family."

"He decided to kill the wives and children of the men who sent the *sicarios* after his family."

Father Crisanto nods.

"Yes. But it wasn't just that. Alejandro wanted to mock the cartels. He knew they would try to hide the murders from the public. They did not want the public to see them as weak. When we were younger, I had excelled at computer programming and I wanted to be a journalist. They were two things Alejandro had always encouraged me to do. As you can probably tell, I had many ambitions when I was younger. And Alejandro remembered this and told me I should start a news hub like many around the country. He said that it would be the best way to get the word out. I must admit the idea interested me. I wondered if I could make it successful. Part of me knew what I was doing—reporting on the murders Alejandro committed—was wrong, but another part knew that the cartels were even more evil. Somebody needed to stand up to them, and I thought perhaps my website could do that."

He pauses again, staring off toward the front of the church.

"Every day I ask God for forgiveness for not stopping Alejandro. I feel the weight of all those deaths on my soul. But I kept telling myself that even if I wanted to turn in Alejandro, what would I say? Who would believe me? As far as everybody is concerned, Alejandro died that night with his wife and children."

Father Crisanto keeps staring off toward the front of the church, and then his brow starts to furrow.

"How did you find me?"

"How do you think we found you?"

"Considering that you came to this church and not to the rectory, it must be because I used the computer here to take down the video of Gabriela."

"The browser wasn't secure. That's how we were able to trace it."

Father Crisanto takes off his glasses and closes his eyes, pinches the bridge of his nose.

"I was too upset to think clearly at the time. I wanted to take that video down as soon as possible. It was only this morning when I realized my mistake."

"Which was why you had the gun."

Father Crisanto nods.

I say, "Father, you realize that if we managed to track you down, others might too."

He nods again, this time more solemnly.

And because God has a cruel sense of humor, it's at that moment the rumbling of several engines approach outside.

Without a word, Nova immediately hurries toward the entrance.

My gun in hand, I quickly stand up and make my way toward the aisle.

Father Crisanto asks, "What's wrong?"

Nova, having peeked out a window by the door, hurries back toward us. The look on his face says it all, but still I ask.

"What is it?"

"Narcos."

"How many?"

"From what I can see, at least a dozen. They have us surrounded."

48

Father Crisanto jumps to his feet. For a moment he just stands there, frozen, and then he hurries toward the middle aisle and then toward the front of the church. He calls back over his shoulder as he runs.

"Follow me!"

We follow him through the door leading to the back of the church. Down a hallway to another door which opens up on a set of stone stairs. Father Crisanto flicks a switch and a faint light comes on. The priest hurries down the steps and races past wooden shelving until we reach an empty bookcase leaning against the wall.

Nova asks, "Why are we here?"

Father Crisanto says, "Help me, please."

The priest grabs one end of the bookcase, and Nova grabs the other end, and they push aside the bookcase to reveal a door.

Father Crisanto opens the door and motions us forward. His eyes are wide, and he keeps looking back toward the stairs.

"Hurry. This will lead you to an entrance to the sewer two blocks away. From there you can climb out."

I dip my head to enter the tunnel but pause.

"Aren't you coming with us?"

Father Crisanto shakes his head.

"No, I must stay here. The narcos expect to find somebody. I must be that somebody."

The meaning of what he says hits me at once, but still I stare at him like I'm not sure what he just said.

Still watching the stairs, Father Crisanto says, "Alejandro is wounded. Two days ago he was shot and stabbed. He does not believe he has much longer to live."

The priest pauses to look directly at me.

"There is only one name left on the list. The man who initially came up with the plan."

I say, "Fernando Sanchez Morales."

The priest nods.

"Alejandro has been saving him for last. Typically he waits weeks or months between attacks, but now …"

Father Crisanto lets it hang there. He doesn't need to say the rest.

Nova pulls out his cell phone, uses the screen to light the tunnel.

"Come on, Holly, we need to go."

Before I can follow Nova, Father Crisanto speaks again.

"Alejandro is suffering. He has been suffering ever since the *sicarios* killed his family. I've tried repeatedly to stop him from killing, telling him how it will damn his soul, but he does not care. Please, if you can, make sure his soul is at peace."

I nod and start after Nova who's already several yards farther ahead. Behind me, Father Crisanto shuts the door and starts pushing the bookcase back in place.

Three minutes later we're out of the tunnel and back on street level. Nova starts toward where we parked the car, but I head back toward the church.

"Holly, stop."

I don't stop. I keep going. My pace slow at first, just a walk, until it speeds up into a jog.

I stop on the corner a block away. There are at least a half-dozen pickup trucks and cars from what I can see. More than a dozen narcos are standing outside the church. A few of the townspeople watch from a safe distance, but for the most part it seems like the town doesn't want to witness what will happen next.

Father Crisanto is currently on his knees in the middle of the street. He has his hands on his head. Three narcos are standing around him. One has a cell phone to his ear, nodding and speaking. Another narco steps forward with a cell phone, holding it in a way which either means he's taking pictures or filming. A third narco keeps asking Father Crisanto something, but Father Crisanto doesn't answer. I can't see his face, but I imagine his eyes are closed and his lips moving soundlessly in prayer.

It's clear what these men intend to do, and I can't let it happen. I even reach for my gun, start to take a step forward, when a heavy hand grabs my arm.

Nova says, "Don't."

I glare back at him.

"Get your hand off me."

"A good soldier knows when not to fight."

"I'm not a soldier anymore. Neither are you."

"You go out there, you're dead."

He's right, of course, but I don't want to admit it. An innocent man—a priest—is about to be killed in front of his church. It's not something I can let happen. Not something I *will* let happen.

Except it doesn't matter anyway, because at that instant a single gunshot echoes through the air.

I turn back to the street just in time to watch Father Crisanto's body collapse in a heap.

My grip on the gun tightens.

Nova's grip on my arm also tightens.

"Let's go, Holly."

I don't move.

He says, "Alejandro is going after Morales next. We need to stop him."

Without a word I turn and start back down the street, pulling my arm from Nova's grip.

He hurries to keep pace beside me.

"How long will it take us to get to where Morales lives?"

"It'll probably take us ten hours. Nine if we drive fast."

"If we drive all night, we'll make it there by morning. For all we know, Alejandro plans to attack tonight, if he hasn't already attacked."

We're a block away from the car now, and I slip the gun in my waistband, pull out the disposable phone.

"I think there's someone who can help us with that."

"Who?"

But I don't answer Nova just yet. Instead I punch in the number and hold the phone to my ear, hoping that Ramon's wife isn't the one who answers this time.

49

Alejandro didn't know how much longer he could hold on.

He had only managed to wrap up the wounds so much, but the bandages kept bleeding through to the point he gave up trying to change them. Usually, walking several miles carrying equipment would be no sweat at all, but now he moved at a slug's pace. What he needed to do was rest. Just take a couple days off, get some sleep, let his new wounds heal as much as possible. But that wasn't going to happen. Not with his mission so close to the end.

It was almost midnight now as he lay in the woods almost three hundred yards away from Fernando Sanchez Morales's house. The equipment he had dragged along—the rifles and extra ammo and RPG launcher—lay on the ground beside him. He currently used a riflescope to watch the men Morales had hired to maintain the perimeter. So far he had counted eight, though there were undoubtedly more inside the house.

Morales had kept his wife and son holed up in that house for over a year now. As far as Alejandro knew, the man hadn't once let his family step outside the gates. He had forced them to become prisoners in their own home. There was something about the idea that gave Alejandro a perverse sort of pleasure, especially considering Morales was the architect behind his own family's downfall. Once Alejandro had learned that Morales was the one who came up with the plan—who had shot down all other ideas because he was certain his was the best—Alejandro knew he would save Morales's wife and son for last. Sure, there was the possibility that Morales would put his wife and son on a plane, send them to some remote country, but Alejandro didn't think so. Morales didn't seem the type to run. He loved his family, yes, but he was too proud to be labeled a coward.

Alejandro set the riflescope aside, placed his forehead against the cold ground, and closed his eyes.

He thought he might just rest for a couple minutes. Gain his strength. He had been mostly lucky the past year and a half. Certainly what he had accomplished hadn't been easy, but he had managed to make it work. As the names on the list started being crossed off, maybe he had become too arrogant, too sure of himself. That's why he had gotten shot when he attacked that convoy, and how he had managed to let himself get stabbed by that narco. And since then, driving here from Michoacán, he hadn't gotten any sleep—not even a few minutes—so yes, resting for a bit should not be a problem. After everything he had been through, surely he deserved some time to rest. Some time to close his eyes. Some time to drift into that welcoming darkness ...

"No."

Alejandro whispered it, opening his eyes and shaking his head suddenly.

No, he couldn't rest. Not now. Not when he was so close to finishing this. Not when he was on the cusp of avenging his wife and children.

He would make his attack tonight because he didn't know

how much longer he had to live. When the attack would occur exactly, he didn't know, but it would happen sometime tonight. It had to.

Alejandro picked up the riflescope again and surveyed the perimeter.

Just a couple more hours, he told himself. Just a couple more hours until this was all over.

For now, he would have to wait until the time was right.

Inside the house, Fernando Sanchez Morales poured himself another shot of tequila.

Jose Luis Guillen said, "Maybe you should slow down."

Fernando threw back the shot. He closed his eyes for a moment, savoring the sweet and spicy taste, and then set the glass tumbler on the tabletop and looked up at his right-hand man standing in the doorway.

"When will they be here?"

Jose Luis checked the time on his watch.

"Soon."

Fernando shook his head and went to pour himself another shot.

Jose Luis said, "If you keep drinking, you won't be able to go."

Fernando shot to his feet so quickly the chair tipped back and clattered to the floor. His jaw clenched as he glared at Jose Luis.

"Are you going to tell me what I can and cannot do in my own goddamned house?"

Jose Luis lowered his eyes and cleared his throat.

"I apologize. But it's important to be in the right frame of mind."

"Don't you think I know that? I'm just having a couple shots. Maybe you should have one too. It will help loosen you up."

Jose Luis shook his head and said quietly, "No, thank you."

Fernando stared hard at his right-hand man. He knew that Jose Luis was a recovering alcoholic. That he had been clean for over a decade now. As far as Fernando knew, the man had almost no vices, which had always worried him. A man with no vices was a man you couldn't trust, his father once said. Now he squinted at Jose Luis and tried to figure out what the man was hiding.

"Do you think you're smarter than me?"

Confusion flashed on Jose Luis's face. It was there for just a moment, and then the man shook his head.

"No, of course I do not."

"I'm your boss."

"Yes."

"You do what I tell you to do."

"Of course."

Fernando took the bottle and topped off the tumbler. He set the bottle aside and with his index finger pushed the tumbler across the table toward Jose Luis.

"Drink it."

Jose Luis didn't move. Didn't say anything.

Fernando said, a bite in his tone, "Drink it now."

Jose Luis stood silently for another moment before he approached the table. He avoided Fernando's eyes as he leaned forward and picked up the tumbler and placed it to his lips to take a sip.

"Don't sip it. Down it. The entire thing."

Jose Luis paused, staring at the tumbler. Then he closed his eyes, tipped the tumbler back, and swallowed it whole.

Fernando smiled.

"Now did that taste good?"

Jose Luis wiped his mouth but said nothing.

Fernando cleared his throat.

"I said, *did that taste good?*"

Jose Luis nodded and whispered, "Yes."

Fernando gestured at the long table spread out in front of him.

"Every night I eat dinner here with my wife and son. And every night we eat in silence. Can you guess why?"

Jose Luis shook his head and whispered that he could not.

"It's because my wife and son have nothing to talk to me about anymore. They haven't for over a year now. What am I supposed to do, ask them how their day went? They hate that I've kept them in this house. They hate me because of it. I can tell them all about the Devil, even show them pictures, but it doesn't matter. For some reason, they blame me. And yes, I know that I am really the one to blame, but they don't need to know that. All they need to know is that the Devil is out there and he wants to kill them. And as for the Devil, I have no control over what he does next. I know he'll come someday, but I have no idea what day that will be. I have no control. Do you understand that? No control at all. So when I have control over something, you better believe I make sure to do everything I can to make it happen. That's why we're doing this tonight. That woman embarrassed me—the entire town embarrassed me—and I will not let it stand. Do you understand? Are my words making sense?"

Jose Luis nodded silently.

"Good. Now I think you're right. I should stop drinking. But there's still more than half a bottle left of good tequila. So we're going to sit here and you're going to drink the entire bottle until it's gone."

La Miserias was quiet and still, just as it typically was in the middle of the night. Almost everybody in town was asleep in bed.

Yolanda was not. She was in bed, yes, but she was not asleep.

She stared up at the ceiling like she did most nights, Dorado asleep at the foot of the bed. When the insomnia had started exactly, she didn't know, but over the course of several months it seemed to be getting worse. Before she would try reading, but the small print in the books gave her headaches. She tried watching TV, but there was nothing interesting on, and she realized she was just wasting electricity. And so she had taken to simply lying in bed as she did now. Staring at the ceiling. Telling her mind to shut down so she could fall asleep. And her mind, as usual, completely ignoring her.

Two young men had been chosen to keep watch. The town had divided up the watch in six-hour shifts. The young men were stationed on the roofs of different houses near the road that led into town. Each of them had a rifle. Each of them had an air horn, which they would use to alert the rest of the town if the narcos returned. The young men understood the importance of their jobs, but they were both tired from working all day. Each of them kept nodding off on their respective rooftops, but neither fell entirely asleep. It was three o'clock in the morning, and they had another hour before others came to take over their watch. All they had to do now was wait.

Ramon had just dozed off when Carlos nudged him with an elbow.

"Don't fall asleep on me."

Ramon shook his head as if to clear it and sat up straight in the seat.

"Did I miss anything?"

Carlos lit a cigarette and shook his head.

"No, you did not miss a single thing. We have been sitting here now for almost eight hours and not one goddamned thing has happened. I think Samantha Lu was full of shit."

They were parked off the main road among a cluster of trees

about a quarter mile up from the drive leading to Fernando Sanchez Morales's house. Like Carlos said, they had been there now for nearly eight hours. Ever since Ramon had gotten the call from the woman who called herself Samantha Lu. He had immediately called Carlos and they had sped all the way up here without a solid plan in mind. So they did the only thing that made sense—they found a secluded spot to park the car and watch the house.

Carlos blew smoke out the window, tapped the ash off the cigarette against the windowpane.

"I think we should call it a night and head home. Try to get a few hours of decent sleep before we both need to be at the office bright and early."

Ramon said nothing.

Carlos said, "I want to catch the Devil as much as you do, but we have other cases that we need to work."

Ramon just stared out the windshield.

Carlos took a final drag off the cigarette and flicked it out into the dirt.

"I honestly don't know what more we can do at this point. We can't get other officers to take our place to watch the house. They'll want to know why we think the Devil is going to attack the Morales family next, and what are we going to tell them? That a woman who claims to be a student from America—and who kicked our asses the other night—says that the Devil is headed here next? No, Ramon, you know just how crazy that sounds. Even saying it out loud now sounds crazy. I'm tired and I'm cranky and at this point I just want to go home. So let's go home, yes?"

Still staring out the windshield, Ramon asked, "What would you do with the reward money?"

"What reward money?"

"For the Devil."

"We're *policía*, Ramon. We don't get the reward even if we

catch him. Maybe a commendation, a nice letter from the president, but no reward."

"The PFM isn't the only ones offering a reward."

Carlos laughed out loud.

"You mean the reward the cartels are supposedly offering?"

"Ten million dollars. We split it down the middle. Half for you, half for me. Though maybe you would feel generous and only take a quarter. What with you being a widower and me with my wife and baby daughter."

"And what would you do with all that money?"

"Leave the country. Start a new life someplace safe."

Carlos laughed again and shook his head.

"A nice thought, but let's be realistic. We're wasting our time here. Let's go home."

For a moment Ramon looked like he was considering it. Then something changed in his face as he stared out the windshield.

Carlos turned his head and watched an SUV come speeding down the drive from the Morales place. It slowed at the road and then just sat there, waiting.

"What the hell?"

That was when the pickup trucks came into view. They came from the south. There were two of them, and packed in their rear beds were narcos. In total there were probably two dozen of them. The pickup trucks' taillights flared red as they slowed, giving the SUV time to jerk forward onto the main road. It sped north, the two pickup trucks directly behind it. They watched the three vehicles for several long seconds until the taillights started to fade.

Carlos said, "Where the hell are they going?"

There was a beat of silence, and then both men answered at the same time.

"La Miserias."

Carlos reached for the cell phone in his pocket.

Ramon said, "What are you doing?"

"I'm calling it in."

"Calling what in?"

"You saw exactly what I saw. They're planning something bad."

"We don't know that for a fact."

"Bullshit we don't."

"And what are you going to tell them when you call? How are you going to explain us being here?"

This made Carlos pause.

Ramon said, "I don't like it anymore than you do, but calling it in might get us in trouble."

Ramon didn't bother adding that there wasn't much the police could do anyway. If Morales and his narcos were up to no good, the police weren't going to be able to stop them. They would just show up later to clean up the mess.

Carlos said, "Fine. But let's get out of here. I'm exhausted."

Ramon settled back in his seat, placing his head against the headrest, and stared out the windshield at the house on the hill.

"Let's give it a couple more minutes. Morales was probably in that SUV. If the Devil plans to attack tonight, he'll do it soon."

50

La Miserias sits about two miles north from Fernando San-chez Morales's house. It's nearly three o'clock in the morning when we pass the town on the main road. I glance at the town as we pass, see that it's dark and quiet, and issue a quiet sigh of relief.

Nova doesn't bother glancing at the town. He has no con-nection to it. He leans heavily on the accelerator, the car's small engine doing everything it can to keep up.

After all this driving, after all this time, we're almost to our destination, but maybe it won't matter. Maybe the Devil will have struck by now, or maybe the Devil won't strike at all. The priest had said Alejandro was wounded, that he may not have much time left, and so maybe he's already been taken out of the game, bled out in some room where his body won't be found for days.

Headlights splash us up ahead, bringing me up out of my thoughts. By the look of it, three cars are coming our way. It's not an uncommon thing—we've passed a lot of traffic on our way here—but it's the way they're tightly grouped together that raises a red flag. I keep an eye on the three approaching vehicles until they're close enough to make out.

At the front of the pack is an SUV, followed up by two pickup trucks.

The backs of the pickup trucks are full of men with guns.

Because of both of our speeds, I see all of it in a flash, but it's enough to send a tinge of dread through my body.

I twist in my seat and watch out the rear window at the receding taillights. Just as they approach La Miserias, each of the taillights starts to glow an angry red.

"Turn around."

Nova says, "What?"

"Turn around! Those were narcos, Nova. They're going to attack the town again."

Without any further prompting, Nova slams on the brakes and twists the wheel, pulling up on the emergency brake as he maneuvers a quick one-eighty.

I pull out my gun. It's fully loaded, but I check the magazine anyway. Ten bullets.

Nova says, "We got any extra firepower?"

"Nope."

"What about extra ammo?"

"Nope."

"Goddamn it, Holly."

"What do you want to me to say, Nova? I wanted to make sure the town had as many weapons as possible in case this happened."

We're almost to the town now, the car doing nearly seventy miles per hour.

"Kill the headlights when you pull in. Maybe we can mow some of them down with the car, take their weapons. They should be carrying AK-47s. That enough firepower for you?"

Nova says, "I guess we'll see."

He makes the turn and kills the headlights as we tear down the unpaved road toward the center of town.

Even without the headlights, we can see the three vehicles ahead of us because they still have on their lights. All of them have stopped, and the narcos have jumped down from the truck beds.

One of lookouts on the roof keeps blaring an air horn while another starts firing down at the narcos.

Because the narcos don't give a shit about being careful, they open fire wildly, spraying the closest homes, shattering windows and tearing through walls.

A pair of narcos is closest to us. Their focus is on shooting at the houses so they don't hear the car until it's too late. Nova runs right over them and then slams on the brakes. I have my door open and am jumping out before the car can even make a complete stop.

I go for headshots and manage to drop three of them before other narcos turn and start firing back at me. I dive behind the car to take cover. Nova has gotten out of the car, too, and he's grabbed one of the fallen narco's AK-47s. He's taken cover behind a wall and waits for a lull in gunfire before stepping out and letting loose.

The man on the roof has given up with the air horn. The only noise filling the night is gunfire.

The townspeople have joined the fight, but they're only half awake and many of them have already been shot and killed. Bodies have started piling up.

When Nova exhausts the rifle's magazine, he takes cover with me behind the car.

"This isn't the Mexican experience I had envisioned it would be."

"How so?"

"I was hoping for tequila and women and dancing."

"You don't strike me much as a dancer."

"I've got moves."

Now that we've taken cover, the narcos have become more emboldened. They keep firing at the car.

I tilt my chin toward the closest rooftop.

"Think you can get up there?"

"Of course. I told you I've got moves."

"I'll draw their fire."

"One problem, Holly."

"What's that?"

"I'm empty."

"Yeah, that is a problem."

I duck down and check underneath the car. The second narco we'd run over is there. So is his AK-47.

Leaning back, I say, "Okay, here's the plan."

The approaching narcos don't let up. The car is being destroyed. Soon we won't have much cover left.

Nova says, "It better be good."

I tell him quick, and he nods, and then I dive down under the car and crawl forward and grab the AK-47 and aim at the approaching narcos. I open up, my bullets tearing into their feet and legs, and as the narcos fall, Nova jumps up from his position and charges the closest narco, grabbing his AK-47 and then mowing down the rest of the men.

He shouts, "Clear!"

I crawl out from under the car and take in the scene. At least six fallen narcos, some of which are still alive. Nova moves forward and shoots them each in the head, and then bends down to grab more rifles and ammunition. Without a word, he tosses me another AK-47 as well as another magazine, and then he turns and disappears around the corner in search of higher elevation.

Throughout town scattered gunfire continues. I hear women screaming and children crying and men shouting.

I hurry behind one of the houses to come around the action from another side. As I do new gunfire starts up in the cacophony, a more controlled *pop ... pop ... pop*, and I know Nova has already made it up onto a rooftop and is picking off narcos.

I race through town, passing by many dead bodies. There are a lot of narcos, but there are even more townspeople. I take out as many narcos as I can, hiding behind walls or other cars for cover. At one point I see Nova off in the distance, jumping from house to house to get in better position. Eventually he'll run out of ammunition, just like me, but for now we need to do whatever it takes to protect the town.

And then I turn the corner and see him.

Fernando Sanchez Morales.

He's standing over an old man, a gun in his hand, and he actually laughs when he shoots the old man in the head.

The old man, I realize a second later, is Antonio.

I start down the road toward Morales who still has his back to me, the gun held loosely at his side, like this is all just a game.

As I approach, I shoulder the AK-47 and slip a switchblade from my pocket.

Morales still hasn't noticed me. He's focused toward the center of town. Where all the dead bodies lie.

He pauses when I'm ten feet away, and starts to turn in my direction.

I throw the knife at his stomach.

The blade hits him dead center as he turns. His eyes go wide for a second, and then he starts to reach for the knife to pull it out.

Now that I'm five feet away from him, I drop my shoulder to loosen the AK-47, and as it falls, I grab the barrel and use the rifle as a bat, swinging it back over my shoulder and then smashing the butt against the side of Morales's face.

He goes down hard.

I step over him and survey the town square. The only movement I see is townspeople. The gunfire has started to die down in the past minute, becoming sporadic, and I realize the last shot I heard was from the rooftop, Nova taking out what might have been the last narco.

Behind me, Morales says, "You bitch."

I turn back to the man.

He's on the ground with a hand on the knife, but it's clear he isn't sure whether or not he should pull it out. His own gun lies only a few feet away, but he barely seems to care.

I walk back to the man and crouch down.

"Want me to take this out?"

I grab the knife and slide it out of his stomach.

He gasps.

I say, "Nah, you should probably keep it where it is."

I stab him in the same spot.

This time he cries out.

I'm aware of people approaching us—the remaining townspeople—but I keep my focus on Morales.

"I told you not to come back here."

His face is a mixture of pain and rage.

"Fuck you."

"Your men are dead."

He grins and says, "So is half of this town."

I nod, listening to the townspeople approaching. Some of them are sobbing, but many of them are quiet.

Morales says, "Are you going to kill me?"

I start to shake my head, but before I can answer, something explodes off in the distance.

I jump to my feet and look up at the house on the hill. A small plume of flames is visible.

I crouch back down in front of the Morales.

"Did you hear that? That's probably the Devil. He's finally come for your family. Just as you knew he would."

Morales grimaces at the pain but says nothing.

"He knows you were the one who came up with the plan. That's why he waited to come for your family last."

This causes Morales to frown.

"How … how do you know this?"

"I know everything."

Down at the end of the street a vehicle screeches to a halt.

I stand up briefly, reaching for the AK-47, but pause when I realize it's Nova in the SUV.

I raise a finger for him to wait a moment and then crouch back down in front of Morales.

"You asked if I'm going to kill you? I'm not going to kill you. You and your men didn't attack my town. You didn't kill my people."

I jerk my thumb back at the crowd behind me.

"You attacked *their* town. You killed *their* people. They're the ones who will get to decide what to do with you. And something tells me it's not going to be pleasant."

I start to stand back up when Morales grabs my arm. His face is suddenly full of fear. Not for him, I realize, but for his family.

He says, "Will you save them?"

I pull my arm from his grip.

"Yes. But not for you."

Before Morales can say anything else, I turn and start through the crowd toward Nova. I only pause when I see Yolanda leaning on her cane. Her face is filled with so much pain and sorrow that it nearly breaks me. We stare at each for just a moment, and then I hurry past her and climb into the SUV.

Nova says, "Time to dance with the devil."

He throws the SUV in gear and punches the gas.

51

Alejandro made his way through the opening in the gate that the RPG had made. He stepped past the bodies he'd killed after firing the RPG—taking out a half-dozen of them with the sniper rifle—and as more men ran around the house he took them out too, picking them off before any of them were able to get off a single shot.

He did not move as quickly as he would have liked. The pain in his side was becoming too much of a nuisance, and though he tried to fight past it, there was only so much he could do.

Alejandro dropped an empty magazine, loaded his rifle with another.

He already knew this would be the end of his revenge. More than likely he would die right after ending the lives of Morales's wife and son. And if that was the case, so be it. As long as he killed each of them, his soul would find rest. It would be eternally damned, yes, but still it would find rest.

He had just reached the house, meaning to enter through the patio door, when the front gate burst open.

He turned and watched a car come speeding up the drive

toward the house. It seemed to pause for a moment, its driver not sure where to go next, and then its engine growled as its driver accelerated and aimed right for him.

Alejandro raised the rifle and let off several bursts. The bullets dented the car's grille and hood and shattered the windshield.

But still the car kept coming, even faster now, and Alejandro realized he wouldn't be able to get out of the way in time. Still he turned and tried to dive to the side, but the car's smashed grille struck him and sent him flying through the patio door.

The car skidded to a stop, and its engine sputtered and died. Both front doors opened, and Ramon and Carlos fell out.

Ramon had taken two bullets to his side, but neither were serious hits.

Carlos wasn't so lucky. One of the bullets had got him in the stomach. He lay on the ground, groaning in pain, and then slowly climbed to his feet. He had dropped his gun when he fell from the car, and he looked around wildly for it, thinking at first it had somehow disappeared. Finally he spotted it underneath the car. Carlos reached for it, his fingers just grazing the metal, and then he managed to grab the gun and used the open door to pull himself upright.

Ramon was already on his feet. He held his side with his left hand as he gripped his gun with his right hand. He started toward the smashed patio door and the inert form of the Devil.

Carlos said, "We need to call this in."

Ramon didn't answer, just kept moving forward.

Carlos said, "I need an ambulance. You need an ambulance. Christ, what were you thinking charging at him like that?"

Ramon still didn't answer. He kept his focus on the Devil. The door had been smashed open enough that he simply walked into the house. He stared hard at the Devil who slowly attempted to sit up.

"Stop."

Ramon said it as he aimed his gun at the Devil. At least, he assumed it was the Devil. The man wore a mask covering his entire head. Only the eyes stared out.

Carlos stumbled into the house behind him. He leaned against the wall to stay upright. Like Ramon, he kept a hand against his wound while his other hand gripped his gun.

"Is that really him?"

Ramon didn't answer. The Devil didn't answer. The house was eerily silent.

Carlos said, "We need to call this in."

Keeping his gun aimed at the Devil, Ramon said, "What if we didn't?"

"Are you fucking crazy?"

"The cartels will pay ten million dollars for him."

"So? We don't work for the cartels."

Ramon turned and shot Carlos twice in the stomach. Carlos stumbled back, hit the wall, and slid down to the ground.

Ramon walked over to Carlos. He bent down and pulled the gun from Carlos's grip and tossed the gun outside.

"Maybe you don't work for the cartels, but I do."

He glanced over his shoulder to make sure the Devil hadn't moved, and then turned his focus back on Carlos.

"I didn't want it to be this way. I wanted to bring you in. I told you we could split the money. But you—"

Ramon's side exploded in pain as two gunshots sounded out. He fell back, glancing toward the Devil again, and saw the Devil with a gun in his hand, pointed right at him.

Alejandro intended to kill both men, but that was when he heard motion behind him. He turned quickly and saw a man standing there, a gun in his own hand. But the man looked drunk, unsteady on his feet, the gun in his hand shaking.

Alejandro twisted around and shot the man.

The man cried out as he fell to the ground. His gun clattered away.

Alejandro checked back on the two men—who were *policía*, they had to be *policía*—and saw that they were both out of commission. The older one had paled considerably in the past minute. It didn't look like he had much longer to hold on. The younger one hadn't paled as much, but he was writhing in pain on the ground.

It took more effort than he thought he had, but Alejandro managed to climb to his feet. He kept telling himself that it was almost over. That soon he would avenge his family. That soon he could close his eyes and never open them again.

Alejandro approached the new man on the floor. He didn't look like a narco. It took Alejandro a moment, but then he realized who this man must be.

"You are Jose Luis, yes?"

The man didn't answer, staring up at him in terror.

Alejandro said, "Where are they?"

The man gritted his teeth, attempted to spit at him.

Alejandro shot the man in his ankle.

The man howled.

Alejandro said, "Where are they?"

The man kept howling in pain.

Alejandro shot him in his other ankle.

The man sputtered, "Upstairs. They are upstairs."

Alejandro had figured as much, but he still needed confirmation.

"Where are they upstairs?"

The man didn't answer, shaking his head, but when Alejandro aimed his gun toward his balls, the man relented with a hoarse shout.

"The master bedroom."

Alejandro looked back over his shoulder to check on the

two cops. Both of them were still alive, but they wouldn't be a problem.

He turned back to Jose Luis and aimed his gun at the man's head.

"Were you at the meeting when your boss made the plan to come after me and my family?"

Jose Luis shook with pain. His eyes were shut tight again, his jaw clenched, but still he nodded, almost imperceptibly.

Alejandro shot Morales's right-hand man in the face.

He turned back to the two *policía*, meaning to put them out of their misery too, when he heard a vehicle approaching outside.

Alejandro couldn't waste any more time. He needed to end this now.

Gripping the gun in his hand, he started for the stairs.

52

Nova shuts off the SUV, and we step out into a heavy silence.

Bodies lie all over the yard.

Nova and I glance at each other.

He whispers, "Too quiet."

I nod.

We start toward the front of the house. But then Nova notices divots in the grass leading toward the side yard. He motions me to follow him, and we round the house to find a car resting on the patio. The car is empty, but we spot two men just inside the smashed entrance.

Ramon and Carlos.

I nod to Nova and we enter cautiously, our backs touching as we sweep different areas of the house. I'm facing the front of the house and don't see anything except the two crime scene investigators who both look like hell. They've been shot several times, but they're still alive.

Nova whispers, "I've got a dead body."

I glance over my shoulder. I don't recognize the man, but he's been shot in the face.

Nova keeps cover as I crouch down in front of Ramon.

"What happened?"

Before Ramon can answer, Carlos shouts, his voice tepid and shaky, "Ramon shot me!"

Ramon doesn't even bother playing stupid. The pain is too much for him to hide his emotions. His glare burns into me.

I stand back up and turn to Carlos.

"Where did he go?"

The man's face is white. He grimaces against the pain, and tilts his face toward the ceiling.

I say to Nova, "Keep an eye on them. I'll be right back."

Nova has already taken a position with his back to the wall so he can watch both entry points and the two men on the ground. He nods to me, and I hurry past him toward the hallway.

I'm halfway up the stairs when I hear a woman scream.

The woman keeps screaming, pleading for mercy, and I follow her screams all the way up the steps and down the hallway to a bedroom.

The door is already open.

I step inside.

Alejandro stands in the middle of the bedroom, the barrel of his gun pressed against the head of a young boy, and the woman—Morales's wife—is in the corner on her knees, her hands folded, begging the intruder to let her son go.

Alejandro has taken off his mask. It lies crumpled on the carpet beside him. In a low, guttural voice, he tells the woman to look at his face, to see what her husband has done to him.

"He did the same thing to my family. To my wife and son and daughter. He sent men to rape them and burn them alive."

So far I've been silent. Nobody in the room has heard me. Alejandro has gone past the point of caution. He's close to death, and all he wants to do is avenge his family before he dies, so he doesn't care that his back is to the door. I could simply take him out now—place a bullet in the back of his head—but instead I step deeper in the room, far enough for the woman to notice me. And because her attention shifts just briefly, it's enough for Alejandro to turn toward me.

I'm not really sure what I expected when Father Crisanto told the story about what happened to Alejandro, but the actual reality of the man's face makes me pause.

I keep my gun trained on him as I say, "Alejandro, don't do this."

There is a tremor of surprise in what's left of his face at the sound of his name, but it's there for only an instant.

"Stay back."

"I spoke to Father Crisanto. He told me what happened to you and your family."

"Stay back!"

"Father Crisanto is dead."

This makes Alejandro pause again. But then, just as quickly, he presses the barrel of the gun even harder against the boy's head. The boy cries out, squirming in Alejandro's grasp.

He says, "They deserve to die."

"No, they don't. Fernando deserves to die, and I've already killed him. So killing that boy and his mother is not going to hurt anyone anymore. Just let them go."

It's hard to read Alejandro's face. It's even harder to read his eyes. For a moment, it looks like he's going to relent, but then he shakes his head and his finger starts to tighten on the trigger, and I have no choice but to follow through with my initial intention.

I put a bullet in the side of Alejandro's head.

His body jerks. The finger loosens on the trigger. The gun slips to the floor. And so does Alejandro. He falls back and tips over onto his side.

The boy immediately runs to his mother. She wraps her arms around him, holds him tight, repeatedly kisses his head.

She keeps staring at the dead body on her bedroom floor, and her eyes shift up to meet mine.

She whispers, "Thank you."

I watch the woman and child huddled in the corner. I stare at them for a long time, and then without a word I lower the gun to my side and leave the room.

53

Nova hasn't moved from the spot I left him in. He stands with his back to the wall and a good view of the house.

I step over the dead man and approach Nova and the two crime scene investigators. The older one, Carlos, looks worse. As for Ramon, it's clear he's in pain, but he does his best not to show it.

Nova asks, "All good?"

I nod and step over to the two men on the floor. I glance at Ramon, who stares straight ahead, refusing to look at me, so I direct my question at Carlos.

"Ramon shot you?"

Carlos's breathing is very shallow. He doesn't look like he has much strength left, but he manages to nod and push out the answer.

"Yes."

"Why?"

"He wanted to capture ... the Devil ... for the cartels' ... reward. Ten ... million dollars."

I whistle at the amount and glance at Ramon.

"That would have been a nice payday, huh?"

He says nothing.

Carlos continues.

"When it became … clear to him … I would not give … the Devil … to the cartels … he shot me."

There are bullet holes in both of them, so it's hard to tell just how truthful Carlos is being right now. But still I crouch down in front of Ramon. He keeps staring past me, refusing to meet my eye, so I snap my fingers in front of his face.

"Earth to Ramon."

He blinks and looks at me.

"Is what your partner says true?"

Ramon's glare is so hard it could probably cut glass. I figure he's not going to answer, but then he grunts out something that doesn't make sense to me at first.

"You should not even be here."

"Say that again?"

"I thought you would be with your friend. There was no reward for you—the cartels don't know who you are so they don't give a shit—but they pay good money for journalists like your friend."

I'm not sure when it happens, but my body starts to shake. It's subtle, but the rage is there, just beneath the surface. At any second it might explode, but before that happens, I need to get more information out of him.

"You sent the tip about Miguel Dominguez's body being found?"

Ramon's glare cracks as he sneers.

"I did not send her to the right scene. I sent her to a place across the city. That was where the narcos picked her up."

He pauses, and his eyes light up with a sort of mischief.

"You saw the video, yes? Then you saw exactly what they did to her."

Ramon sees my rage, and it causes him to smile. Not sneer as he had done before, but *smile*.

He says, "You could have been in the video too. You could have been a star."

Nova moves away from his position against the wall.

"This isn't productive. We need to leave."

I hear his voice and I hear his footsteps, but both are distant. I keep my focus on Ramon.

"How much?"

He raises an eyebrow, like he doesn't understand the question.

I say, "How much did they pay you?"

Now that he understands, he smiles again, and coughs out a laugh.

"Two thousand dollars. *American* dollars."

He pauses again to see my reaction, but the rage is still just beneath the surface, so he continues.

"It's not the first time I sent a journalist like her a tip. I've done it before. There are many things I have done for the cartel. The money is easy. All I have to do is—"

I've finally had enough. I stand up and raise my gun and shoot him in the face. It should be more than sufficient—the man is obviously dead—but I fire three more rounds into his face until there isn't much left of his head.

"Stop!"

I glance back at Nova, see that he's impatient to leave, but I'm not ready to go just yet.

I turn back to Carlos.

The older man can barely keep his eyes open. But he slowly shakes his head and offers up a weak smile.

"I guess nobody … should piss … you off."

I crouch down in front of him.

"I was the one who attacked Ernesto Diaz's compound. I found the woman and the two children inside the house, and I took them with me up the coast. I dropped them off at that building. I intended on leaving the country, but I felt the woman and children still needed help, so that was why I returned to the house. I didn't get a chance to verify it upstairs, but somebody who knew the Devil said those murders were not done by the him."

Carlos's eyes fall shut. He forces air into his lungs to speak.

"When you helped … them leave the house … did the woman … have an earring?"

"No, she didn't. Why?"

Carlos's head tilts to the side.

"In my … pocket."

I reach into his pocket and pull out a familiar crumpled photograph.

Carlos says, "Who … is that?"

"I don't know who she was, but she was a prostitute. Her friend said she had been working that street the previous night but never returned home."

"Do you see … her belly?"

I do. She wears a halter-top exposing her midriff and a belly button ring.

"What about it?"

"The coroner … found only one … earring … on the body. But I … do not think … it was an earring."

I stare at the picture for several long seconds before I frown at Carlos.

"So you think Miguel Dominguez got a call at the motel and he grabbed the prostitute and took her to the building and … what? He swapped out her body for Maria's?"

This causes Carlos to frown again. His face has somehow grown even paler, and his breathing has worsened. He barely has a minute to live, and I'm worried he's going to die before I learn what I need to know.

When he speaks next, his voice is barely a whisper.

"Who is … Maria?"

"The children's nanny."

Carlos closes his eyes as his head slowly moves back and forth.

"She ... was not ... a nanny."

I glance back at Nova, and then I lean forward to hear Carlos better.

"Then who was she?"

54

Daniela felt like a prisoner.

For four days now she hadn't been allowed to leave the ranch house. She was allowed to leave her room, of course, but that was only to wander down the hallway to the bathroom. If she was hungry, food was provided. If she was thirsty, drink was provided. If she felt like smoking, cigarettes were provided. At one point, just to be a bitch, she asked for cocaine, but the men keeping an eye on her—whom she had come to think of simply as her guards—just shook their heads and ignored her.

She hadn't seen her father since the day he brought her to the ranch house. Several times she asked the guards to call him for her, to put him on the phone, but the answer was always the same: he was busy and would return when he felt it was safe.

Safe. That was a word Daniela had always taken for granted. She knew the company she'd kept was not the best, and there had always been the threat of some kind of danger, but she had never felt in fear for her life. Not like that night at the compound when the shooting started and Ernesto ordered her to hide with the children. That was the very first time she felt true fear. At that moment, *safe* was a mythical concept.

Could she run? Probably. While her father had stationed guards around the ranch house—older men he could trust, retired *policía* no doubt—she didn't think they would shoot her if she attempted to escape. They would chase after her, yes, and they might even manage to catch her, but they would not hurt her. At least, she didn't think so. The men had been pretty indifferent toward her so far. None tried to make conversation with her. None even asked her questions. They simply brought her food and water and cigarettes and told her that her father would eventually come every time she asked them to call.

The ranch house sat out in the middle of nowhere. There was electricity but no Internet. Books and magazines were provided, but she was never much of a reader. Still she would page through the magazines, looking at the same pictures and text, but absorbing none of it. Mostly she lay in bed and stared at the wall and smoked.

That was what she was doing on the fifth morning when her father finally returned.

When the door opened, she expected it to be one of the guards bringing her breakfast, but in walked her father. He was already an old man, but he looked as if he had aged a decade in the past several days.

He stood there for a moment in the doorway, simply watching her. Daniela stared back. A younger version of herself may have rushed forward, wrapped her arms around him, but that wasn't the relationship they had. Not anymore. Whatever close ties they once shared had long since been severed, but in the end he was still her father and she was still his daughter, and like most fathers, he would do anything to keep her safe.

Her father said, "Let's go."

She wanted nothing more than to leave this ranch house and

never return. But still the stubborn part of her—the part that created the rift between them—forced her to stay motionless.

"Where have you been?"

Her father shook his head, impatient.

"We do not have time for this. Let's go."

She didn't move.

"Where are you taking me?"

"Out of the country."

She had assumed this was the plan from the beginning. There was no way she could stay in the country after what had happened. She wasn't that well known, but word spread quickly. If someone in the country happened to recognize her, it would cause a lot of trouble. Her father didn't need to do this, not after how awful she had been to him, but again she was his daughter and he was going to do whatever it took to help her. Even if it meant putting his career on the line. Even if it meant putting his *life* on the line.

When she didn't move, her father grunted in frustration.

"We do not have time to waste, Daniela. You have no idea just how much shit has happened in the past two days."

This made her pause.

"What happened?"

"Fernando Sanchez Morales is dead. Over two dozen of his men are dead. Half the town of La Miserias is dead. Two of my crime scene investigators are dead. The whole thing is a mess. We need to leave *now*."

The stubbornness keeping her in place finally snapped. She nodded and stood and started toward her father. She had taken only three steps when the gunfire started.

At first Daniela wasn't sure what she had just heard. It was only one shot, distant and almost indistinct, but then more quickly followed. She had never fired a weapon herself, but she could tell that the current gunfire was coming from several different guns.

Her father stepped into the room, slammed the door shut. He locked it, though she didn't think the simple lock would do much to stop whoever was outside. He moved past her toward the single window in the room. It was high and narrow, making it nearly impossible for them to escape.

She said, "Don't you have a gun?"

He simply shook his head.

The gunfire continued outside. It started to become sporadic, dissipating, until a few random shots rang out and then there was silence.

Out in the hallway, slow, steady footsteps echoed off the hardwood floor.

Daniela looked toward the high and narrow window again. Maybe she could squeeze through it after all. Her father couldn't, but maybe he could give her a boost and then she could—

The door was kicked open with such force she jumped and cried out.

A man entered, an American, his gun sweeping back and forth between her and her father while he scanned the room. When it was clear to him Daniela and her father were not armed, he stepped to the side and shouted.

"In here!"

Another set of footsteps came down the hallway. A lighter set. They did not hurry. They took their time. Just as the footsteps were right around the corner, Daniela closed her eyes. She knew these people were here to kill her, and for an instant she wanted to believe this was all a bad dream.

Then all at once the footsteps stopped, and a woman spoke.

"Hello, Maria."

55

The woman just stands there, her eyes closed. She's acting like a child trying to keep the boogeyman away. If she can't see the monster, the monster can't see her. The only thing she doesn't get is that she's the monster in this situation.

"Or should I say hello, Daniela?"

The woman opens her eyes. Stares at me for a long moment. Her mouth opens up a bit but no words come out.

Her father says, "Who are you? What do you want?"

"It doesn't matter who we are. What matters is that we know who you are. You are Comandante Geraldo Espinoza. You oversee the *policía* in this part of the country. And this is your daughter Daniela Diaz. When I first met her, she told me her name was Maria and that she was a nanny."

Espinoza frowns, clearly not following.

"I'm the one who attacked Ernesto Diaz's compound. I'm the one who saved your daughter and Javier Diaz's children. I took them up the coast and I left them at that brick building in the middle of nowhere. I left them there, and then your daughter killed the children."

Espinoza doesn't respond. Neither does Daniela.

"You see, Javier threatened me and my family. So I killed him. I knew the only way to keep my family safe from retribution was to come here and take out Ernesto. So the research I did was mostly on Ernesto. I must admit, that was my own fault. Had I looked close enough, I would have learned about how Javier's first wife died giving birth to their second child, and how a year later he married Daniela."

Still no response.

"The way I figure it, Daniela, you thought telling me you were the children's nanny would make it less likely that I would kill you. The truth is, had you told me you were the children's mother—or stepmother in this instance—I probably wouldn't have done anything to hurt you. Those kids needed you, especially after what had just happened. But then, well, you went and killed them."

"No."

Daniela nearly barks it. Her face has reddened, and she shakes her head adamantly.

"I didn't kill them."

"Okay. You didn't kill them. But Miguel did."

The flatness of her eyes tells me I'm right.

"So here's how I see things played out. After I left you at that building, you ran up the drive to the phone. Maybe you thought about calling your father, but most likely not. After you married Javier Diaz, you became estranged from your father. Went years without speaking to him. So you didn't call your father that night. You called Miguel Dominguez, who was either an old friend or boyfriend or maybe drug dealer. Correct me if I'm wrong."

Daniela says nothing.

"So you tell Miguel what happened. How the Diaz compound was attacked and how you ended up a couple miles up the coast. How you don't know what to do now. You ask Miguel to come get you, and like a loyal friend—or maybe a guy who has always had a thing for you and will ask how high whenever you tell him to jump—he leaves his post at the motel. As he leaves, he runs into a prostitute on the street. Maybe the idea came to him, or maybe … maybe you came up with the idea."

Still nothing.

"See, that's the one thing I'm not sure about, whose idea it was from the start. But one of you had the idea of copycatting the Devil. Miguel managed to get the prostitute in his car and brought her out to the building. I'm thinking at that point she probably wouldn't have gone willingly, so maybe he had to stuff her in his trunk or something. But then he shows up, and he manages to kick down the door into that brick building, and then … what happened, Daniela? If you didn't kill the children, did you at least watch Miguel when he did it?"

She just glares at me.

"So you cut the prostitute's and the children's throats and you leave them there in the building. Maybe it was Miguel's idea after all, but I don't think so. Remember when we were on the beach and you asked to come with me? At first you said *I* but then hesitated and changed it to *we*. See, it didn't mean much to me then, but now I've had time to think about it. Something tells me you've always resented the children. They weren't yours, after all, not really, and besides, they probably kept you from having a more exciting life. So when you saw the chance to eliminate them—to start over a new life all by yourself—you jumped at the chance. Told Miguel to pick up a prostitute and bring gasoline. Tell me, Daniela, was it him who lit the bodies on fire or was that you?"

Still no answer.

"Doesn't matter in the end. Somebody lit the bodies on fire. But before you did, you didn't properly search the prostitute. I'm guessing when you were hiding with the children in that closet you took off all your jewelry because already the idea of claiming you were the children's nanny had entered your mind. So you wanted to make sure the prostitute didn't have on any jewelry either. But you missed her belly button ring. How am I doing so far, Daniela?"

No response.

"Anyway, Miguel drives you away. He puts in an anonymous call acting like the Devil. He says he just killed a woman and two children and tells the *policía* where to find the bodies. Because crank calls like that come in all the time, only one car went out initially. Then your dad eventually showed up—I recognize you now, Comandante Espinoza—and despite your strained relationship of course he was devastated. And then when he heard about the phone call and how it went to the motel and the crime scene investigators determined Miguel had been working there, I'm guessing the name rang a bell to your father. And once it became clear Miguel had gone missing, your father decided to hunt him down. How long that took, it's hard to say, but it couldn't have been more than two days because that was when Miguel's body was found. Did your father tell you how he cut up the body into different pieces and stuffed them in a trashcan? Probably tried to make it look like some narcos did it. In the end it doesn't really matter, because he got information from Miguel and found you and then brought you out here to this ranch house in the middle of nowhere. And now that Fernando Morales is dead, I bet your father decided it was time to come get you. And since we've been keeping an eye on him, we followed him all the way here."

Daniela says nothing.

"I'll admit, you and Miguel almost got away with it. As far as anyone was concerned, the Devil killed you and the children. There was no way you could have known about the list."

This last part piques Espinoza's interest.

"What list?"

"The Devil was killing the wives and children of certain cartel families as retribution for what happened to his own family."

Understanding flashes in the older man's face.

"So it was really—"

I nod and cut him off.

"Yes, it was really the Devil who attacked the Morales compound."

"Where … where is he now?"

"Dead. I killed him."

"When?"

"Two nights ago. He went after Fernando Morales's wife and son."

Espinoza frowns, shaking his head.

"But there was no body. There were dead narcos and there were my two investigators and a few other bodies, but not the Devil."

"That's because we decided to take the body with us when we left. We buried it out in the middle of nowhere."

"But … why?"

"If the public learned who he really was it might cause too many problems for President Cortez. Besides, the president sounds like a good man. He already lost his son once. He shouldn't have to lose him again."

Espinoza looks from me to Nova and then back to me. He takes a deep breath.

"If you are going to kill us, then get it over with and kill us."

I smile at him and glance back at Nova who has kept his gun trained on them this entire time.

Nova has a bag strapped over his shoulder. The gun not once wavering in his hand, he lowers his shoulder to let the bag drop to the floor and kicks the bag over to me.

I stuff my own gun in the waistband of my jeans and then crouch down and zip open the bag. Before I pull out the contents, though, I glance back up at Daniela.

"Whose idea was it to kill the children, yours or Miguel's?"

She doesn't answer. Her eyes remain flat. Which, in a way, is all the answer I need.

I pull out the two sets of handcuffs, the two cans of lighter fluid, and the pack of matches. I line them out on the floor and stand back up and clap my hands together. I ignore Espinoza and focus all my attention on Daniela when I ask my final question.

"So, are we going to do this the easy way or the hard way?"

CODA

We drive north. The border is maybe six, seven hours away. Time doesn't seem to have much meaning anymore. I've hardly gotten any sleep the past couple days. Which is why Nova drives Geraldo Espinoza's car. We've switched out the plates with one of the other cars at the ranch house just in case.

We don't talk much. Hell, we don't talk at all. It's been at least two hours since we left the burning ranch house. Two hours since we tied all the loose ends.

The silence, it starts to unnerve me, so I decide to break it.

"I don't think I would do it."

Nova glances at me, says, "Do what?"

"Kill Hitler as a baby."

"Where is this coming from all of a sudden?"

"I've just been thinking about it. It's been bugging me."

"Why?"

"Because I couldn't bring myself to kill Morales's kid."

Nova says nothing to this.

After a beat of silence, I take a deep breath.

"After I had killed Alejandro—after Morales's wife had embraced her son and looked at me and said thank you—I stared at them for a long moment. I stared at the woman who had married Morales. Who may have never taken part in the man's crimes but who was complicit all the same. And then I stared at the boy in her arms. The child whose path was to no doubt take up his father's business one day. Who might become even more ruthless than his own father. The boy could grow up to become one of the worst drug lords in the country. The boy could be responsible for thousands of deaths and even more unknown terrors. Part of me thought I could potentially save all of those people by killing him and his mother. It would be so easy. Just two quick squeezes of the trigger, and thousands somehow could be saved."

I shake my head, staring out my window.

"But then another part of me thought about how the boy could grow up to be completely different. The exact opposite of his father. He might become a doctor. Instead of killing thousands of people, maybe he would help thousands of people. Just because his father was a drug lord didn't mean he would follow the same path."

Nova says, "Do you know what somebody once said about that baby Hitler time travel thing? That maybe Hitler would have grown up being a perfectly normal human being. Maybe he would have been a saint. But then all these time travelers kept showing up trying to kill him, and that soured him on humanity and he decided to be a giant dick."

There's another beat of silence, Nova letting the joke hang there, and then I bust out laughing. I can't help it. I can't remember the last time I laughed like this, and it feels good. For a moment I don't think about the charred bodies of Javier Diaz's children. I don't think about Gabriela and her grandmother. I don't think about Yolanda and Antonio and all the rest of the townspeople of La Miserias. For a moment, my mind is simply filled with the rush of laughter, and it's bliss.

Then I wipe at my eyes and settle back in my seat and glance again at Nova.

"So what's your plan once we return to the States?"

Nova doesn't answer right away, his focus once again on the highway. His grin has faded, and his face has gone all at once somber.

I say, "Did I hit a nerve?"

He shakes his head.

"No. It's just, well, something happened recently that made me think about my old man."

"You know, in all the time we've known each other, I don't think you ever once told me about your parents."

"Nothing to tell. My mom died a long time ago. My dad ... well, he's just a son of a bitch."

"I'm sorry to hear that."

"It's not your fault. But when Atticus called me about you needing help down here, I asked him to do me a favor."

"What's that?"

"Try to track down my old man."

"You want closure, huh?"

"Something like that."

There's another lengthy silence. I go back to staring out my window. I know what I need to tell Nova now, but part of me wants to stay quiet. To keep what I need to tell him a secret.

"Nova?"

"Yeah."

"I talked to him."

"Who?"

"My father."

Nova's quiet for a beat, and then he glances at me, incredulous.

"You're joking."

"I'm not."

"When?"

"The night after all that shit went down with Zane and Walter's children."

I say it like it happened years ago when in reality it hasn't even been two weeks. Zane kidnapping Walter Hadden's children because he wanted me to steal something. I stole that something, but I didn't give it to Zane. Instead, I killed Zane.

"Zane had a phone on him. I didn't tell Walter. I didn't even tell Atticus. There were three numbers on the recent call list—my apartment number, the number to a cell Zane had waiting for me in my car, and a foreign exchange. After you came to clean up Javier Diaz and his men's bodies in my apartment building, I went to see my mom before I headed south. But before I saw her, I called that foreign exchange number."

"And your father answered."

Nova doesn't bother making it a question.

I close my eyes and think about sitting in my car outside my mother's house. Zane's cell phone to my ear, the phone ringing four times, and then somebody on the other end simply answering *Yes?*

When I don't immediately answer, Nova asks, "What did he say?"

"Nothing. I did all the talking."

"And?"

"I told him Zane was dead. I told him he disgusted me. I told him he was no longer my father. I told him he should have killed me back in that alleyway in Paris, because the next time we met ..."

"What?"

I shake my head.

"That was it. I let it hang there. He's smart enough to know what I meant. I disconnected the call and turned off the phone. Then I went and saw my mother and acted like I hadn't just learned her husband was still alive after all these years."

Nova opens his mouth, starts to say something, but then shakes his head.

I ask, "What?"

"It's nothing."

"Say it, Nova."

"You quit, Holly. So did I. We both walked away from what it is we do best, and now your father is out there doing God knows what."

"Your point?"

"You can't feel good about that."

"Of course I don't feel good about that. But what do you want me to do? Beg Walter for my job back? He's not too happy with me right now. Shit, I'm not too happy with him either. He knew about my father this entire time and didn't tell me. No, I think it's a good thing I quit. Maybe I can actually start having a normal life."

Nova snorts at that.

I give him a dirty look.

"What's so funny?"

"You having a normal life. I'm sorry, Holly, but in case you didn't realize it, people like us don't have normal lives."

"A girl can dream, can't she?"

"Speaking of which ..."

Nova reaches into the backseat, fumbles with the luggage bag, pulls out the Holy Bible, and tosses it in my lap.

"I think it's time we find out your new identity."

I stare down at the bible. The ID and passport are inside the flaps. All I need to do is tear them out. It would be so simple.

Nova says, "Well?"

I pick up the bible. I heft its small weight in my hands, and then I shake my head and toss the bible in the backseat.

Nova says, "Not ready yet?"

"Not yet."

I settle back in my seat, lean my head against the headrest, and stare out the window.

I think I'll stick with being Holly Lin for just a little bit longer.

ABOUT THE AUTHOR

Robert Swartwood is the *USA Today* bestselling author of *The Serial Killer's Wife*, *The Calling*, *Man of Wax*, and several other novels. He created the term "hint fiction" and is the editor of *Hint Fiction: An Anthology of Stories in 25 Words or Fewer*. He lives with his wife in Pennsylvania.

www.ingramcontent.com/pod-product-compliance
Lightning Source LLC
Chambersburg PA
CBHW021210250626
47155CB00008B/2756